A DATE WITH MY WIFE

BRIAN McCABE is the author of two other collections of stories – *The Lipstick Circus* (Mainstream) and *In a Dark Room with a Stranger* (Penguin), a novel, *The Other McCoy* (Penguin) and three collections of poetry, most recently *Body Parts* (Canongate). Every book he has written has received an award. He lives in Edinburgh with his family.

A Date with My Wife

BRIAN McCABE

CANONGATE

First published in Great Britain
in 2001 by Canongate Books Ltd,
14 High Street, Edinburgh EHI ITE

Copyright © Brian McCabe, 2001

The moral rights of the author have been asserted

The publishers gratefully acknowledge subsidy from
the Scottish Arts Council towards the publication
of this volume

British Library Cataloguing-in-Publication Data
A catalogue record for this book is available on
request from the British Library

ISBN 1 84195 140 4

Typeset in Plantin by
Palimpsest Book Production Limited,
Polmont, Stirlingshire

Printed and bound by
Creative Print and Design,
Ebbw Vale, Wales

www.canongate.net

Contents

Acknowledgements

Acknowledgements and thanks are due to the editors and producers of the following publications and programmes: *The Herald* (November, 2000); *From Glen to Glen* (Argyll Publishing, 2000); *Nerve* (2000); *Product* (2000); *Scotland Into the New Era* (Canongate, 2000); *Shorts* (Polygon, 1998); *Shouting It Out* (Hodder & Stoughton, 1995); *Some Kind of Loving* (ASLS, 1997); *Storyline* (BBC Radio Scotland). An earlier version of *A New Alliance* was broadcast as two radio plays produced by Gaynor MacFarlane for BBC Radio 4 (1998). An earlier version of *Conversation Area One* was produced as a play for the Traverse Theatre's *Sharp Shorts* (1996). An earlier version of *The End of Something* was produced for BBC Radio 3 by Patrick Rayner.

The author would like to thank the Scottish Arts Council for a writer's bursary in 1998 and the Hawthornden Foundation for a fellowship in 2000, both of which helped him complete this book.

Welcome to Knoxland

SEARCH RESULTS:
You have found **666** *pages:*
Site Matches 1 – 10 [Text Only]

100%   FREE Guilt sex shame Scottish hardcore XXX
presbyterian hangups.
Resume: And ye shall roast in the fires of hell –
CLICK HERE for Scottish presbyterian repression
– FREE downloads – LIVE vid. feeds – Mutilations
– Burnings – Hangings – Beheadings – Castrations
– Murders – Suicides and MORE – JOHN KNOX
XXX HARDCORE SERMONS – REFORMA-
TION FETISH/http//www.guiltshame/knoxboy.html

98%   WEE FREE hot shame of the body Scottish Sex
Perversions
Resume: Scottish punishment extreme hardcore
XXX self-denial – masochism thumbnails – self-
laceration and MORE – Live vid. feeds 1000s of
FREE liths. CLICK HERE for extreme hardcore
presbyterian HAIR SHIRTS self-denial lithographs
– men fuck sheep bestiality – cattle buggery and very
original sins. http//www.guilt/shame/perv/knox.html

95%   FREE PROTESTANT FUCKTHEPOPE WANK
SITE
Resume: Click here for Catholic Idol worship and
bestiality FREE pics naked idol celeb crucifixions
– FUCK THE POPE JOKES – Rangers in Europe

sportslink – barely legal pregnant papish teensluts confess their sins LIVE to you and more . . .
http//www.guilt/shame/perv/knox.html

92%   The Wee FREE Scottish Presbyterian Hardcore Repression self-denial site to end all Wee FREE Scottish Presbyterian Hardcore Repression self-denial sites on the web
Resume: Click here to see the dirtiest hardcore religion on the net AND BE SAVED BY GOD'S GRACE FROM ETERNAL DAMNATION.
http//www.guilt/shame/save/grace/knox.html

87%   Salvation is Real – Real salvation is Real
Resume: Did you know that SALVATION is real? Salvation is very real and salvation is FREE for the chosen few – visit this site to become one of the ELECT – and get direct access to God's Grace. Please visit our sponsors. Hardcore shame guilt repression and predestination free preview.
http//www.guilt/salvation/grace/knox.html

83%   Join the Elect
Resume: Click here IF YOU WOULD LIKE TO BE ONE OF THE ELECT members only chosen few who are saved by the Grace of God. This is the most exclusive hardcore religious site on the net. Visit this site for extreme XXX Protestant Chat – Click here to chat to God.
http//www.guilt/salvation/elect/knox.html

79%   The best Presbyterian Wanksite on the Web
Resume: FREE orange walk download of nude Rangers managers singing the sash my father wore – I-spy hidden cams show corrupt pope Innocentus IV signing papal bull authorising torture in the Spanish Inquisition – Live vid. feeds of Bruno burning at stake in the Piazza de Forintini. Shamed

2

priests and nympho nuns commit and confess original sins live. http//www.guilt/shame/perv/knox.html

72% <u>SOUTAINE FETISH AND CONFESSION BOX LIVE ACTION</u>

Resume: Choirboys abused by priests take the host in their mouths in more ways than one – LIVE – crucifixions and extreme Catholic perversions – stained-glass windows of nudecelebs – SPICE GIRLS bare all – MADONNA blowjob – the three main tenets of Calvinism – monstrous regiment of women vid. feeds. http//www.guilt/shame/perv/knox.html

69% <u>KNOXLAND</u>

Resume: Welcome to Knoxland the hottest Presbyterian site on the net – Click here for kalvinist klingons wee free skandals – latest news: The Great Wee Free Split Personality – rebel ministers give the V-sign to General Assembly – Lewis lolitas join the elect only WEE FREE TRIAL MEMBERSHIP GOD'S GRACE FORGIVENESS SALVATION & MORE . . . http//www.guilt/shame/salvation/grace/forgiveness/knox.html

67% <u>Orange Walks King Billy sash my father wore Protestant links</u>

Resume: Orange Walk Archive and streetplanner for future marches – King Billy Biog – Rangers in Europe Link – CRAIG BROWN leaves a message on his under-21s ansaphone outlining his game-plan – Forfar teenslut bites your bridie – FREE KING BILLY SCREEN-SAVER! http//www.orangewalks/sectarian/hardcore/presbit/knoxboy.html

[Text Only]   Next

Refine your search:

3

WELCOME TO

KNOXLAND

XXX

Welcome to Knoxland
The Hottest Presbyterian Site on the Net

No image No image No image No image No image

Connecting to server: http//www.guilt/shame/perv/knox.html

4

Welcome to Knoxland
The Hottest Presbyterian Site on the Net

<u>(WARNING: This is an adult hardcore religion site)</u>

PROTESTANTS <u>ENTER HERE</u>

CATHOLICS <u>ENTER HERE</u>

ATHEISTS <u>EXIT HERE</u>

AGNOSTICS <u>FREE PREVIEW HERE</u>

HERE'S what you get!

CHAT TO GOD *click here*
HAIR SHIRTS *click here*
KALVINIST KLINGONS *click here*
MEN-ONLY BURIALS *click here*
SABBATH SLAVES *click here*
XXX SELF- DENIAL *click here*
FREE CHURCH SKANDALS *click here*
ASHAMED TEEN PRESBYTERIANS *click here*
KATHOLIC IDOLATRY *click here*
TRANSVESTITE ELDERS *click here*
MONSTROUS REGIMENT OF WOMEN
click here
MARY GIVES HEAD *click here*
WORK ETHIK SLAVES *click here*
SAVED SOULS *click here*
JOIN THE ELEKT *click here*
KISS MY PAPAL RING *click here*
REFORMATION FETISH *click here*
RANGERS IN EUROPE LINK *click here*
UDF LINK *click here*

Receiving online image: jpg elect/joinform

Become one of the Elect Now!
Submit:

I am a Protestant:

YES NO

I wish to be saved:

YES NO

My credit card number is:

My e-mail address is:

My password is:

JOIN NOW TO BE SAVED
OR ROAST IN THE FIRES OF HELL

NEXT >

knoxland

CHOSEN   *click here!*

DAMNED   *click here!*

FREE PREVIEW   *click here!*

I ACCEPT THE TENETS OF
PREDESTINATION

click anywhere!

NEXT >

Receiving online image: happy well-adjusted adult/jpg 004/html *knoxland – free tour*

I am a happy, well-adjusted adult and I wish to
leave Knoxland now
click here

I am a screwed-up Scottish alcoholic with deep
problems to do with my Protestant upbringing. I
am already a member of Knoxland
click here

I am a visitor to Knoxland and would like a
free tour
click here

I am a Catholic who wishes to be converted to
Knoxland.
click here

Monstrous Regiment of Women
click here

John Knox Sermon Archive
click here

Salvation
click here

< BACK   CONTINUE TOUR >

After insulting his corpse, they hung the body over the castle wall for the inhabitants of St Andrews to see, and held the castle against the government. This sordid affair was just the beginning.

'These are the works of God, whereby He would admonish the tyrants of this earth, that in the end He will be revenged of their cruelty, what strength so ever they made in the contrary.'

< BACK   CONTINUE TOUR >

knoxland – free tour

THE MONSTROUS REGIMENT OF
WOMEN PICTURE GALLERY

Click on the image to censor it!

(Image) Mary Gives Head

(Image) Floating and Sinking Witches

(Image) Papish Pregnant Teensluts

(Image) Sash Fetish Archives

(Image) Dirty Historical Underwear

(Image) Predestined in Paisley

(Image) Servile Sandwich Makers

(Image) Forfar Flute Girls

(Image) Lewis Lolitas

< BACK   CONTINUE TOUR >

Browser alert:

The application is running low on memory. Quitting applications or closing windows may help.

Okay

WARNING:

The information you send to this site may be intercepted by a third party in the Free Church of Scotland.

Don't send   **Send**

Transferring file: http//salvation/elect/chosen/knoxboy.html

Unknown Host

Description: unable to locate the server named 'god.saviour. com.tw'. The server does not have a DNS entry. Perhaps there is a misspelling in the server's name, or the server no longer exists. Double check the name and try again.

Forbidden

You don't have permission to access godsgraceforgiveness.html on this server.

CLICK HERE TO LEAVE

Something New

JACK CAME OUT of the 'Scotland' search almost as soon as he'd found the site. He accessed some of the stuff he hadn't gone into and saved it – he might browse through it another night. He really should find out more about his ancestors, but after working all day as a researcher for *The Human*, the last thing he felt like doing when he got home was research. Well, he'd found out something, at least: they'd got their own parliament in 1999. Strange. He supposed it couldn't have achieved very much, coming so late in the day – just a decade before the Unification of Europe in 2009.

He put the screen into mirror mode and saw himself naked on the bed: his new cock looked good, long but not ludicrously so like some of the cocks on the market. Only last week he'd gone to a party where the host had come into the kitchen with a really horrible 3-G, a special-offer king-size monster rearing from his thong like a late-twentieth-century dildo. Who knows what state that body part would be in now? Such cheap and nasty geneplants were notorious for turning bad in a matter of days. There had been investigative pieces in *The Human* about the genetic transplant companies who grafted horse-genes on to human genes to produce such obscenities. Sometimes the grafts didn't take and sometimes they did but went wrong. He had read about cases of 'centaurs', totally unlike the proud, wild creatures from Greek mythology they were named after.

Jack wondered if there really had been centaurs in Ancient

Greece, but didn't feel like going into a search. He had a feeling that maybe they'd been made up, just to imagine what a cross between a horse and a man would be like. Now they were finding out – most of the cases he'd heard about were cursed with an impossible anatomy for the rest of their lives, which were always very short because of spinal problems. He had never actually seen a centaur, but he'd seen plenty of their mythical opposites: sitting in doorways, their heavy heads sagging between their knees. They didn't die but went on living as a constant reminder of how things could go drastically wrong with 3-Gs – genetic genital grafts.

Still, everyone did it because it was possible – it was the future. What most people didn't realise was that it was also the past. When you asked the Genie – the gene-searcher – for a new body part, the search offered you something from the past, even if it used genetic elements from many different generations. What you were getting was a finger from the past, if a new finger was what you had ordered. He had sometimes felt disconcerted by the way a new body part could be grown with such alarming speed. Many people had expressed their misgivings about the fact that the genetic past was finite, and that people would eventually exhaust all their Go, their genetic options. According to some scaremongering prophets, the result would inevitably be a spiralling recession into the past, and the universe would implode.

Jack was aware of the dangers of 3-Gs. He had chosen carefully from his GB, his personal gene-bank. It had used up most of his credit, but now he congratulated himself on a good investment. His new cock was pale, because all the accessible options in his GB were pale. He suspected that some of the more expensive options were fiction, invented by some Fantasy Consultant for a fat fee. They used the impossible to tempt you to buy the possible. His male ancestors – from Scotland, before the Unification of 2009, the Genie had been pretty clear about that – were pale-skinned people. Anyway, it was certainly a vast improvement on the one he had been born with.

The trouble was it didn't quite go with the rest of him, or at least with his other geneplants. But then there were so many, it was sometimes difficult to remember which parts of his body were his own. He'd more or less replaced everything you could see, and a lot you couldn't: heart, lungs, liver and quite a few bones. Some things had been replaced many times. His face had undergone so many changes, he sometimes accessed and enhanced ancient facial images of himself, searching for an original face. It was impossible to find his real face, because ultimately all that came up was the face he'd had as a baby, before his carers modified it according to their tastes. It was difficult to remove himself from their version of him, without a very expensive search. He had found only one image of himself as a baby: as naked as he was now, lying on a bed. It was the face that fascinated him: even although it had probably been genetically designed to some extent, it had a haunting quality. Sometimes the eyes that stared at him from the screen seemed infinitely wise and thoughtful, as if the baby he had once been was looking at him across time and was trying to tell him something.

Jill was taking a long time in the aurum. He wished she would hurry up and come to bed.

His new cock didn't go with his hips, but maybe that was just as well, because in the last six months or so his bum had become wide, sagging and rubbery. The enormous crease between his buttocks was beginning to exude a peculiar, almost reptilian odour. The tight bottom he'd bought on impulse had lost its firmness in a few weeks, then it had spread at an alarming rate, becoming thick and lardy, eventually affecting every other part of his body – not only in an aesthetic way, as a horrible visual contrast, but also in terms of its weight. It had become a ponderous burden, a centre of gravity, and now he suspected that it was ready to go old on him. That was the trouble with geneplants – depending on the quality, they could age in anything between a week and a year or two. All the bigger companies were at work on the problem. Still, his new cock was good for the moment. He took it in his hand and was pleased to find that there was feeling in it.

He was also very pleased with his new breasts. Compared to some they were modest, small and firm and pink-nippled, with a delicate purity that made him think of rain and Scotland. He squeezed them together between his hands, then let them go and saw them spring back into their alert, outgoing attitude. It was reassuring to know that one of his distant cousins in time had probably grown such wonders all on her own without having to apply for them and pay for them. And he was getting her breasts before they had matured, before they had had to suckle babies. Who knows how many men had lusted after these breasts, just wanting to see them or touch them or give their mouths to them? Now they were his, but they were still strange to him – and what would Jill make of them?

She was depilating – he could hear the faint buzz of the depilator. She'd probably come out with a pudenda as bald as a billiard ball. Once she'd nodded off during depilation and had slumped in the seat. She had come out of the aurum without eyelashes and eyebrows and a drastically receding hairline. The next day she had finished the job and gone completely bald.

The buzz of the depilator ceased, then he heard the faint hum of the massager. So she was using the oils. When she used the oils on her body, it usually meant she was feeling adventurous. She had certainly hinted that tonight would be special, she was going to do something new.

Maybe, like him, she'd had one or two new geneplants, but he was hoping that it would be something else. He was hoping that tonight they would leave aside the VR equipment completely and experience real touch. He had wanted it since the night his visorscreen had been out of order and he'd had to rely completely on the network of feeling sensors in his VR suit and gloves. There was a name for it. It was called 'doing it in the dark' – people did it, sometimes, as a harmless kind of perversion. Real touch was something else. People didn't do real touch, or at least they didn't usually admit to it, but Jack was sure it was more common than *The Human* would have people believe.

Secretly, he'd wanted to touch Jill for a long time now, to touch her skin, and to have her touch him, to touch his skin, but he didn't know how to ask her for this and was afraid of how she'd react. He'd joked about it in such a way that she might get the message that this was what he wanted. Maybe she had, and maybe tonight this would be the 'something new' she had in mind. In any case he decided not to put on the VR suit and gloves just yet. But they were there, on his side of the bed, connected up to Jill's, on her side of the bed. He propped himself up on his elbow and popped the pills from their vacuum-pack.

They weren't Instants. He'd gone to great expense to get a Deep Multiple Bliss for her and a Rodeo Rider – 'Hold on as long as you can!' – for himself. It was important that she took hers before he took his. He could wait until she'd had her first climax before he popped it, then she'd have her second before being drawn inexorably into his. And he certainly would hold on as long as he could. Maybe they would even come together.

There was such a range of orgasm pills and injections and sprays on the market these days, it was always difficult to choose. He'd done a piece about it for *The Human* – a round-up of the options available legally and illegally, with a bit of overview commentary thrown in about the morality of it all, which had unfortunately been cut because there wasn't enough space. Still, at least they'd kept in his description of a group-orgasm he'd witnessed in a public park – a bunch of students celebrating the end of term – and they'd kept another bit he liked about a woman he saw having a quiet but unmistakably pill-induced orgasm as she ordered some banapples at the fruit-bank. Public orgasm had become a fad of life, and though it was more prevalent among those who were rich enough to stay young, some poor decaying people had started to do it too.

He laid the pills out, poured two glasses of highland water, selected some ambient Scottish Music – it sounded like a personal alarm device that wasn't working right – dimmed the lights, then pulled the sheet over his breasts. He didn't want the changes in his body shape to come as too much of a shock to Jill. It would be better if she discovered them gradually, during the dual virtual foreplay. Why was she taking so long? Jack wished she would hurry up and come to bed. His new cock seemed fine, but he hadn't taken it for a test-drive. Also, he was tired. He had had a hard day being groomed and packaged for his new site in *The Human*, which the editor had made clear was going to have to be about the most recent developments in virtual sex. If only he'd got the food site, things would be so much easier. It would just be a case of taking Jill out to eat and making fun of the food and the restaurant and the other diners.

While he was waiting for her he put the screen into sensory mode, slipped on the gloves and the visor and indulged in some solo virtual foreplay. He could use his own body, with its new parts, to stimulate the images. He stroked a breast with the fingerpads of his thinly gloved hand and watched as the milky skin dappled with sunlight began to form before his eyes. He began to see and hear and smell and taste and feel them, the memories of the breasts.

It was a cold sunny afternoon. The breasts were in a grave-yard. They were being fondled by a hand. He couldn't see the hand, or its owner. All he could do was feel it. And he could smell his breath, like a foul dishcloth. Then something else came: something sweet and nurturing, smelling of skin and milk and saliva. Then he saw the baby's head, swelling beneath his breast. So he was feeding a baby. The baby sucked and sucked until it was falling asleep. But just as it was falling asleep, the baby opened one eye and looked at him as if from very far away, with that same wise, thoughtful look he'd seen in his own baby image – my God, was he seeing himself? Had they given him his own mother's breasts?

He reached for his water and guided the glass to his lips. In a piece he had done recently for *The Human* he had used an analogy to describe what it felt like to do things in the real world while you were living in the virtual – he'd said it felt like being a blind man at the cinema. That had been it.

Maybe he should find out where the graveyard had been.

He pressed the search button on his hand-set. He knew from his genebank transactions that his ancestors had come from Scotland, but since Scotland no longer existed it was difficult to know what to look for.

When Jill dimmed his visorscreen, he saw that she was lying on the bed beside him. He was a little disappointed that she didn't seem to have changed – except that it was the first time she hadn't changed for a long time, and this in itself was a change. She looked exactly like the woman he had

gone to bed with last night, but maybe he was being com-
placent. There might be hidden changes he would discover
only during virtual lovemaking – maybe she had changed her
sexual needs – and at least she was naked, rather than wearing
any of those video transfers. Maybe he was right: tonight the
'something new' might be the thing he'd been craving. He
could feel the heat of her body next to him. He began to
unfasten his gloves.

'What are you doing?' said Jill.

'I think I know what it is,' said Jack.

'What what is?' said Jill.

'The something new,' said Jack.

'What?' said Jill.

'Touch,' said Jack.

'Touch?' said Jill.

'Real touch,' said Jack.

He held the gloves up by their spaghetti of wires before
discarding them. He turned to her, his naked hands rising
towards her naked neck, then he saw her mouth turning down
at the corners with disgust.

'No,' said Jill. 'Please don't, Jack.'

'What then?' asked Jack.

She moved aside to show him what she had brought from
the aurum: two syringes, one filled with a bloody liquid, the
other empty. A little disk. Even before he saw the GB logo
he knew it was a catalogue from the Gene Bank.

'I want to choose a baby,' said Jill.

Losing It

HE KNEW IT would do him no good to smash the monitor, but that didn't stop him. In one fluid movement he scooped up a heavy object – a glass ashtray, he found out later – and flung it at the screen, which burst with a strange popping noise as it imploded. There was the crash of broken glass falling inside the machine, then a light somewhere inside went out. That was it done: the computer monitor was fucked. He couldn't believe he had done it – he who depended on computers for his living. It would do him no good – unless it already had.

He was on his feet, breathing hard, shaking with anger. The computer went on making its neverending noise, even though the monitor was now completely fucked. He tried to remember the key command to shut it down – how the hell did you turn the thing off when you didn't have a screen? He reached for the computer manual on the shelf. What a hateful book it was, with its trite step-by-step explanations and its thick blue spine and its stupid, macho words like 'trouble-shooting'. He threw it at the wall and watched it splay open in mid-air and slap against the photo of his daughter Scarlet on the wall, before falling open at his feet like a shot bird. He kicked it across the room. A dangerous solution presented itself. Why not? The work was gone anyway, the work was lost. He bent down and wrenched the adaptor with all its plugs and wires from the socket. The buzz of the computer stopped, the anglepoise on his desk went out and the music he had on lurched to a stop. All that could be heard in the room was his own hoarse shout:

'Fuck you, bastard!'

He stabbed a finger at the monitor, as if to say it had got what it deserved. Then he began to shudder with a strange laughter: it burst in his chest like an underwater explosion and his throat was crowded with it as it rushed to his mouth and spilled out in a froth of giggles. Possessed by this glee-less laughter, he marched back and forth in the room, shaking his head and flailing his arms as if having to swim upstream. He lurched back to his desk and sagged into the chair. He looked at the monitor, at what he had done. He had lost it. He had lost it completely. Completely lost it. He couldn't believe that all that careful, detailed work over the course of weeks, months . . . Almost a year's work had gone, had van-ished into cyberspace in a split second.

He covered his face with his hands and groaned. It was unbearable to think about all the time he'd spent editing and re-editing, designing and re-designing. It was almost finished – at least, he was getting towards the end, even if he'd have to go through it again. Now it wasn't there to go through again. It was gone. Had he taken copies on disks? Not for weeks, and the last time he'd tried to use those disks, they hadn't let him in. The computer had given him a message that the disks had become unreadable. He remembered feeling annoyed about this at the time, but had he taken other copies?

He rummaged in the open drawer and found a box of disks. Some of them had labels on them with 'Accounts' or 'New' or 'c.v.' or 'working documents'. Others had blank labels and others again had no labels, they were just disks that hadn't been used yet or disks that had been used and had stopped working, had become unreadable. Unreadable – it sounded like a criticism and this made him all the more furious as he flicked through the disks in the box but didn't find the damn ones he was looking for. When he had flicked through all of them he snapped the box shut and threw it back into the drawer. He was fucked. He was completely fucked. All that work, for nothing. All that work he would have to do again, like Sisyphus and his stone.

He thought of Sisyphus shouldering his stone, trying to get it to the top of the hill. But just as he's about to get there, the stone gains so much inertia and feels so heavy that it's impossible to push it any further. Then Sisyphus feels the stone rolling back down the hill a bit. Of course, he tries to stop it, but there comes a point when he can't – because of certain laws of physics and gravity and because he's fucked. And at this moment when Sisyphus decides or realises that there's no point in trying to push, there is a choice. The choice is: he can either jump out of the way and let the stone go, or he can stay where he is and keep pushing, in which case the stone will crush him in its downward path. It's not much of a choice, but it is a choice. And every time Sisyphus gets to this point, it occurs to him that there is this choice between life and death.

Of course, Sisyphus is a fly guy. He's outwitted death before, locking Hades in his own handcuffs with the oldest dodge in the book – 'Hey, show me how they work, sir . . .' – so Sisyphus jumps out of the way and lets the stone roll back down the hill, because even if he's doomed, he's out-witted death again. Sisyphus wants to stay alive, at any price. Even if it means rolling a fucking stone up a fucking hill for the rest of his fucking life. So he picks himself up and walks back down the hill – and this must have been the only good bit of Sisyphus's life since he'd got the stone-rolling job: the downhill stroll. At a leisurely pace, with rests.

He smiled a bitter smile, and felt a strange elation. He'd

let the stone go. Maybe now it was time for the downhill stroll. He had to admit that it felt good to have let his anger out, let go of it completely. He couldn't remember losing it so completely for years – not with his kids, not with his wife, not with anybody. Not since he'd been in a fight in the playground at school. Sitting on another boy's chest, drumming his fists on the other boy's head. And he hadn't been able to stop, because he was out of control. He'd lost it then. But he was an adult now. He had learnt the virtue of restraint, if it was a virtue.

To lose it with a computer like that . . . but maybe it wasn't the computer, maybe he'd lost it with himself. How could such a thing have happened? All that carefully compiled information had melted into nothing. It was gone. Had he at least taken a printout of the data involved? Yes, but the last time he had taken a printout had been before he'd decided to reshape and reorganise the material completely and he wasn't even sure if he still had it. He tugged open another drawer and rummaged among the clutter of letters and calculators and screwdrivers and photographs and batteries and lightbulbs and bankbooks – what a fucking mess that drawer was. Of course it wasn't in there. He didn't keep printouts in that drawer. That drawer was for everything else. He'd probably lost that printout, and anyway, that printout was so incomplete he'd be better to start again, start from scratch.

As he put a cigarette in his mouth and lit it, he noticed that his fingers were shaking. So he had smashed the monitor. So he'd have to buy a new monitor. But that was the least of it. He would have to start again. Virtually from scratch. If he could get into those disks, the ones that wouldn't let him in, he would be halfway there. He would be where he had been six months ago, if they let him in. If not, it was gone, it was all gone. What would Louise think when she came home? What would Scarlet think, when she came in from school? What would they think when they saw the smashed monitor? What had happened to the ashtray? He reached into the guts of the monitor and found it, intact.

Though it was only half past three, it was beginning to get dark when he loaded the cardboard box into the boot and drove around the city looking for a skip. He did see a couple, but they were being used by workmen, and he didn't like the idea of asking them if it was okay if he could dump something in their skip. Anyway, there were a lot of people around – people hurrying home from work, or hurrying to work, hurrying because it was getting dark and it was cold and outside was no place to be.

At this very moment Scarlet would be on her way home from school. He hoped she had her key. If not, she'd have to wait until Louise got back. He took out his mobile and switched it on. It rang immediately, but he had to put it down on the passenger seat while he turned a corner and looked for a skip. He pressed the button and heard a woman's voice. It was his boss, asking him in a very measured way how he was and hoping the work was going well. He would have to tell her it was gone, that he'd need another three months min-imum. It wasn't so outrageous. She would probably under-stand. When you told people that you had a problem with your computer, they tended to be sympathetic, as if you'd told them you had the flu.

He pulled out his mobile and thought about paging Scarlet – but of course, you couldn't do that from a mobile, so he pulled over at the first phone box he saw, turned his head-lights off and climbed out of the car. In the phone box he took out his wallet and rifled through a wad of bills, receipts and money until he found the little piece of paper with his daughter's pager number on it and the list of number codes. He punched in Scarlet's number and heard the woman's voice thanking him for using this service, then instructing him to say his number, one digit at a time, after each tone. It was a cheap pager that used number codes instead of text, and now he paused as he ran his eye over the list of codes . . . 604 – 'hugs and kisses' . . . 216 – 'stuck in traffic' . . . 1664 – 'fancy a beer?' . . . 220 – 'where are you?' . . . until he found it: 4164 – 'I'll be late home'. He spoke the numbers after the tones. The woman's voice read the numbers back to him and asked him to say 'yes' if they were correct or 'no' if they weren't after the tone. He said 'yes' and listened to the woman's voice telling him his message had been accepted, then he hung up, stuffed his papers back into his wallet, his coins into his pocket and went back to his car.

Would Scarlet have her pager switched on anyway? Would she switch it on, when she got out of school? Would she re-member the number code? Would the message get through? Even if it did, what difference would it make? If she had her key, she'd let herself in anyway. If she didn't, she'd have to wait.

He pulled back on to the street and looked for a skip. Wouldn't it look odd, a man stopping his car and lifting a heavy box out of the boot and dumping it in a skip? He headed out towards the bypass. He'd been to the city dump once before, to get rid of some stuff the bucket men wouldn't take, some rubble and bricks from knocking the arch from the kitchen to the dining-room, stuff they called builder's waste. He couldn't remember where it was exactly, but it was out towards the bypass somewhere.

As he accelerated he noticed that there was a new noise coming from the car, from somewhere underneath. The exhaust. A strange growling noise, as if something had cor-roded to the point of coming off. He'd have to have it replaced with a spanking brand new exhaust – but what did the garage do with the old one? And what happened to the files you dumped from the computer? You put them in the wastebasket and then you emptied the wastebasket, but then where did they go? Limbo files. In his first computer, there had been a thing called 'limbo files'. You could retrieve something you had erased or thrown away. Maybe the work was still there in the computer's memory, in the dump for discarded files. Maybe he could pay somebody to go through his mountain of trashed files, looking for the ones he wanted back, needed back. He couldn't believe all that work had ceased to exist. It had to be out there somewhere still. The growling was definitely there, persistent – underneath, towards the back of the car – he wasn't just imagining it.

He came to a mini-roundabout and didn't know which way to go, so he kept on going. He passed the car dump where he'd tried to get rid of his last car – a godforsaken place surrounded by a twenty-foot-high fence. He'd driven into it one afternoon, when it was clear that it was time to get rid of his car, thinking that he'd get a taxi back into town once he'd sold it for scrap. He'd stopped the car in front of a wasteland of dumped cars, but he hadn't got out, because a lean alsation leapt from the doorway of a hut and ran around the car barking fiercely. Sitting there in that grim place with the angry dog, in a car he wasn't sure would start again, he'd felt his heart panicking, like an animal trapped in his chest. When no one appeared and the dog kept on barking at him, he had started up the car and driven out of there. He'd got rid of the car somewhere else, a few days later.

A couple of miles out of town, he saw the sign: Waste

Recycling Unit, and the city council's logo. He pulled off the road and followed the track up to the gates. He was just in time – a man in a fluorescent boilersuit was just about to close them, but he pulled the gate back and waved him in. He followed the signs past the bottle banks and the recycling unit for car batteries. He found himself in a queue of cars, and he switched the engine off while he waited. Every time he started the car to move forward, the exhaust sounded worse. It was definitely the exhaust. He would have to get the car to a garage. The exhaust was fucked. He might even have to call the AA. He was going to have to get the car fixed, before he did anything about the lost work.

The dark machines glinted in the yellow overhead lights as they ground and crunched and squashed the stuff men threw into them. The machines seemed to be vehicles of some sort – at least, they sat on what looked like tram-tracks. When his turn came, he opened the boot and lifted out the box with the fucked monitor in it. A man in a fluorescent boilersuit, a cap with ear flaps and gloves that made his hands look huge pointed to one of the machines. He carried it over to the machine and threw it in, then he stood back and watched the great metal jaws eating it and forcing it down.

He got back in the car and turned the key in the ignition. The exhaust sounded like anger itself as he changed gear and accelerated out of the place, with its infernal machines masticating in the darkness. Back in the town, when he was stopped at the lights on the way to the garage, he took his mobile out and switched it on. He pressed a button and heard a woman's voice telling him that he had no new messages, then he pressed the button to get his own number. He phoned his own number and got the answer-phone. He heard his own voice trying to be as neutral as possible as it told him: 'Hello, this is John. I'm sorry you got the machine. If you have a message for me, Louise or Scarlet, please wait until you hear the tone.' He waited until he heard the tone. He was about to leave the message when he lost the signal completely.

The Host

'SO. HOW. WAS. The. Film.'

I was speaking in words but I didn't know what I was saying and my voice sounded thick and moronic and my mouth was dry and my heart was hammering and my skin felt like a cold chamois leather as I touched my face with my fingers – no doubt the way I would normally touch my face with my fingers if I was asking somebody about a film they'd been to see but nothing was normal because here in my room was a man with two heads.

For a horrible moment there was no response from anyone. Had the words come out of my mouth at all or had they come out sounding so strange that no one could make sense of them? Was it my drugs? Had I forgotten to take my drugs? No, I had taken them earlier. Had I got the dosage wrong? No, I distinctly remembered taking the correct dosage.

'Well, I thought it was not a bad film, but the book—'

I felt a surge of gratitude to Jim. He had heard my question and he was answering it. He was talking about the film, thank God, so for the moment the attention of the room was not focused on me. Had nobody noticed that I was trembling and sweating and finding it difficult to speak?

I tried to pick up my glass and get it to my mouth. I couldn't help turning a little to check that the man who had been introduced to me as Douglas really did have two heads. I had seen the other head quite clearly when he'd come into the room and shaken my hand – lolling on his shoulder, as if it couldn't quite support itself. I'd had to look away as I'd said my pleased-to-meet-you.

It was there all right, I hadn't imagined it. In the dim light of my room it was difficult to see the crumpled features of the face, which was as pale as a cauliflower, but I could make out two screwed-up eyes, closed tightly under wispy, whitish eyebrows. I could see no clearly defined nose, but the lips were unmistakable – they looked dry and cracked and unnaturally old. Unnaturally old – that is the meaningless phrase that came into my mind. The face had set into an expression which was both sour and aloof. The way the lips curled down at one side and up at the other made me think of a kind of bitter relish, as if the owner of the mouth might take pleasure in sarcasm. At the same time there was something dreadfully vulnerable in the face's frozen sneer and the way the head lolled against the back of the armchair Douglas was sitting in – to all appearances a dead appendage. And no one seemed to have noticed it. Douglas himself appeared to be completely relaxed, as if utterly unaware of his encumbrance. He struck me as a congenial sort of guy, probably in his early thirties. Apart from his other head, his appearance was quite ordinary. He had longish brown hair and a neat beard. He looked mildly interested in the world and had a constant, rather vacant smile. He wore a dark blue jacket, jeans and a casual, checked shirt.

But he had another head.

A red-haired woman I didn't know and whose name I hadn't taken in was disagreeing with Jim about the film and there were one or two comments interjected by the others – including Douglas. He didn't say much – as far as I could make out, he was agreeing with the general drift of the discussion about the film. He was quietly spoken, maybe even a bit shy, but it was the kind of shyness which hints at an inner confidence.

THE HOST

They were having this good-natured, not-too-serious sort
of debate about the merits of the film they'd been to see –
for all the world as if nothing was out of the ordinary. I felt
a moment of relief. The hammering of my heart was slowing
down to a steady, heavy pounding. Although I'd raised my
glass of wine to my lips I still hadn't taken a drink. Now I
gulped some of it down in the hope that it would steady my
nerves.

Was I over-reacting? I was with friends, after all. Jim was
a friend, a good friend, I had known him since my school-
days. He often did my shopping for me, and that meant a lot
to me. One or two of the others had been coming to see me
for over a year now. There were strangers, but Jim often
brought people back after a late-night film. It was supposed
to do me good, help me cope with my agoraphobia, which he
thought he understood. At least he understood that it wasn't
just the fear of open spaces. He knew that it went hand in
hand with claustrophobia. He understood that my fear was
the fear of people. So he brought them round. It was supposed to encourage me to overcome it – or so I'd thought.
Tonight he'd gone over the score. There were too many of
them tonight. I couldn't see them clearly one by one as people,
they were blurred into the same animal. I kept seeing movements of the feet and the hands but I didn't know whose they
were. But although I saw them as one, at the same time I felt
desperately outnumbered. It was difficult to hold on to myself.

Had Jim brought all these people round out of a spirit of
charity or therapy? Maybe it was also convenient for him.
Maybe he didn't want to take them all to his place. Here he
was, acting for all the world as if he was doing me a favour
by crowding out my house with the entire membership, I
shouldn't wonder, of the local film club – one of whom had
an extra head.

I glared at Jim, hoping to convey my displeasure with him in no uncertain terms, but he went on elaborating on some crucial discrepancy between the book and the film. He'd never brought this Douglas back before, I was certain of that, but people in the company seemed to know him, or if they didn't, they seemed to have accepted the fact that he had two heads with no trouble at all. Or maybe they were being polite. Maybe everyone in the room was doing his best not to look at it or talk about it, but inside they were panicking just as much as me. Or could it be that they were being quietly supportive? After all, an extra head, one which seemed to serve no purpose, must be a dreadful disability and Douglas seemed to be coping with it incredibly well. Maybe later on, I thought – but only if Douglas brings the subject up and wants to talk about it – maybe then I'll ask him if he has ever thought about the possibility of having it surgically removed. Oh God – no! I couldn't possibly ask him that – what was I thinking of?

Douglas leaned forward to flick his ash into the ashtray on the coffee-table. The head sprang forward to hang over his shoulder. With a start that set my pulse racing and almost made me yelp with fright, I noticed that one eye had opened a little and seemed to be peering at me as if from a great distance. When Douglas leaned back slowly – apparently he was listening to the post-mortem of the film with interest – the other head still hung forward, leaning one cheek on the collar of his jacket. I shuddered as I made out for the first time the tiny, creased nostrils. The head had, I was sure of it, taken a breath.

'So what do you think?'

Jim had turned to put this question to me and everyone now looked to me, their host, for an opinion.

'Well . . . I mean, obviously . . . not having seen it—'

'But would you go to see it, on the basis of what we've said, or have we put you off going?'

'Well, I wouldn't want to go to a cinema, but—'

What was I doing? Trying to make light of my own condition? Or drawing attention to it, to spare Douglas the attention of the room? But then, no one was looking at him, everyone was looking at me, and I didn't know how to go on.

Jim smiled and said: 'You asked us what we thought of the film.'

'No, you don't know what . . . I wasn't asking you what the film was *about*, what I *meant* was . . . what was it like to go and see a film, to sit in a place in the dark with . . . a crowd of other . . . I mean . . .'

I trailed off, trying to use the glass and the wine as an excuse to interrupt myself. I truly could not go on, not only because I was talking nonsense but also because the image of a crowded, darkened cinema had come into my mind, with its rows of silhouetted heads. One or two people laughed, apparently under the impression that I was being deliberately obtuse out of a sense of mischief. Jim looked at me in a pointedly puzzled way. I spluttered on my wine. I made the most of it, pretending that it had gone down the wrong way and I was having a coughing fit. Someone sitting next to me obliged by thumping me on the back, but in the middle of it I began to wheeze with disbelief. The head had now opened both eyes and was looking around the room.

Douglas took the cigarette from his mouth and, without even looking at what he was doing, placed it carefully in the other head's mouth. The other head sucked on it with some difficulty, then Douglas removed the cigarette and went on smoking it himself. A thin jet of smoke came from the other head's mouth, which was as desiccated as a shelled walnut, then it gave a little cough. How can I explain how this little cough made me feel? It was like a baby's cough, alarming because it hints at an articulacy and a history no one would expect of it. The sound of it made me shudder inside, as if on the verge of tears. I had to suppress a heavy sob welling in my chest. But now it was doing something else: I watched the head's mouth in awe as its dark, liverish tongue licked its cracked lips before speaking:

'That was very interesting.'

The eyelids of both eyes had parted, but were still stuck together at the corners in a way that looked extremely uncomfortable. The eyes, deep blue in colour, looked enormous in the shrunken face. But it was the look in the eyes . . . How can I describe it? There was infinite depth and distance in it, as if it was still looking at something in another world it had just come from. Yes, that was it, the head was waking up. The eyelids blinked rapidly to unstick themselves completely and now the dark eyes looked directly at me.

'I don't mean what you were saying, but the way you were pretending to cough. Most people don't cough unless they have to, do they?'

The voice was rather thin and chesty, with a squeaky quality that made it sound slightly comical. It was like the voice of a very old man, but it also sounded like the voice of a child, made harsh by some bronchial illness. The other head smiled with one corner of its mouth, then uttered another babyish cough.

I couldn't answer. I was aware of the babble of voices around us. Apparently Jim was being witty and people were laughing. No one was paying the slightest attention to me or the head which had just addressed me. They were having a good time, apparently, but I was breathing hard and trembling and my hands were sweating so much they felt gloved in oil as I tried to find something to say to this head, this other head growing out of a man's neck.

I looked to Jim to rescue me, but he was engrossed in some kind of intellectual duel with the red-haired woman. Of course, it was transparent to me that they were flirting. If only that had been all that was going on in my room – but no, there had to be a man with another head that wanted to talk to me. Douglas himself showed no interest whatsoever in the head even though it had woken up so conspicuously. He seemed completely preoccupied with stubbing his cigarette out, refilling his glass and following the conversation.

The crumpled face was waiting with an infinitely patient sadness. I had to say something.

'I'm sorry. It's just that I . . . don't know how . . . I've never met a person with . . .'

'Two heads? Is that what you're driving at?'

'Well . . . I suppose so.'

The head, hanging at an angle so that it seemed to be peering around a corner, did its best to nod with resignation.

'It's more common than you think.'

'What is?'

'Two heads.'

'Really? I had no idea.'

'Lots of people have two heads. Ask him.'

The other head indicated Douglas with a movement of its eyes and gave out a sharp little giggle. I glimpsed a row of neat, square teeth. Douglas raised the wine glass to his other head's lips, taking care not to spill it. This he managed to do without so much as glancing at the other head. Even so a drop of wine dribbled from the corner of the mouth. Douglas put the glass back down and took a tissue from his jacket pocket, with which he dabbed the other head's chin – though there was little in the way of what would normally be called a chin. All this he performed while staring straight ahead, apparently quite engrossed in the discussion about the film.

For a moment I saw Douglas and his other head as a music-hall double-act – the ventriloquist and his dummy. As if by telepathy, the other head looked at me and said: 'A gottle a geer.'

It chuckled at its own joke and the sound of its gargling laughter made me want to cry again. I had to fight back the shuddering sobs which wracked me inside and threatened to burst out at any moment. I call the other head 'it' because that is how I thought of this extraordinary phenomenon, but now I was forced to confront the fact that 'it' was a thinking, feeling being – 'it' was, I had to admit, a person. Had the poor man been someone's other head all his life? It was an intolerable thought.

The small, puckered face smiled up at me.

'How old do you think I am?'

My attempt at congenial laughter, as if we were engaged in the everyday social game of guess-how-old-I-am, left a lot to be desired. The small face with its vast, deep eyes watched me steadily as I brayed unconvincingly, waiting for my answer.

It was very difficult to tell how old he was. The eyes were as steady and watchful as a child's, yet they had a terribly knowing quality, as if they had seen the worst atrocities of humanity – the kind of thing most of us only read about in the newspapers. I could no longer meet their consuming gaze, and I studied Douglas – his main head and face, I mean, but also his clothes and his hands – before venturing:

'Well . . . younger than me – thirty? Thirty-one?'

The other head snorted briefly and said:

'That's *his* age. What about mine?'

'I have no idea when you . . . came about.'

'Came about? Oh, you make the mistake of thinking I grew out of *him*. No, my friend, you have it all wrong . . .'

I was alarmed by the way one of Douglas's hands suddenly stabbed a finger emphatically at his own chest.

'You see, *he* grew out of *me*.'

The hand now flew up to the uppermost side of the other head's face and scratched a loose flap of skin – it must be, I realised, an earlobe – then it swooped to the coffee-table and, in one fluid movement, lifted Douglas's glass of wine to the other head's mouth.

'My God, *you* did that!'

The other head drained the glass, set it down carefully on the coffee-table and smirked at me with pride, as if it had proven its point beyond question.

'My God. I see.'

The head nodded to me then, and with a look of profound sadness said softly:

'*Now* you see.'

And I did see. I saw Douglas in a completely new way, now that it was clear that his other head could control his body. His main head, his normal head – or the one I had taken to be 'main' and 'normal' – now looked gross, a bland and doltish growth which had brutally usurped the other head's place, pushing it aside and, for all I knew, drawing succour from it, like a fungus sapping the life of the tree from which it has swollen. His open, rather vacantly smiling expression now appeared to me as abhorrent as the sated leer of a callous parasite. The other head looked weak, drained of life, dying.

'Yes, he's taken over. I'm on the way out.'

'That's terrible!'

The other head smiled at me sadly.

'Oh, not so terrible. He's better-looking than me. He's nicer, he'll get on all right. Less intelligent, of course, and less honest – but that will be to his advantage. It was nice to meet you. You've been a very good host. But you look pale – you should get out more often.'

The other head yawned, winked at me, then the fragile eyelids drooped and closed. He snuffled a little before his breathing slowed to a barely perceptible whisper in the air.

Douglas leaned back and the head swung behind his neck and subsided among the shadows of the armchair. His dominant head turned to look at me, as if he expected me to speak. Everyone was looking at me, waiting for me to speak. Jim had asked me a question and now he was repeating it:

'Are you all right?'

I tried to pick up my glass but my hand shook uncontrollably. Thankfully the glass was almost empty. Someone relieved me of it, there were other people's hands and faces everywhere, then Jim said something about there being too many for me.

'One too many, just one too many.'

I looked at Douglas meaningfully as I said it and his eyes widened with baffled alarm. He stood up, and there was a sudden consensus in the room: everyone was standing up, draining glasses, putting coats and scarves on. The blur of all that activity made me feel nauseous, dizzy. Voices kept offering me their apologetic thanks.

Jim, crouching down beside my chair, asked me again if I was all right. This really was the last straw. He brings enough people to my house to fill a small cinema – one of them a double-header into the bargain – then he asks me if I'm all right! I stood up, pushing him aside, and shouted:

'*I'm* all right. Ask your friend there how his other head is. Ask him if *he's* all right!'

But Douglas was already shuffling hurriedly into the

hallway, where a few of the others were waiting to leave. Jim looked at me with puzzled concern.

'Take it easy now. We're going.'

'About time too.'

Jim turned and raised his eyebrows to the woman with the red hair. It was evident to me that they had formed an unspoken pact. It would be back to his place, or hers, for sexual congress. But would it bring them closer to each other, or even to themselves? Somehow I did not think so. I suspected that their transaction between the sheets would leave both of them feeling lonelier than they had felt before, if either of them had ever felt truly lonely.

Jim said he'd call round in a day or two, thanked me for my hospitality and said they'd see themselves out. That was just as well, because I didn't feel particularly like standing around in my own doorway, exposed to the elements as I exchanged farewells with him and his army of film buffs. Let them go out into the street, under the empty sky. It was all right for them, they could do that with their eyes wide open and their heads held high, without the dread and the panic and the keeping near the wall and the scurrying for cover like a beetle when its stone is overturned.

When the front door eventually closed, I breathed more freely. The room seemed to settle into place around me, it became familiar again, but I felt exhausted by the evening's events. I wanted the warm cocoon of my bed. In reality it would be cold, unless I filled myself a hot-water bottle, and I felt too tired to do that. It was hard work, being the host. It was all I could do to tidy up the glasses and bottles and ashtrays before going to the bathroom to clean my teeth.

As I pulled the switch-cord, the sudden bright light made my reflection jump out of the mirror at me. The roar of the

Xpelair couldn't drown out my gasp of outrage at what I saw. It was there, no matter how often I wiped the condensation from the mirror with my sleeve, a mushroom-like swelling on my neck: the face was not fully formed, but already I could make out the mildly interested eyes and the constant, rather vacant smile.

Petit Mal

THE THESIS WAS already a year late and he was sick to the back teeth of predestination and the eternal recurrence. He wanted to get the damned thing finished so that he could begin to think about what he was going to do next. Part of the problem was that he'd been jilted by his girlfriend Helen six months ago, and it still felt like a defeat to be on his own. Was their separation predestined? Maybe not – she'd just got a job in Newcastle, and met someone else. That was the cruel thing about it: it was just ordinary. It wasn't because they couldn't stand to see each other any more or anything dramatic like that. It was just geography. Geography had come between them, and a Maths post-grad from Durham. So they had split up. It was pathetic, so pathetic that it made him wonder if their relationship had been worth anything in the first place. Perhaps, after all, she had jilted him because of his epilepsy. That thought had been growling at the back of his mind all summer, while he worked as a barman in the post-graduates' union, skinning what he could from the takings and eventually saving enough to rent the cottage for the winter – one of a row of six which had at one time housed farm workers. She had seen him having a *grand mal* only once – at a post-graduate party, unfortunately – but no doubt it had stayed in her mind.

The unfinished thesis was spread out over the table behind him as he looked out of the window beyond the farm to the firth. He watched the rain sweeping over the landscape in a series of waves, a pattern that must be caused by something. If everything was caused by something apart from a First Cause, then everything was random. Or rather, everything formed a kind of logical pattern, but this pattern was based on something quite random and unpredictable, if it was based on anything. Although he had stopped believing in God and had refuted the design argument more than once, here He was again, glowering at him from the heart of his thesis.

He turned from the window and looked at the clock on the mantelpiece. He should have taken his medication before now, but he felt suddenly hungry. He had been trying to eat only as a matter of necessity, but now he felt ravenous. He went into the kitchen and opened the fridge. The little brown bottles jiggled in the rack other people might keep salad dressing in. He should take the Phenytoin, but he felt the need to eat first, and there was nothing left of the food he'd brought with him when he'd moved in a week ago, apart from half a carton of milk and two slices of greenish bacon. He looked in the cupboard above the fridge and found a packet of cornflakes and a rusting can of spaghetti hoops left by the previous tenant. There were a few slices of stale bread in the bread bin he could make toast with, a couple of potatoes in the vegetable rack, but it didn't add up to a meal.

He heard a hen clucking outside the back door. Of course! There were eggs to be had on the farm – he remembered the farmer's wife telling him – from one of the sheds opposite the farmhouse.

Outside, the weather hit him: a howling gale, the same howling gale he had grown up with on Lewis, and which seemed to follow him wherever he went, as if the weather was in his bones as well as the theory of predestination which seemed to underpin Presbyterianism. If only he'd done a thesis

on the philosophy underpinning Buddhism, or Hinduism, anything but the one he'd grown up with.

Holding his collar up around his ears, he hurried down the
muddy track to the outhouses opposite the farmhouse. There
were various doors, some padlocked shut. He found the egg
shed after the one for rubbish. When he drew the bolt and
pulled the heavy door open, a bird flew out of somewhere in
the dark rafters, passing so close to his face that its wing
whirred against his cheek. He jerked aside and his head
clunked against the door frame.

Then it came on: as if he was on the ferry and the sea was
rough enough to make atheists pray. Was he leaving or
returning? It made no difference, because the sea was rising
up and swallowing him, sucking him down into its black
depths.

When he surfaced, he steadied himself against the door
frame, seeing dark spots swarming in front of his eyes. He
veered and convulsed, but there was nothing to throw up. His
stomach lurched as the hull was sucked into the trough and
he gasped. A sentence he had written that afternoon came
into his mind: 'Chaos is everywhere, and we fool ourselves if
we think that our order has made sense of it.' What did it
mean? He would have to erase it. The thoughts surrounding
this sentence in his mind, the ones he had yet to put to paper,
had been erased forever by the fit, which left him shaking and
splayed in the doorway like a puppet whose strings have been
dropped, the puppeteer having lost interest.

He could make out dismantled bikes and bits of farm
machinery on the ceiling below, except that it wasn't the ceiling
and he wasn't above it. It was the wall and he was sitting
opposite it. There was a rancid animal smell, as if something
had died here. Or maybe the smell was coming from him:
had he pissed himself? He felt his crotch with his hand. It

was dry, but even a *petit mal* took a bit of you away for good, it always did. It was alarming to be robbed of consciousness, and yet it was something that happened to everyone every night of their lives, when they went to sleep.

As a boy, he'd thought they were caused by God, that God was sending a bolt of electric wrath through him as a punishment for something he'd done or had not done. Once, he tore a page out of his bible in school, to see if doing something wrong would bring on a fit. And it did. Less than an hour later it had come on, a *grand mal*, and no doubt the whole class had watched him as he spasmed and gnashed his teeth and pissed himself, kicking and thrashing out at the desk and chair he was trapped in.

He stood up and moved around in the dark outhouse like a blind man in a strange room. The eggs were laid out in a cardboard tray on top of an old chest of drawers, alongside a square biscuit tin with 'Hen Money' written on it. He pulled the lid off and found a smattering of coins, a hardbacked notebook and a biro. He opened the notebook but could barely read the names and the amounts written by the others from the neighbouring cottages who'd bought eggs. He felt in his pockets and realised he'd come out without money. Okay, he could pay later.

The wind spat an icy rain in his face as he slogged his way back up the muddy track. The sky had darkened, and there was going to be no moon tonight. He thought about Helen, about making love to her, as he reached the cottage and opened the door. He walked in, shaking the rain from his hair, still thinking about her as he kicked off his boots in the hallway, how she sometimes liked to change position in the middle of things, bending one leg up to turn over underneath him, until her back was to him, then she'd raise herself up on her knees and push against him . . . As he crossed the living-room and put the eggs on the table, he noticed it was covered with a batik tablecloth that hadn't been there before. Had the farmer's wife, deciding that he needed a tablecloth, come and put one on the table while he was out for the eggs? There was also a vase of wild flowers on the table and propped against the vase there was a note. It was written on some kind of thick, creamy paper and the message had been carefully printed with a calligraphy pen. It said: 'I don't hate you. I love you.'

My God, he thought, the farmer's wife doesn't hate me – though it had never occurred to him that she might – no, she loves me! He had only met her twice, when she'd showed him the cottage and when he'd moved in. Both times she'd seemed to him a very pleasant woman, but she was his landlady and she was married to the farmer and she had children and she must be twenty years older than him and now she was in love with him. Such things happened, sometimes. Destiny overtook people, it plucked them like wild berries from a bush.

He was startled to see an oval mirror above the fireplace that hadn't been there before, and in fact the fireplace itself was different. Instead of an open hearth, it was fitted with a wood-burning stove. Now that he looked around, he saw that the entire room was different – the carpet, the curtains, the furniture – everything had been changed and rearranged. There were house-plants in every corner of the room – on the windowsill, the bookshelves, the coffee-table, the mantelpiece, everywhere.

He stared into the oval mirror and saw his own face change expression from confusion to realisation: he was in the wrong house. He had come into the wrong cottage, the cottage next door, his neighbour's cottage. Maybe it was the fit. It had knocked him sideways. His concentration had gone, it had been erased. He was confused. He needed his drugs. He should have taken the Phenytoin hours ago.

Everything was different, but in essence the room was a replica of his living-room, with the same alcove by the window and the same arrangement of doors. He tilted his head as he stared at everything in the room, as if trying to decipher a message in mirror-writing. Part of his brain was still reluctant to admit that he wasn't in his own cottage, and was still clinging to the impossible: yes, the farmer's wife had fallen in love with him, so much so that she had taken it upon herself to completely redecorate his cottage and write a love-note to him – and all while he was out getting the eggs!

There was a dirty, metallic taste in his mouth as if he'd been sucking a coin, and his fingers shook as he picked up the note. 'I don't hate you. I love you.' Who had written it? Who was it for? Not for him, but something in him still clung to the notion that this was a message for him, even if it had been intended for somebody else.

He propped it back up against the vase of flowers.

He let out a panicky laugh as he picked up the eggs and hurried into the hallway. He tugged on his boots, grabbed his coat and whirled out the door, hearing the hollow yowl of the wind as it roamed over the empty hills and amplified in the firth. He didn't think he'd been seen.

He kicked his boots off in the hall and came in, throwing his coat over the couch and putting the eggs on the table beside his thesis. He sat down in the armchair by the fire and covered his mouth with a hand. To go into the wrong house like that – what would the woman who lived there think if she knew? What was her name? He couldn't remember. He'd met her only once, on the day he'd moved in, and now he found it difficult to remember anything about her. He'd gone out of the back door to get logs for the fire and she'd been hanging some wet underwear on a washing line she'd rigged up between two trees. He'd looked away as they'd chatted, away from her and the underwear which, although plain enough, had embarrassed him, and he'd felt all the more embarrassed about being embarrassed by something like that, at his age.

A car drew up outside the cottages. He went to the window. He saw a gaunt, grey-haired man wearing a long dark coat getting out and hurrying into the cottage next door. He listened for the man's movements but could hear nothing. He imagined the man picking up the note and reading it: 'I don't hate you. I love you.' He went into the kitchen, switched on the radio and cracked three of the eggs into a bowl. He started to whisk them with a fork, then he heard the door opening next door and the man going outside. He walked to the front window and caught sight of him throwing a suitcase into the boot of the car before driving off.

He was eating the last of the omelette when he heard another car drawing up outside. He rose quickly and stepped over to the window. He caught a glimpse of her scarf blown back by the wind as she ran to her door. He heard the door crashing shut, then nothing.

In bed, he listened: surely he would hear something – the shattering of a glass against a wall, a stifled sob. He lay with his eyes wide open, not moving, listening. There was nothing to be heard except the wind, battering against the windows as if demanding to be let in.

When he woke up the next morning his neck and shoulder were stiff because of the awkward position he'd slept in. He heard something – a whisper of something slipping over the floor outside his bedroom door. He put on his jeans and a T-shirt, stepped out into the chilly hallway and saw, between his bare feet, the cream-coloured envelope on the floor.

★ ★ ★

The rain made such a loud drumming on the roof and against the windows, he found it impossible to concentrate. He'd been mad to think that moving to a quiet, country place would help him to work. He pushed the papers aside, stood up and walked to the window. He watched the rain falling in windswept sheets above the fields, all the way down to the firth. He looked down at the windowsill, saw the envelope with the key and her note and picked it up. He read through her note again, telling him that she'd be away for a couple of weeks and asking him to water her plants. She'd only been gone two days – her plants would hardly be in need of water yet. He took the key from the envelope and raised it to his lips.

He pushed open the door into the living-room and stepped inside. It seemed warmer than his cottage, even without the fire lit. He switched on an anglepoise which stood on a little table beside one of the armchairs and was pleased by the effect of the bright light. It would be good to sit down there, surrounded by plants, and read through his notes. He looked at the table – the vase of flowers was still there, without the note, of course. The note had been read by whoever it was meant for – him, or her? Somehow he knew that she had written it. If a man were to write such a note, surely he wouldn't use a calligraphy pen.

He padded into the kitchen, moving as if afraid he might disturb somebody or something by his presence. He had been here before, by accident, and still felt like an intruder. He looked at some photographs which had been arranged in a clip-frame and hung on the wall above the fridge. They were of her at different ages, some with her parents, one with a dog, and in some she was with a man, probably the one in the long dark coat: sitting at a dinner-table with a lot of other people; standing on a sunlit beach somewhere abroad, both of them wearing sarongs; standing outside the cottage together, arm in arm and smiling. There was a whole version of her life there in the clip-frame. He opened the fridge and reached for a bottle.

He poured himself a gin and tonic and added some ice cubes from the ice tray. He topped up the tray with water before he put it back, then replaced the bottles. He wandered through to the bedroom with the drink in his hand. When he noticed the CD player on top of the chest of drawers, he pressed the 'play' button and some slow, throbbing music came on.

It was good here. It was very good. He felt as if he had been here before – and of course he had, by mistake, so the feeling wasn't a *déjà vu* exactly. It was more the sense that his mistake was something predestined. Something had fated him to come into the wrong house, and this had put a twist into his life, like the twist in a möbius strip which made it a one-sided, one-edged, infinite loop. In the story of his life, going into the wrong house would always be there, and who knows what it might lead to? If it was predestined, if it was part of an eternal recurrence, he'd have to live through this moment again and again. The absurdity of this idea struck him and he uttered a scornful laugh.

He put his drink down on the chest of drawers and slid the top drawer open. He put both his hands into the drawer, closed his eyes and explored the tangled mass of her underwear. It was a long time – six months, to be exact – since he'd touched a woman's underwear. He breathed deeply as he ran his fingers over the cotton and the satin and the silk and the nylon and the lycra and the lace. There were so many good things here, it was going to be difficult to make a choice.

Conversation Area One

HE'D SPOKEN TO her before, this boy who thought he was God. He'd come up to her only the week before last and said he was God and she was an angel. It was the look in his eyes, like he really believed it. Now she saw him sitting there on his own staring into his empty plastic cup, wearing a shirt that looked like it needed a wash, and her heart hurt for him. He was just a poor young man who'd lost the place like her own son Michael, and he didn't even have a visitor to talk to.

When she walked up to where he was sitting and stopped, he didn't so much as look up at her, just went on staring into the empty cup.

'Excuse me, son,' she said.

She didn't have time to say anything else, because he stood up from his chair and looked her straight in the eyes. Then he said, 'The Son and the Father and the Holy Ghost. I am the Resurrection and the Life.'

Gertie took a step back from him and asked him if he knew where her boy was. The way he looked right through her made her blood run cold. Then he said, 'Mrs Houliston' – she had no idea how he knew her name, unless he knew Michael was called Houliston and knew she was Michael's mum – 'I think you will have to look very long and very hard to find your boy.'

There was something far wrong with him, you could tell that, but she had to admit he was very well spoken.

'Oh,' she said – she was being polite – 'Why is that?'

Then he leaned forward and stared into her eyes like he could see right into her and knew everything that had ever happened to her in her life and he said, 'You'll have to go to hell to find your boy, Mrs Houliston, because that is where your boy is. Your boy is in hell, Mrs Houliston.'

It worried her that he knew her name. Then he started raving at her – bits of the Bible all jumbled up with other things like adverts on the TV – but luckily a nurse came and led him away. She was going to ask her if she knew where Michael was, but she thought better of it – the poor girl had her hands full enough with that one, so she went into the table-tennis room, but he wasn't there. Nobody was, just the empty tables and, over in the corner, a plant that looked like it needed water. When she came out into the corridor again, another nurse – Sister Nimmo, her badge said – came up and asked her if she could help her.

'I'm looking for my boy,' Gertie told her. 'His name's Michael Houliston.'

'Oh. Yes . . . Michael,' the sister said. She was bonnie, with her fair hair and blue eyes, but she was that thin you could've played a tune on her ribs, and as pale as a pint of milk, and she had dark marks under her eyes – one of them was darker than the other one, turning purple. Somebody had done that to her – one of the patients as likely as not. There was that strained look in her eyes as well, like she'd been trying to read something in tiny wee writing, like the phone book or the Bible. 'Michael is in Conversation Area One,' she said, 'I've just been talking to him there.'

'Oh, is that right?' said Gertie. 'Conversation what?'

'Conversation Area One.' Then she gave her the directions. Up the corridor, through a set of double doors, up the stairs, turn left, along another corridor and through another door.

She was out of breath by the time she got there. He didn't

notice her, sitting with his eyes shut and his earphones on. She
didn't think a personal stereo was a very good idea for somebody with mental problems. It was just a way of cutting himself off from the world around him and hiding behind whatever
he was listening to. She took a look at the room. It was just a
room with a few chairs in it and a coffee-table. It didn't have
a window, and all that there was on the wall was a noticeboard
with nothing on it except a sign somebody had printed in big
letters saying 'This is Thursday'. Michael sat there with his arm
thrown over the back of the chair, shaking his head and moving
his feet in time to the music he was listening to on his wee
black earphones. It was that loud she could hear it when she
sat down beside him and put down her bag. He opened his
eyes and saw her and took the earphones off.

'Hi, Ma,' he said.

'Hello, son. How are you this week?'

'Okay.'

She fished her hanky out of her sleeve. It wrung her heart
to see him again and she just wanted to greet. She always
wanted to greet when she saw him because he wasn't happy
and because it was terrible to think he might be mad. There
had never been any madness in her family, at least none that
she'd heard about, but she'd seen it before, when she'd worked
as a cleaner in the infirmary. Some of the cases that came in
there were mental, and not just the suicides either.

'How are you, Ma?'

He'd taken the earphones off his head, making the noise
coming out of them louder, and now he was looking at her
like he didn't even recognise her.

She sniffled and blew her nose. 'Ye didnae hear me there,
did ye? Wi they things in your ears. I don't know how you
can listen to that damned rammy. It would drive me batchie.
Switch it off, son, eh? It gies me the willies.'

He switched it off and leaned back in his chair. His mouth hung open and it was like he was looking at nothing. He didn't say anything else and he didn't look at her. He was on something, she could tell that by the way his movements were slow and tired, like he was in slow motion. He looked like he was trying to remember something, then he said: 'Me as well. It gives me the willies as well, Ma.'

'Well, why d'ye listen to it, then? What is it, anyway?'

'It's just some jazz, Ma.'

'Is that what ye cry it? Well, it gies me the willies.'

'If it didn't give you the willies, it wouldn't be jazz, Ma.'

'Sounds like the monkey-hoose in the zoo at feeding time, if ye ask me.'

She was trying to make him laugh, or at least give her a smile, but he just looked at the wall as if he couldn't see anything there and said, 'They're happy, then.'

'What, son?'

'The monkeys. At feeding time. I expect they're happy then.'

She had no idea what on earth he meant by that, but she agreed with him, anyway. At least he was talking again. A few weeks ago she had come to visit him and he hadn't said a word. Since then, most weeks he'd not said much. It had been like trying to get blood from a stone to get him to answer a question, but tonight he was talking, at least that was something.

'Have they stopped yer medication, Michael?'

'They changed the tablets, Ma.'

'So what is it they're gi'en ye now?'

He didn't seem to hear the question. He just stared into space and fiddled with the wires on his earphones, winding them round and round his fingers then unwinding them again. When he didn't speak it always made her talk too much. She knew she was doing it but she couldn't help herself.

'Sorry I'm late the night, son. My watch is stopped. It's never done that before. What a job I had finding ye the night, Michael. I went into the television lounge, but there was naebody in there. The TV was on, though. A waste of electricity. Not only that, it's public money they're frittering away. Anyway, ye werenae in there. I thought ye might be watching the film. I saw the start of it before I came out the night. It was about somebody just like you, who goes to the university . . . and he cannae get on wi his studying. It was philosophy he was studying as well, and not only that, it was the very same philosophy you were studying – would ye credit that, Michael? What d'ye cry it again?'

'What, Ma?' He was miles away.

'You know. Thon philosopher wi the funny name.'

'A lot of them had funny names, Ma.'

'Tell me some.'

She was trying to get him talking as much as anything else, but he took so long thinking about it before he said, 'Kant. Heidegger. Schopenhauer. Nietzsche.'

'That's it. They were studyin that Neechie. They were studyin one of his books . . . what was it called again? What books did he write, Michael?'

If she could get him talking about the books he read at the university, she might find out what it was that had turned his mind and changed him into somebody you couldn't have a normal conversation with. But he just yawned and said, 'He wrote a lot of books, Ma.'

'Tell me some, then.' You had to keep at him to get anything out of him, that was the thing.

'The Anti-Christ. Thus Spake Zarathustra. Beyond Good and Evil.'

'That's it. Be and Good and Evil. An this boy, a student, him an his pal read this Be and Good and Evil an it goes to their heids, Michael, it drives the both of them yon way. An they turn intae right bad buggers the pair of them. They murder a bairn. A wee lassie. Oh, the very thought . . . It made me feel ill. I didnae see the end. I hope they hung them. I was thinkin it was earlier, ye see, because my watch stopped. Then I nodded off in my chair and when I woke up I looked at the clock. Quarter past six, it was. I says tae masel, Godalmighty – is that the time? I'll be late for Michael.'

She knew she was talking too much but what else could you do when the other person just sat there not even nodding their head at what you were saying, not even looking at you? She shut up and waited for him to say something, but he didn't. If she waited much longer it was going to make her want to greet again. She could feel the tears like needles jabbing at the backs of her eyes.

'I wasn't expecting you, Ma.'

'Well, ye should've been. Ye know I come on Thursdays. Did ye forget I was coming?'

'No, Ma. I forgot it was Thursday.'

It was a bad sign if he was forgetting things, forgetting things like the day of the week – mind you, she did it herself sometimes – him that used to be able to remember so much, whole pages of things he had to remember for his exams at school, and he'd been that good at it as well. A lot of good it had done him by the looks of it.

'How could ye forget it was Thursday? Look, up there. They've even written it's Thursday up there on the notice-board.'

'It always says that, Ma.'

But he didn't look up at the noticeboard. He just went on fidgeting with the wires of his earphones and licking his lips like he was thirsty. He didn't look at things any more, his eyes were like windows with the blinds down. He looked like he was always looking at something away in the distance, but like it was somewhere inside him, away in the distance inside himself.

'Well, then, ye shouldnae have forgotten then, should ye?'

He didn't have anything to answer to that. She looked up at the sign on the noticeboard. This is Thursday. Of course, if it always said that . . .

'Oh . . . ye mean it always says it's Thursday? Ye mean it's wrong?'

'Not always, Ma.'

'That's a relief. Ye mean it says it's Thursday when it's Thursday.'

He stopped fidgeting with the wires for a minute and frowned, like he was trying to work out something really difficult in his head. Then he said: 'It says it's Thursday when it's Thursday, Ma. But it isn't always Thursday. But since it always says it's Thursday, it's not always wrong. It's right once a week, Ma – when it's Thursday.'

'Oh, Michael, you've lost me there. Either it's right or it's wrong. I had to look for ye high and low the night. I went intae the canteen and I met that boy that thinks he's God. He knew I was lookin for you like, he's no that daft. He knew my name – how did he know that, Michael?'

'God is omnipotent, Ma.'

'Is that what's wrong wi him? You wouldnae think it, to look at him. Anyway, I looked everywhere. I looked in the table-tennis room, but ye werenae in there.'

'No?'

She looked at him – was he being cheeky? It would be good if he was. It might mean he was getting back to his normal self, the boy who used to play practical jokes on her, putting things in her slippers and tying the legs of her tights in a knot.

'No, ye werenae. Because ye dinnae play table-tennis. Mibbe ye should take it up. It's a sport.'

'I know it's a sport, Ma.'

'I had to look for ye somewhere, Michael. Then I met sister what's-her-name, ye know, that yin wi the fair hair.'

'Sister Nimmo.'

'Aye, her. She's a very bonnie lassie, d'ye no think, Michael? Only she had a nasty black eye. And she said she thought ye were in Conversation Area One. I felt that stupid. I had no idea what she was talking about, Michael. Ye never told me about these conversation areas. So I said, oh, Conversation Area One? Where is that, again? I didnae want to let on I'd never seen it. Then she sent me up here. So is this it?'

'What, Ma?' He was miles away again.

'Conversation Area One. Is this it?'

'Yes. This is Conversation Area One.'

'Fancy that. How many are there, then?'

He had to think about that one for a long time. Then he said, 'Two.'

So there were two of them. She wondered what the other one was like. This one was all right, except it didn't have a window. She liked a view, even when it was dark. She cleared her throat. It was her turn to speak. 'What's the other yin like?'

'What?'

'Michael, try to pay attention, son. I'm no here for long. I'm sayin, the other Conversation Area, number Two – what's it like?

'I don't know, Ma.'

'Ye don't know? Have ye never seen it, then?'

'No, I've never been in it.'

'Well – mibbe we should try it. Next Thursday.'

He didn't say anything to that, didn't look interested one

way or the other. He just went on winding the wires round his fingers and then unwinding them. She had to bite her tongue to stop herself telling him off for it.

'It's nice to see ye talking, son. Have ye been out this week?'

'No, I've been in.'

'Ye should get out in the grounds. Lovely hydrangeas. And the rhododendrons need to be seen to be believed. I'm always telling ye to get out, but ye dinnae listen to yer mother.'

'I can't go out, Ma.'

'Why no, son?'

He looked down at his feet then, like when he was a wee laddie and he'd done something wrong. It was terrible to see your own son, twenty-five years old, with all his education and everything, looking like a wee boy who's done something wrong. 'I lost my privileges.'

'What privileges, Michael?'

'My walking privileges.'

It was the first she'd heard of 'walking privileges'. 'What, you mean they won't let you go out? Not even in the hospital grounds? Why not, Michael?'

'I argued with Sister Nimmo.'

'Oh, Michael, ye shouldnae argue wi the staff. Ye'll only make it worse for yersel. I hope it wasnae you who gave her the black eye.'

No answer one way or another.

'Michael, ye shouldnae sit all on your own like this, ye should be a bit sociable wi the others. They're all in the same boat as you, after all. Ye were miles away when I came along.'

'I was thinking, Ma.'

'I don't know how ye can think wi they things on yer ears, that jazz cannae be good for yer brain. Ye think too much anyway, Michael, ye always did.'

'I was thinking about Christmas. I was remembering, one Christmas . . . I came downstairs to get my presents . . . and there weren't any. Mary had hers . . . a nurse's uniform, a doll, games, she had all kinds of presents. And Dad said to me: "Santa must've forgotten to leave yours this year."'

She couldn't remember that at all. Mibbe he was just making it up, or mibbe he really did remember it. It did sound like the kind of thing his dad might've done, mind you, big clown that he was sometimes.

'He said to Mary that I hadn't got any presents and he got her to give me one of hers. She gave me the doll.'

'A doll . . . oh, ye wouldnae like that.'

'I smashed its brains out on the fireplace.'

'Oh Michael, ye didnae. That was a bad thing to do.'

'Then Dad told us it was a joke, and he brought out my presents.'

Fancy him remembering all that, if he wasn't making it all up. 'That reminds me, I brought you something.'

She bent down to pick her bag off the floor and unzipped it. She'd forgotten about the wee present she'd bought him in Woolies yesterday. She'd been attracted by the picture on the box, then she'd thought it would help him pass the time. When she pulled it out of her bag and saw it was still in the Woolies bag, she thought she should really have wrapped it.

'Here ye are. It'll help ye pass the time, son.'

The way he looked at it when she handed it to him, like he was scared to take it off her, like she'd put a bomb in his hands.

'What is it, Ma?'

'A wee surprise.'

'I thought it was. Thanks, Ma.' Then he took it off her and just laid it in his lap quite the thing as if that was that.

'Are ye no gonnae open it, at least?'

He picked it up again. He looked worried by it, as if a wee present was something he didn't know what to do with.

'I bet ye cannae guess what it is.'

He shook the box and heard the pieces moving about inside. 'It's a jigsaw, Ma.' He was still a clever laddie even if his mind had turned.

'Ye always liked the jigsaws. Used to spend hours doing them when ye were wee.'

'Did I?'

'Oh aye. Ye must remember that. Ye were jigsaw-daft. Ye always liked to fit the last piece, to finish the picture.'

'Thanks, Ma.'

He was just going to put it down again and leave it at that.

'Take it out the bag at least, Michael. See what the picture is.'

When he took it out and saw the picture on the front, he looked like he was reading his own death sentence.

'What's the matter, Michael – d'ye no like it? It's called "Sunflowers". It's by Van Gogh.'

'Thanks, Ma.'

'That's all right, son. There's nothing like flowers to brighten up yer life. Ye should get out in the grounds.'

He leaned over and put the jigsaw down on the floor. She saw the back of his head, with the hair tapering into the nape of his neck, and it made her heart hurt.

'I will when I get my walking privileges back.'

'What were ye arguing wi her about, anyway?'

'Who, Ma?'

'Nurse what's-her-name.'

'Sister Nimmo. We had a disagreement about the nature of the human condition, Ma.'

'Oh, ye didnae, did ye? Ye should leave the human condition well alone, Michael, if ye want to get on in life. Ye see, there's no the demand for philosophers like what there used to be. See that Neechie? When ye studied him. It didnae make ye want to . . . do somethin like they boys in the film, did it?

'What, Ma?'

'To kill a bairn, like that.'

He looked like the question had got through to him but he didn't know how to answer it.

She explained the story to him: 'They didnae even know her. Ye could mibbe understand it if it was somebody ye knew, somebody at yer work, somebody ye'd fell oot wi – but a complete stranger, and a bairn . . . the very thought makes me feel ill. All the same, if you ask me, that Neechie's got a lot to answer for. What did he think, anyway? What did he say in his books that made they boys want to do something like that?'

'God is dead.'

'Eh?'

'He said, "God is dead."'

'He did not, did he? That's a terrible thing to say. It should be banned, if ye ask me. Anyway, how can God die? He's eternal and everlasting, everybody knows that. Even I know that. So how could he die?'

'I don't know, Ma.'

'Well, he was wrong, wasn't he? I mean . . . I just met God, in the television lounge!'

She tried to laugh, but when she did laugh a bit it hurt so much she had to stop. She looked at her watch. Her stopped watch.

'I keep forgetting the damn thing's wrong.'

Michael moved around in his chair and looked at her, as if he'd just noticed she was there. He rubbed his eyes, as if he was waking up. 'Not always, Ma. Your watch. It's right twice a day, Ma.'

'That's not much guid tae me, is it? Anyway, it must be time I was away. I've never been in one of these Conversation Areas before. They're nice, though, aren't they? Nicely . . . set out. And they're very quiet, aren't they, Michael? Michael?'

He had settled back down in his chair. He was miles away again.

'I'm saying they're quiet, aren't they? These Conversation Areas. Very quiet.'

'Yes, Ma. Very quiet.'

''I daresay the other yin's quiet as well. I daresay it's much the same as this yin.'

He took a long time to answer, then all he said was: 'Yes, I expect it is.'

Waiting at the Stairs

THIS WAS THE bit he hated. This waiting at the stairs. He looked at his watch. Ten to. The taxi had been quicker than usual, as if the driver, a committed normal, wanted him off his hands – literally – as soon as possible. So he would have to wait ten minutes. It was raining but he didn't mind. It felt cool on his bare arms, which he liked to show off because they were tanned, tattooed and very muscular. You had to flaunt what you had, even if it was just your arms and your shoulders and your torso, although lately he'd given up wearing the tight, weightlifter-style vests in favour of looser, sleeveless T-shirts. One of the things he had noticed about the normals: a lot of them had their work clothes and their play clothes. They changed out of their work clothes after work and got into their play clothes. Not all of them, of course. Some of them just wore the same clothes all day. He moved himself along the street a little, as if this was a way of avoiding the rain. Not too far – not out of sight of the doorway. She had to be able to see him when she came out, or she might go back in again.

A man hurried round the corner and collided with him. He had to let go of the wheels to catch the man in his arms to stop him from falling, then quickly grab the wheels again, before the two of them toppled backwards down the steps. He stared at the man's tense red face as he leaned over him and muttered his apologies before hurrying down the stairs and in the door.

It was okay for him – he could just go in on his own. In an ideal world, he might have asked that man to bump him down the stairs. They were going to the same place for the same thing, after all. But of course he couldn't ask him, because no normal, able-bodied man would want to see themselves as being in the same position as somebody like him. And then, maybe they would have other reasons for not wanting to be seen bumping somebody in a wheelchair down the steps to a sauna. It was hard enough going into the place without being seen.

The sex wasn't the problem. It was getting the wheelchair down the stairs to the door of the sauna. He could easily have lowered himself to the ground and bummed it down the stairs – his arms and his biceps had already won him two silver medals and three bronzes in the Paralympics – but who wanted to go into a sauna on the floor? Also, he'd have to leave the wheelchair at the top, and it might be stolen. Who were the people who stole wheelchairs? Probably the same people who stole bikes. They saw a good wheelchair and they knew how much it was worth – a lot more than a bike, if it was motorised. His wasn't, because he liked to spin the hoops himself for the exercise. Even so, his wheelchair was worth an arm and a leg. It was out of the question to leave it on the street, even if he padlocked it to the railings.

He didn't like to wait in the taxi, squashed in there sideways in the wheelchair, lowering his head under the roof and conscious of the meter ticking away. It was an expensive business, being a cripple. But it wasn't the discomfort or the expense that put him off – he was used to these things; it was the scenario of being a parcel, a human parcel handed over by the taxi driver to the girl who came out to bump him down the stairs. That was what put him off waiting in the taxi.

It had happened once, and once was enough. Although the

taxi driver and the girl had been okay about it all – the taxi driver had helped her down the stairs with the wheelchair, with him – the whole thing had created a spectacle for people who were passing by, people seeing him being unloaded from a taxi and dumped into a sauna.

No, it was better to get here early, get out of the taxi and pay the driver, watch the taxi leave and wait. Early but not too early. Waiting at the stairs wasn't ideal either. People walking by were beginning to notice him. Maybe they thought he was just waiting for somebody to pick him up, or waiting while whoever was in charge of him had gone into the corner shop next door.

A few weeks ago an old woman had thought he was begging on the street and she'd offered him some change from her purse. He had thanked her and taken the change, because he didn't have the heart to disillusion the old bat. She thought she was doing some good, so he thanked her.

There were too many people on the street at this time of night. He could see from the looks on some of their faces that they made the connection with the sauna and felt disgusted. Not disgusted with him. Not disgusted with the sauna. What they were disgusted with was the idea of somebody like him having sex, that was what disgusted them. He felt like shouting at them something they already knew: no good sex is entirely wholesome.

He took out his packet of chewing gum and busied himself with taking a piece out and unwrapping it and putting it in his mouth. He wanted to look engrossed in what he was doing, so that people would ignore him. The rain was dripping from the ends of his hair and trickling down his neck and his chest, wetting the ribbons of his medals.

The first time he'd come, nobody had appeared. Nobody had come out to bump him down the stairs. He'd wheeled himself halfway home, then submitted to a taxi. When he'd phoned to complain the next day, the girl had given him a polite apology and an explanation to do with somebody's shift coming to an end and the appointment book, but since he'd pre-paid, he was welcome to come back whenever it suited him, and she would make sure someone would be there to deal with the stairs.

He had to admit that the girls at the sauna were much better at dealing with his disability than most people were in the social services – and not just because they were willing to have sex with him. It wasn't just the sex that he was coming for, and the girls knew that. A lot of men were lonely, not all of them disabled.

He looked at his watch and had to wipe the rain off the face to see the time. There was still five minutes to go. He moved the chair, turned it and wheeled himself along the pavement for a few yards, then he turned and wheeled himself back. He went on, wheeling back and forth on the street. He realised that what he was doing was the wheelchair equivalent of pacing up and down. He sensed that people walking by and crossing the road were looking at him curiously. Sooner or later, if he didn't watch out, somebody would stop and ask if he needed help.

It was at moments like this that he would curse himself for coming to a sauna with stairs. Why he hadn't gone to a place without stairs in the first place was hard to say. The stubborn determination to be admitted to the places that didn't have disabled access, maybe. And now that he was coming here, he didn't want to change – they'd got used to him, and he'd found one girl in particular who understood what he wanted and didn't seem to bother at all about his condition. Nina, she called herself – probably not her real name. Nina had been administering hand-relief to him for the past three months, expertly. No one else had ever done that for him, and it made him feel that happiness could sometimes be a physical thing.

He stopped wheeling himself back and forth and looked at his watch. Two minutes to eight. The rain had come on heavier. Soon, his clothes would be completely soaked. He felt impatient to be inside, to be out of the chair and on the bed, with Nina asking him where he'd got the tan, and he'd tell her, at the solarium, then she'd ease his T-shirt over his head and she'd see the medals. She'd lift them by their coloured ribbons over his head and place them carefully on the locker beside the bed, then she'd oil her hands and get down to work, working downwards from his neck and his shoulders.

When she'd made him come, she'd smile and say something like, 'I hope you enjoyed that,' and she'd leave him to clean himself up with the tissues the sauna provided for that purpose. She'd put on some of her clothes, then she'd help him on with his. Finally she'd hang each medal – two silvers, three bronzes – around his neck again, then it would be time to get him back in the chair and take him out to the reception area. She'd say goodbye to him, and the girl on reception would call his taxi. When he was finished he wanted to get out and they wanted him out, there was a kind of understanding about it. They didn't want him to wait in the reception area where other clients might see him, and he didn't want to wait there being seen either. So the girl on reception would haul him up the stairs. Then he'd be here again, waiting for the taxi. This was the bit he hated. This waiting at the stairs.

Out of Order

SOME NIGHT. WHAT? No that great. It would've been okay if it hadnae been for Eddie Leckie and his fuckin jacket. I know you think he's got a problem. You're right. Tony thinks he's got a problem as well. He said that the night. He says: I think your friend's got a problem. I says, wait a minute, Tony. He's your fuckin friend as well.

Kids okay? Any wine left?

Aye, but it's no just that. It's no just a drink problem. I mean, he's got problems with his relationships with women, for a kick-off. And he's in debt. And he's in his forties but he's no had kids yet an he's wonderin what the fuck his life's about. And he hates his job, cannae stand his boss. And he's still got this problem wi his upbringin and that, I mean his dad was a transvestite Elder in the Wee Free Kirk, for fuck's sake. I mean he says he's free of the Wee Free thing but if ye ask me he's still a fuckin Presbyterian prisoner.

He's a fuckin mess, that's his problem.

The thing is, there was the three of us. Snooker's never that great wi three. Sometimes it's okay, dependin on the three guys involved. I mean some guys are quite happy rackin up the balls and markin up the board and gettin the drinks in while the other two play. Just watchin the game. No Eddie, though. He's so fuckin restless. Pacin up an doon like somebody in the labour ward waitin to find out if it's a boy or a girl or a fuckin gorilla.

I know it's worse for the woman.

But it's better if it's just the two of you. Because snooker's like that. It's intimate. What? I don't see what's so fuckin funny about that. It's a game for two people. The place has got an atmosphere as well. Low lights, smoke. Very quiet. Not a lot of talking. Just the noises of the cues hitting the balls and the balls hitting each other and sometimes – no very often, the way we play it – a ball dropping into a pocket. There's an atmosphere of . . . how can I put it? Scholastic intensity. There is an atmosphere of scholastic intensity, if I can put it like that.

Go on, then, fuckin laugh.

Originally I'd just arranged to meet Tony there. I mean, me and Tony sometimes just like to meet and play snooker for the night. You can think it's pathetic if you like – for two grown men to meet and knock balls into holes, but d'ye want to hear what happened, or no?

Well, listen, anyway. So Eddie phones up. I know Eddie likes a game of snooker, so I says, I'm meetin Tony at Marco's, come along if you want. It's only when I'm walkin along Dundee Street that I think, wait a minute, what if Tony doesnae want to meet Eddie, or Eddie doesnae want to meet Tony? Because the thing is, although me and Eddie go back a long way, and although me and Tony get on okay these days, Tony and Eddie are no what you'd call bosom buddies. In fact, they just tolerate each other because of me. So Eddie knows I'm meetin Tony, because I says to him on the phone. I says, I'm meetin Tony. Come along if you want.

I didnae really get the feelin Eddie fancied it that much, anyway. When I'd spoke to him on the phone, it was like he was sayin, I might drop in, I might no. I'll see how things go, he says. I got the distinct impression that the snooker was on the back burner. I daresay on a Friday night Eddie's usually got other fish to fry.

So I'm walkin along Dundee Street past the brewery, an I thinks, fuck it, I've got enough on my plate. I mean, I've got kids, they've no. If they dinnae get on, that's their problem. Fuck them. I'm gonnae enjoy a game of snooker anyway.

Yes, I am aware that it is late. But d'ye no want to hear what happened? I mean, are we communicatin here or what? I know we can communicate in the morning. But we'll not. We'll not communicate in the morning.

So I thought: two of us can play, the other can mark up the board, etcetera. It'll be okay, I thought.

It wasnae, though.

Me and Tony went through the usual rigmarole. The tenner deposit, the waitin till a table was free, so we had a pint in the bar till we hear my name announced on the tannoy – because I'm a member, like. So we takes the balls and the cues through and gets on the table and racks up and Tony breaks the first frame. It's busy and we're no talkin much, me and Tony, we're just gettin on wi it. He's playin some good shots – compared to me, like.

Then Eddie turns up, wearin this new leather jacket. A wee grey leather jerkin kinda thing, wi wee poppers instead of buttons. Said he got it from Gap. Me and Tony are that engrossed in the game by then, I mean we were really gettin into it, really concentrating on the position of the balls. What? Engrossed. That's what I said. I said we were engrossed. Concentrating. The position of the balls was . . . unusual.

Fuckin laugh if ye like.

Anyway, we were. So when Eddie appears, we just sortae nodded and said hello and went on wi the game. We didnae pay that much attention to his new leather jacket. So Eddie starts markin up the board and respotting the colours. Or that's what he's supposed to be doin, but half the time he's up at the bar. By the time the game's finished – Tony won, like – Eddie's already half-cut. So then Tony plays Eddie and I mark up and get the drinks in.

It was my round, like.

The thing is, me and Eddie go back a long way. We're close. I mean, we've got absolutely nothin in common, but we can talk to each other. He's in a totally different situation from me, because he's single and he doesnae have kids. He envies me, by the way. He's said that. Sometimes I think he's lucky. Free, single, etcetera. It's a case of the fuckin grass always bein fuckin greener.

So, anyway, while I'm up at the bar, I'm aware of some kind of commotion behind me, a dispute of some kind taking place. I just ignore it. I don't even turn round to have a look. But I can see in the mirror behind the bar that something is taking place. Then a bouncer runs past me. Basically I'm hoping that Eddie an Tony havenae fell out. Fallen out. Okay then, I'm hoping they havenae fuckin fallen out.

Anyway, I takes the drinks back to the table. And to my heartfelt relief the pair of them are playing away quite the thing, in an atmosphere of almost religious transcendence. So then when Tony wins, I play Tony an it's Eddie's job to mark up the board and get the drinks.

I was winning for a change, I made a forty-eight break an then I lined up a nice wee snooker for Tony. I was working my way through the colours when Tony says, where's Eddie? Sure enough, he'd fucked off. So then the lights start flashin and the bouncers move in – that always happens before you've got time to clear the table – and they clear the snooker hall and we go through to the bar.

So me and Tony take the balls and the cues back and get the deposit. Then we get a last drink in and we actually get a seat and Eddie reappears drunk as a fuckin skunk. He says: where's ma jacket? Where's ma new leather jacket?

He was lookin at Tony. Tony looks at me, starts to say he's sorry. I says, wait a minute, Tony. Eddie's jacket is not your responsibility. Then I says to Eddie: Eddie, your jacket is your responsibility.

He says, aw aye, fuckin great mates yous two. If a mate of mine left his jacket, I'd've looked after it for him.

I didnae notice you left it in there, says Tony.

That's no the point, I says. Why should you?

We were playin snooker thegither, says Eddie. For fuck's sake. It's no just the jacket. It's what's in it. My wallet. My banker's card. Driving licence. Some fuckin mates yous two.

So I says to him to his face: Eddie, you are way out of line here. You are seriously out of order.

Me out of order? he says. It's you who's out of order, no me.

Then he goes away to look for his fuckin jacket and Tony says to me: I think your friend's got a problem. I says, wait a minute, he's your fuckin friend as well, Tony.

Tony looks at me as if to say: no he's no. Then he thinks about it an he says: mibbe he's right, mibbe we should've brought his jacket through, but I didnae see him takin it off, did you?

I says, that's no the point, Tony. Fuck him an his fuckin jacket.

When Eddie came back, he was wearing it. It didnae suit him. If you ask me, he got the wrong size. He sat there in the huff, then he left before me and Tony had a chance to drink up. Then we drank up. Then we left.

It's just. Sometimes I think. For fuck's sake. As if I havenae got enough on my plate. Snooker's really a game for two. It's never that great wi three.

What? Sorry. I've been telling you this because I love you.

Shouting It Out

HE COULD DO it in the dark, with Christine there beside him, surrounded by everybody just sitting there watching the film, when the only sound was the soundtrack, so loud it was like somebody whispering in your ear. He knew how to wait for that moment when everyone was totally into the film, when nobody was coughing or giggling or whispering or eating popcorn. A moment like now, when there was just the eerie music and David Bowie taking his first step on the planet Earth. Without having to think about it, he shouted it out: *'Step we gaily, on we go, heel for heel and toe for toe!'*

Christine thumped him on the chest and told him to shut up, but it had worked. Although she was embarrassed, she was laughing. Everybody was laughing – or it seemed like everybody. Really it was probably just a few folk here and there across the cinema, but in the darkness it felt like the whole cinema was laughing. Now would be good to get them on the tail-end of the laugh with something else, but already the usher's torch was looking for him among the seats and Christine was telling him to keep quiet. He huddled down in the seat as the beam of the usher's torch tried to find him.

'Keep it quiet along there!'

Christine punched him lightly on the arm. He liked it when she hit him. It felt so different from being punched by one of his pals. There was something very light and playful about it – it made him feel bigger and stronger than he was. He liked it when she touched him in any way at all. Even if she just touched his sleeve, it was like he could feel the touch on his skin. And although his friends said she was hackit, a dog, he liked her big brown eyes, her thick dark hair, her wide mouth with the deep corners that twisted up so quickly when she smiled – everything, really, except the nose. She didn't like her own nose either, and sometimes covered it a bit with her hand. At first her nose, and what his pals said about her, had really bothered him, but now he was getting to like being with her – they'd been going out together for nine weeks – and in a funny way he'd started to think her nose wasn't so bad. It made her look foreign – Greek, Spanish or Italian. He liked the way sometimes a little crease wrinkled the side of her nose when she laughed. It suited her.

He watched the film for a while, but then, just as David Bowie was arriving in the small town in the middle of nowhere in the desert, he couldn't help himself. He had to shout it out: *'Excuse me. Ah'm lookin for Mairi's weddin'!'*

Laughter. But this time the usher's torch trapped him in its beam and Christine hid her head behind his shoulder. He could feel her shaking, shuddering against him as she held in her laughter.

'Right, you – out!'

'Who? Me?'

He went through the routine of protesting his innocence until the usher gave up and went away, with the warning that if there was any more of it he'd be out.

Christine hissed into his ear: 'What a red face! Can you no just watch the film, like everybody else?'

'Okay.'

Like everybody else. He slumped forward in the chair, made his mouth hang open and stared like a zombie at the screen.

Christine shook her head, thumped him on the arm and

laughed. That was one of the things he liked about her – he could make her laugh.

He'd been coming to the same cinema since he was seven or eight years old. He could remember a whole gang of them coming to the Saturday matinee, sometimes bringing their rollerskates to skate down the aisle until they were thrown out. Buying cinnamon sticks at the chemist's and smoking them behind the cinema before they went in. The old man with the cap hanging over one eye who sold the Kia-ora. He was so old and bent and wrinkled, they were scared to buy his juice. Climbing over the seats, drumming your feet on the floor when the film broke down, cheering when the cavalry arrived . . . Then there was that really scary film called *The Time Machine* with the monsters called Morlocks. They were big and blue and hairy, a bit like gorillas except they lived under the ground. Above the ground was a kind of paradise. The people just played around all day and wore futuristic clothes and ate exotic fruits, till they heard the siren. When the siren sounded, they all froze and became like zombies, the zombies of paradise. They had this glazed look in their eyes as they walked, hypnotised, to the caves that led down into the underworld where the Morlocks waited for them, stirring the cauldrons – and guess what was for dinner. Although it seemed like a hoot now, the film had given him nightmares for weeks as a kid. He could remember checking in the wardrobe and under the bed at night, checking for Morlocks. And after his dad had come and put his light out and told him to get to sleep, he had sometimes shouted it out into the darkness of the room: *'Go away, Morlocks!'*

But in his dreams the darkness of the cinema had blurred with the underworld the Morlocks lived in, and the Morlocks were coming down the aisle like wild ushers with flaming torches in their paws, and the old man who sold the Kia-ora had turned into a Morlock although he still had his own face and the cap hanging over his eye, and when the siren sounded he was stirring the Kia-ora in the Kia-ora machine and all the kids were queuing up to buy it.

For a while the nightmares had bothered him so much that he'd stopped going with the gang to the matinee. He could still remember those Saturday afternoons without the gang, kicking a puckered ball against the wall of the house, playing at patience, throwing stones at nothing in particular . . . Then one Saturday he'd plucked up the courage to go back to the cinema, although he was still scared of the Morlocks and the darkness that would happen when the lights went down and the golden curtains opened. And it had been all right, the film had made him forget all about the Morlocks – until now.

He looked along the row at all the faces bathed in the bluish light from the screen, staring up at the film. They looked so stupid, so dumb and stupid and hypnotised. They were like the zombies of paradise, their mouths hanging open, their eyes staring up at the screen. When the film finished, when the siren sounded, they'd have to go and meet the Morlocks who waited for them at home, stirring the cauldrons . . .

He started laughing silently to himself at the idea of it. Christine felt his chest shaking, turned to look at him and said: 'What is it?'

He shook his head and said, 'Nothing.'

But she could always tell when he was keeping something to himself. She persisted: 'What is it? Tell me!'

When he still wouldn't tell her – it was too long and complicated and anyway she wouldn't find it funny – she pretended to be annoyed. It looked like she was acting. Acting was something they did together all the time. She acted sad; he acted concerned. Or he acted moody and she acted cheerful. Or she acted annoyed and he acted like a fool to get her out of it. It wasn't like real acting, the kind they did in films. It was a different kind of acting, because the feelings were real, but it was like the two of them were trying the feelings on for size, like clothes to see if they fitted, and to see if they suited them.

He quite liked it when she was annoyed with him. It did suit her. She had dark eyelashes, and when she was being annoyed she looked down, so that all you could see was the eyelashes and the wide mouth turning down at the corners. It made her look mysterious.

Once, he'd made her cry. What his pals had been saying about her had been getting to him, so he'd decided to chuck her.They'd gone for a walk in the graveyard. It had been a lovely sunny evening. Everything had been fine except that at the back of his mind he knew he was going to have to tell her it was finished. They went into a bit of the church that was sort of half inside and half outside. In the cool shadows they'd kissed and canoodled as usual. Then he'd told her. She'd turned away, but he'd seen the long black mascara tears trailing down her cheeks.

He'd felt so bad about her crying and had missed her so much that a few days later he'd knocked on the door of the girls' bogs at dinnertime and asked for her. When she'd come out, he'd taken her along to the maths corridor and asked her if she'd have him back. She'd thrown her arms around him and looked happier than he'd ever seen her before.

Maybe it wasn't all acting, even if they didn't know how they should do it or say it.

He noticed that she'd stopped chewing her gum and was still looking really annoyed. He asked her: if she'd finished with it, could he borrow it?

It didn't work.

In the end he had to tell her. About the rollerskates, the cinnamon sticks, the Kia-ora man, the Morlocks in the wardrobe and the zombies of paradise. About the nightmares and being scared of the dark when the lights went down at the matinee. What he couldn't tell her about, what he couldn't find words to explain, was the idea that all the folk around them were just like the zombies of paradise, and when they left the cinema it was like the siren sounding. The Morlocks would be waiting for them . . . but he couldn't tell her all that. She knew it anyway. She knew that if she missed her bus and had to walk home and got in late, the Morlocks would be waiting for her, stirring the cauldron.

She listened to it all and when he'd finished whispering it in her ear she moved away from him and said, 'Is that all?'

But she kissed him quickly on the cheek, looked at him as if she was looking from far away and smiled. It was just a little kiss, but one of the things he liked about Christine, although everybody said she was a dog, was that she was a great kisser, she had all these different kinds of kisses. All of her kisses made him feel good inside, made him feel like himself, like he was acting in a film but the part he was playing was himself. It was magic, and sometimes when he was with her he wanted to shout something out but he didn't know what.

He put his arm around her and let his fingers play with the gold chain of her locket. She went back to the film, her mouth opening and closing as she chewed her gum.

David Bowie was watching fifty televisions at once, all showing different programmes. He kept changing all the channels with his remote. Christine's hand covered his mouth before he could shout it out: *'Nothin much on telly the night!'*

Anyway, it wasn't very funny. Not worth getting thrown out for. But Christine was laughing because of what she was doing, putting her hand over his mouth to shut him up. She was still laughing a bit when he moved his hand up to her neck, pulled her closer and kissed her on the mouth. Then the laugh died away in her throat as they started kissing seriously. He could taste her lipstick and her chewing gum, feel the tips of her teeth and her moist, soft tongue. He stroked her neck, then ran his hand down over her collarbone . . . before he could go any further, she caught his hand in hers and squeezed it.

After a while they broke apart and watched the film.

David Bowie was having his nipples removed with a scalpel. Christine hissed: 'Don't you dare!'

Anyway, he couldn't think of anything very funny to shout out, except maybe: *'Ohyah!'*

What would it really be like to fall to Earth? Sometimes he wondered about that. Sometimes he could even feel that he really had just fallen to Earth, like when he looked along the row and saw all the faces staring up at the screen. It was like seeing people for the first time. Not one at a time, the way you usually looked at them, but sitting there in a row, like a line of aliens, like the zombies of paradise.

They held each other close in the newsagent's doorway, waiting for the bus. They kissed, but his mind was only half on what he was doing. He wanted to tell her that she wasn't like the others, not a zombie of paradise, and that she suited her nose or it suited her, and that he liked her eyes, her mouth, her hair, the way she laughed . . . He wanted to tell her something he'd never told anybody else.

Why couldn't he just say it to her, just look her in the eyes and say it? Of course, it wasn't like saying something ordinary, although going by the films, people said it to each other all the time. He should forget about looking into her eyes when he said it. He should just, after a really long kiss, a serious kiss like this one, whisper it in her ear, and it would sound as loud and as real as the soundtrack of a film. Or just say it, say it like he meant it, say it like he wasn't acting at all.

'Here it comes.'

She snatched another quick kiss and broke away from him and hurried to the door of the bus. She turned to him, smiled and waved as the bus door opened. Then she went on, paid her fare and found a seat next to the window so that she could smile and wave again. It was only when the bus started to pull away from the stop that he panicked inside and he didn't care who heard as he shouted it out.

Out

HE WAS WONDERING if he could really carry off the jacket – a white catering jacket he'd bought in an army surplus store and dyed lime-green – when his mother came in. In the dressing-table mirror he saw her face sag when she clocked what he was wearing.

'Victor, you're not going out looking like that, are you?'

He didn't answer. He wasn't required to. It was always the same. You're not going out looking like that. Oh yes I am, just watch me. The trouble was, if she objected to something, he'd feel obliged to wear it on principle, but he wasn't sure about this lime-green jacket himself. It didn't go with the white T-shirt or the grey jeans. Basically lime-green was a difficult colour to wear. If he'd been black it would be different. Sometimes he envied the black guys in his year at school. They could wear vermillion, turquoise, canary yellow, even pink and no one turned a hair, because it looked fine. Of course, they had other problems.

'Your father would turn in his grave if he saw you, Victor.'

'Oh, he's probably spinning in his grave by now, Mum.'

'At least put a tie on, son – for my sake.'

'A tie with a T-shirt? Now that would get the neighbours talking, wouldn't it?'

'Wear a shirt, son. It's freezing cold outside. You can't go out with only a T-shirt on and that thin jacket. It's the middle of winter.'

He turned to her, took her face between his hands and

kissed her with an audible *mmmmwa!* on the forehead.

'Mother, you're absolutely right. What I need with a lime-green jacket is a black shirt. *The* black shirt.'

He moved her out of the way carefully – she was getting a bit doddery, poor old dear. He didn't want to knock her over accidentally – she could bang her head on the corner of the table and die. The jury would find him guilty of manslaughter, of course, and he'd spend the next fifteen years in jail with all those twisted men wanting to rape him.

The future would soon be here. Soon it would be all right for him to be the way he was. As soon as he left school. As soon as he left home. As soon as he got out.

He threw off the jacket, reached into the wardrobe and slid the black shirt from its hanger. He took the T-shirt off and put the shirt on. Yes, it felt better already.

'Now a tie, son,' said his mother.

'Which tie would you recommend, Mother?'

'The stripey one, Victor. It makes you look smart.'

'It makes me look like a schoolboy.'

'You are a schoolboy, Victor.'

'That's why I don't want to look like one, stupid.'

'You wouldn't talk to me like that if your father was here.'

'But he isn't. He's getting dizzy in his grave.'

'Oh, Victor. Don't talk like that, please.'

He saw her face tighten in the mirror. Oh God no, he didn't want to reduce her to tears. He wanted to settle her down in her armchair, bring her her magazine and a cup of tea. He wanted to go out feeling that she wasn't going to sit there worrying about him all night. When it was time to go to bed she'd lie awake worrying until she heard him come in the door, then she'd get up and start fussing around him.

'All right, I'll wear it.'

She smiled at him. It was all so pathetic. 'Where are you going anyway, Victor?'

'Out,' he said. 'Just out.'

Now all he had to do was get the bus to town, meet Louise at the station, then take the train to Edinburgh. They'd wander around, have a drink somewhere, then catch the train back in time for the last bus home. It was a bit pathetic, but it was more or less what they did every Friday night unless there was a film they both wanted to see. The important thing was to get out, go somewhere else, get away from Murkirk for a couple of hours. He stepped outside and shut the front door. It was a cold, clear night. The frost glistened on the pavement under the streetlights. None of the householders in Park Street were out – that was a relief. He closed the garden gate behind him and walked briskly down the street.

The bus stop was next to the public toilet, and when it came into view he saw Jimmy Kidd – at school he was nicknamed Gym-kit – and his sidekick, a younger boy everybody called Caspar, hanging about inside the bus shelter. They had nothing better to do on a Friday night. He slowed down, hoping to time his arrival at the bus stop so that it more or less coincided with the bus coming. That was the trouble with leaving so early – there weren't other people waiting for the bus into town. He heard Kidd saying something and Caspar laughing. As he crossed the road to the bus stop he was aware of the two of them watching him in silence.

'Look who comes.'

'Who is she?'

'The queen of Park Street.'

He didn't say anything. He wasn't required to. He stood outside the shelter, as far away from them as he could. He looked at his watch. He was early because his mother had made him early. And no doubt the bus would be late. Now he had to wait for the bus. That was all he was required to do.

He started to shiver with the cold. He should have taken the scarf his mother had offered him as he was on his way out. He heard Caspar laughing behind him and knew that Gym-kit would be doing the mincing walk and the limp-wrist routine behind his back. Now both walked around him until they stood on the pavement in front of him.

Gym-kit took a half-smoked cigarette from his jerkin pocket and lit it. 'Ah like the tie. What d'ye think of the tie, Caspar?

'It's shite.'

'Hear that? Caspar thinks your tie's shite.'

'Caspar can think what he likes.'

'Hear that, Caspar? Queen Victoria says ye can think what ye like.'

'The jaiket's shite tae,' said the younger boy, moving close to Victor and tugging at the pocket of his jacket.

Victor moved away sharply and hissed: 'Piss off.'

'Ooo!' mocked Gym-kit. 'Watch out, Caspar, she might scratch yer eyes out!'

Caspar opened his eyes wide and whined in a parody of fear. It annoyed Victor that this little runt felt he could take the piss just because he was with Gym-kit. If he'd been on his own – a different story then. Even Gym-kit, on his own, wouldn't have had a go at him like this.

'Waitin for the bus, are you?'

'It seemes a reasonable thing to do, at a bus stop. You should try it.'

'You've missed it.'

'Not according to my watch.'

'It was early. The bus was early, eh, Caspar?'

Caspar kicked a stone and said, 'Yeah.'

Gym-kit flicked the hair out of his eyes and drew on the last of his cigarette. Years ago they'd been friends, had walked to school together and even gone round the village together on their bikes. They'd drifted apart at secondary school and now Gym-kit had something to prove. 'Did ye hear me? Ah said you've missed the bus.'

'Yeah, sure.'

Gym-kit leaned forward and said: 'You callin me a liar?'

He didn't say anything. He wasn't required to.

He saw the bus turning the corner to come down the street as the fist cracked against his mouth and made him stagger backwards.

'Even if I am,' said Gym-kit, 'don't fucking call me it.'

A kick from the younger boy caught him on the back of the leg before the two of them ran off into the night whooping and laughing.

His lip was bleeding. He took out the handkerchief and pressed it to his mouth. When he got on the bus, the driver noticed the blood but didn't say anything as he paid his fare. He leaned his face against the bus window as it lurched into motion and he watched the ugly village slide by until the last of its streetlights was swallowed up by the night. Then it was completely dark, but if he stared hard enough through his own reflection he could make out the black fields stretching for miles and, in the distance, the dirty orange glow in the sky above Murkirk.

He felt his lip beginning to smart and swell. There were spots of blood on the collar of the lime-green jacket. Louise would ask him what had happened, and he'd have to go through the whole stupid episode again. She'd sympathise, but it would just confirm something for her – at school, she'd had to defend herself against the taunts of the other girls. He'd been telling her for so long that he wasn't like that, that he just liked clothes and wasn't into being macho. Maybe tonight he'd tell her the truth. The blood had hardened on his lip, and he wet the handkerchief with his spit and tried to do something about the spots on the jacket, but this only smeared them into bigger stains. He settled back in his seat and closed his eyes. When he came home, Gym-kit might be there again, hanging around at the bus stop. It didn't matter, none of it mattered. All that mattered was that it was Friday night and he was out.

Relief

THE SINS OF the flesh are innocent, compared to some.

Who had said that? Somebody must have said it. Or maybe the thought had just floated to the surface of his mind. Could you have thoughts without thinking them in the first place? Maybe thoughts arose of their own accord, or were set in motion by external forces. And what about beliefs? Maybe they too could rise from the depths of one's being unbidden, like serene corpses of the drowned.

He doubted if they would be serene – they'd be horribly bloated. All the same, it might be true about the sins of the flesh, and he comforted himself with that thought as he hurried down the steps to the door of Sensations, the sauna he favoured. Unlike the others he'd tried, it was discreet. Lurking in a quiet lane just off London Street, in a basement with blacked-out windows, with the barely legible name hand-painted on a board above the door, Sensations was tacky, but it had a low profile. All there was was a door that was barely open, the padlock still hanging from the bar.

He stopped a moment in the hallway to get his breath and shake out his umbrella. There was barely a spit of rain, but the umbrella had been useful as a shield against curious glances. For a city, Edinburgh was still a big small town and there was always someone who knew your face and wanted to place it. And he had the sort of face people felt the need to place. For as long as he could remember, people had looked at him in this way, as if they remembered him from somewhere.

He suspected it was something that set him apart from them, had always set him apart. But what was that? That he was too clean-shaven, and smelled too clean? Maybe that was enough to set you apart from other people. It was a kind of respectability people didn't trust. They could recognise the thin, astringent smell of his ruined celibacy. He shook out his umbrella.

A delicious guilt ignited his innards, like the first mouthful of a pakora. Later, when he was home, if things panned out the way he hoped they would, he would lie down on his bed and feel that same sensation of mingled transgression and satisfaction spreading through the cells of his entire body, like the afterburn of a good lamb bhuna. A carry-out was definitely the next thing on tonight's menu.

He took off his glasses and wiped them clean with his hand-kerchief, then he stepped through the doorless doorway into the inner sanctum.

The cubicle wasn't warm enough. The oil felt tepid on his skin. She had strong hands, large enough to encircle his ankles. As she worked her way up, he felt the unpleasant prickle of her nails against his calves. Although he felt cold, he was sweating. As she spread the lukewarm oil up the backs of his thighs, he began to feel peculiar, like some amphibious creature coated in slime. The music wasn't helping. Usually they had some slow reggae stuff throbbing away in the background. Tonight it was something harsher. Like a slowed-down tape of someone trying to howl while having a car crash. Nothing was working. When she massaged the loose flesh around his middle, she kneaded it too hard, like someone trying to squeeze the inner tube on a bicycle wheel into the tyre.

'Would Sir like to, y'know, turn over?'

Her voice had a shadow of something in it, behind the

professional politeness. She slurred her words a little, not as if she was drunk but as if the habit of drunkenness had sloshed over into her sober hours.

He rolled on to his back and looked at her through half-closed eyes. He had taken his glasses off before lying down, and he saw her as a dyed-blonde blur in a low-cut top. Then, as she leaned forward, she almost came into focus. Even without his glasses on, he could tell that her face was unnaturally puffed, and her eyelids looked swollen under the mascara – as if she'd been crying, or had had too much to drink, or hadn't slept. Or maybe it was a combination of all three. Her movements seemed reluctant as she poured more oil on to her hands and began to rub his shins.

This wasn't how it should be at all. There was something wrong here. She seemed nervous. If anyone should feel nervous, it should be the client, not the girl doing the massage. But he could feel the tension in her hands as they circled around his knees. Was she new? She didn't look new. Was there something bothering her – the fact that he was at least twenty years older than her, maybe? His misgivings didn't affect his cock which, despite everything, stretched and hardened in anticipation as the tips of her fingers, slick with oil, coasted up the insides of his thighs and skimmed his balls. Her hands hesitated around his groin and then travelled on up to his stomach, where they began to fuss around his navel, as if they didn't know what to make of it.

He sat up a little and cleared his throat, then reached for his glasses. When he put them on, something lurched in the pit of his stomach as she loomed into focus. He knew her face. It was shockingly blank of expression, but he knew it. He didn't know where he'd seen her. Church? More to the point: if he knew hers – wouldn't she know his?

She looked at the ceiling and asked: 'Any extras?'

She pulled her top open. Between her dangling breasts swung a thin gold chain. She had tied it in a knot, and a small crucifix hung to the side at an odd angle.

When she noticed him looking at it she said: 'I have to tie it up so it doesn't get in the way when I, y'know, do this.' She lowered her face so that her mouth was in position, then looked up and asked: 'Is that what Sir would like?'

'Thank you, no. I just want . . . relief.'

'Sure. You want relief, right?'

She made a question out of the word as she went to work on it, and he wondered why. It was what they called it, after all. Yet now the word sounded odd to him, and faintly obscene. Relief – was that what he was coming for? Was it just a question of emptying his balls? Or was it relief from his position, relief from the instinctive distrust people felt towards him when they caught a whiff of his loneliness? Was he coming here and doing this, or rather having this done, as a way of humbling himself, declaring himself to be no different from an ordinary man with ordinary needs? But that was sophistry. An ordinary man, even if he frequented the sauna with the monotonous regularity he practised, wouldn't always crave it on a Sunday.

The Sunday thing was, it had to be admitted, in the nature of a turn-on. After mass there was the congenial afternoon drink with a few of the younger Catholic intellectuals, all intent on trying to be liberal and loud, as if Christianity was a new fashion, arguing the toss about whatever ethical dilemma had surfaced in the papers that week, whether it was cloning or decriminalising cannabis or that old favourite, abortion.

When he went home at night, he felt the need for something else. For a long time he had simply made himself a meal and fallen asleep in front of the TV, or while praying. He had gone through a phase of using videos, which were easily obtained by mail-order from advertisements in *Escort* or *Penthouse*, but they made him feel ashamed of himself, the shame of his loneliness, and of course he had to throw them out or hide them. It worried him that he might have hidden something like that somewhere in the house and forgotten about it. One day, somebody might find it. In the meantime he had found a solution to Sunday night, and it was called Sensations.

The askew crucifix dangled on the knotted chain between her breasts as she worked on him – too energetically for comfort.

'Slow down,' he admonished.

The blank eyes didn't look up from what she was doing, but she slowed down. 'How's that feel? Is that slow enough, Father?'

He sat up and convulsed, as if he'd been winded by a punch in the gut. Her hand tightened around his balls and he felt the sharpness of her nails.

Her puffed face was an inch or two from his as she spoke in a bitter whisper: 'Don't worry, Father. I'm not into blackmail or any of that shit. Lie down, now, lie down.'

Although she was whispering, it sounded like an order. Her grip relented as he sagged back on the bed. Not that it was really a bed. It was more like a doctor's examination table. He felt too far from the floor. She spread her left hand over his chest, as if holding him in place. Her right hand went on doing its work down below. She had raised her eyebrows and lowered her eyelids, as if she faintly disapproved of him.

He had to stop her. She knew him. She knew he was a priest. 'My child . . .'

'Don't "my child" me, Father.'

'How do you know me?'

'Just you lie there and relax. C'mon, smile, Father, smile.'

He obeyed, then felt the smile congeal on his face as he looked at her: she wasn't smiling back. Her eyes had hardened on his mouth, and the coldness of her look scared him.

She answered his question before he could repeat it: 'You came to see my dad. When he was dying.'

'Your father? Did he come to my church?'

'No, he was like – lapsed. He'd stopped going to mass and all that years ago. I think he turned against it, y'know, when he got a book out the library on the Spanish Inquisition and read about this scientist guy called Bruno.'

'Bruno?'

'I think it was Bruno. They tortured him.'

Bruno. He couldn't believe that the girl giving him a massage was talking to him about a sixteenth-century scientist who had been burned at the stake in the Piazza Campo di Fiori because of his belief that space was infinite.

'Bruno. The Inquisition. I see. The Catholic Church has been responsible for many terrible things, but I'm sorry if that shook his belief in God.'

'It didn't. He asked for a priest, one of you, on his deathbed.'

The way she said 'one of you' made it sound like something cheap and disdainful. As if priests were ten-a-penny, prostitutes working for a pimp called God.

'What was his name?'

When she said it he remembered. A narrow living-room in a ground-floor flat in Easter Road. A bed made up on the couch. A pale, gaunt man watching the racing on Saturday afternoon, his newspaper and his tea and his cigarettes on a coffee-table in front of him. He had heard his confession, unremarkable as far as he could remember, and had recommended a hospice on the way out. That's when he'd met her – she'd been looking after him.

She poured more oil on to her palm, rubbed her hands together and smiled down at him.

'I'm sorry.'

'What for? You do your job, I do mine, right? Just relax.'

Her hands resumed doing what they were doing – stroking and restroking, pulling slowly and squeezing with a slow rhythm.

He looked up at her and tried to guess what she was thinking. She was smiling, but he found it impossible to know what her smile meant. It could mean she was going to phone the *News of the World* tomorrow and tell them her story of the priest who came to her for relief. She didn't know where he lived, but they'd sniff him out. Or maybe she was smiling because she was thinking of phoning him up any time she was short of money. She'd said she wasn't into blackmail, but what if she changed her mind about that? To get rid of her, he might have to involve the police. But no, he was in no position to do that. Maybe that's what the smile meant.

'How's that feel, Father? Just relax.'

He wished she wouldn't call him Father.

She smiled down on him with her lipsticked mouth, the crucifix dangling between her breasts.

She would never go away, this believer from hell. She would watch over him whatever he did, this unholy Madonna, and he would pray to her for forgiveness as he prayed to her now and heard her answer his prayer, calling him Father, telling him just to relax.

He let himself dissolve into the orgasm as the fluid catapulted out of him and spattered on his chest, like the first spots of a downpour.

There would be no relief.

An Invisible Man

SOMETIMES ON DARK winter mornings he watched them before
the doors were opened: pressing their hands and faces against
the glass, a plague of moths wanting in to the light. But you
couldn't look at them like that, as an invading swarm. To do
the job, you had to get in among them, make yourself invisible. You had to blend in, pretend to be one of them, but you
also had to observe them, you had to see the hand slipping
the Game Boy into the sleeve. Kids wore such loose clothes
nowadays, baggy jeans and jogging tops two sizes too big for
them. It was the fashion, but it meant they could hide their
plunder easily. You had to watch the well-dressed gentlemen
as well – the Crombie and the briefcase could conceal a for-
tune in luxury items. When it came down to it, you were a
spy.

He was in the Food Hall and they were rushing around
him. He picked up a wire basket and strolled through the veg-
etables, doing his best to look interested in a packet of
Continental Salad, washed and ready to use. It was easy to
stop taking anything in and let the shopping and the shoplifting
happen around you, a blur, an organism, an animal called
The Public. The Public was all over the shop: poking its nose
into everything; trying on the clean new underwear; squirting
the testers on its chin, on its wrists, behind its ears; wriggling
its fingers into the gloves; squeezing its warm, damp feet into
stiff, new shoes; tinkering with the computers; thumbing the
avocados.

He was watching a grey-haired woman dressed in a sagging blue raincoat, probably in her sixties, doing exactly that. The clear blue eyes, magnified by thick lenses, looked permanently shocked. A disappointed mouth, darkened by a plum-coloured lipstick, floundered in a tight net of wrinkles. There was something in her movements that was very tense, yet she moved slowly, as if she had been stunned by some very bad news.

She put down the avocados – three of them, packaged in polythene – as if she'd just realised what they were and that she didn't need them. He followed her as she made her way to the express pay-point and took her place in the queue. He stacked his empty basket and waited on the other side of the cash-points, impersonating a bewildered husband waiting for the wife he'd lost sight of. He watched her counting her coins from a small black purse. The transaction seemed to fluster her, as if she might not have enough money to pay for the few things she'd bought. A tin of lentil soup. An individual chicken pie. One solitary tomato. Maybe she did need the avocados – or something else.

The pay-point wasn't the obvious place to catch shoplifters, so they used it. It was like declaring something when you went through customs, in the hope that the real contraband would go unnoticed. Or offering a small sin at confession, hoping that it would distract God from his ferocious omniscience. An amateur tactic. It was easy to catch someone with a conscience, someone who wanted to be caught.

He ambled behind her to the escalator down to Kitchen and Garden. When she came off the escalator, she waited at the bottom, as if not sure where to find what she was looking for. He moved away from her to the saucepans and busied himself opening up a three-tiered vegetable steamer, then he put the lid back on hastily to follow her to the gardening equipment. She moved past the lawn-mowers and the sprinklers until she came to a display of seed packets.

It wasn't often that you had this kind of intuition about somebody and it turned out to be right, but as soon as he saw her looking at the seeds, he was certain she was going to steal them. He moved closer to her, picked up a watering-can and weighed it in his hand, as if this was somehow a way of testing it, then he saw her dropping packet after packet into the bag. He followed her to the door and outside, then he put his hand on her shoulder. When she turned round he showed her his ID. Already she was shaking visibly. Her red-veined cheeks had taken on a hectic colour and tears loomed behind her outraged blue eyes.

'Please,' she said, 'arrest me. Before I do something worse.'

He took her back inside and they made the long journey to the top of the store in silence. For the last leg of it he took her through Fabrics – wondering if they might be taken for a couple, a sad old couple shopping together in silence – and up the back staircase so that he wouldn't have to march her through Admin.

It was depressing to unlock the door of his cubby-hole, switch the light on and see the table barely big enough to hold his kettle and his tea things, the one upright chair, the barred window looking out on a fire-escape and the wall-mounted telephone. He asked her to take the packets of seeds out of her bag and put them on the table. She did so, and the sight of the packets, with their gaudy-coloured photographs of flowers, made her clench her hand into a fist.

He told her to take a seat while he called security, but when he turned away from her she let out a thin wail that made him recoil from the phone. She had both her temples between her hands, as if afraid her head might explode. She let out another shrill wail. It ripped out of her like something wild kept prisoner for years. It seemed to make the room shrink around them.

'Now, now, no noise, please,' he said, like a dentist who'd just drilled into a nerve. He cursed himself inwardly for bringing her here alone – he should have collected a security guard on the way. Now he was on his own with her in the cubby-hole and she was wailing. If the people in Admin heard, it might be open to all sorts of interpretation. His job was under threat as it was, what with the security guards and the new surveillance cameras.

She wailed again – a raw outpouring of anger and loss. Christ, he had to get her out of here. He stooped over her and reached out to take one of her hands away from her head, then he thought better of touching her at all. His hand hovered over her as he spoke: 'Look, you don't seem like a habitual shoplifter –'

She blurted out that she'd never stolen anything in her life before, but it was hard to make out the words because she was sobbing and coughing at the same time, her meagre body shuddering as if an invisible man had taken her by the shoulders and was shaking her violently.

'I'm sure it was just absent-mindedness. You intended to pay for these –' He motioned with a hand to the scattered packets of seeds on the table, but she was having none of it.

'No, I stole them. I don't even like gardening –' The words came out in spurts between her coughs and sobs but there was no stopping her now that she'd started: 'It's overgrown, weeds everywhere. It was him who did it. He was mad about his garden. He spent all his time there, morning till night, out in all bloody weathers –'

He let her talk. Her husband had been obsessed with his garden. It had been his way of getting away – from her, from everyone and everything. He'd withdrawn from the world into his flowering shrubs and geraniums. She hardly saw him, and when he'd died all there was left of him was his garden. Now the weeds were taking over. When she'd seen the seed packets, with their pictures of dahlias and pansies and rhododendrons . . . It made a kind of sense. Why had she stolen them rather than pay for them? He should have known better than to ask. He got the whole story of her financial hardship now that she was on her own, including the cost of the funeral. It was an expensive business, dying.

When she'd finished, she fished a small white handkerchief from her coat pocket to wipe the tears from her eyes. It was the way she did this that reminded him of his mother, the way she had to move her glasses out of the way to get the handkerchief to her eyes. He told her to go home. She looked up at him in surprise, then clutched the handles of her bag, realising she should get out while the going was good.

When she stood up her blue eyes were alert with curiosity. 'Why are you doing this?'

'I don't know.'

He had made thieves of so many people. But this one reminded him of his mother. He absolved her with a wave of his hand. Still she made a fuss of thanking him, reaching up to touch his collar. When she'd gone, he noticed the crumpled handkerchief on the floor and bent down to pick it up.

He had stepped into the lift and pressed the button for the ground floor before he realised that the lights weren't working. The doors hissed together and he was alarmed to be shut inside a box of night. He crossed himself without thinking, although he hadn't done so for years. He heard the machinery of the lift working – a slight gasp of the hydraulics he'd never noticed before – then he began to descend slowly through the darkness. He imagined that the lift was his coffin and he was descending into the earth. Then he wondered why they didn't bury people upright, what with cemetery space being at a premium. When his mother had died, hadn't he had to take out a personal loan to cover the funeral and the cost of the plot? As the woman had said, it was an expensive business.

The lift came to a halt, the doors slid apart, but no one was waiting to get in. He looked out at Lingerie. From the crowd of people shambling around the counters rose a line of perfect legs sheathed in stockings and tights, their toes pointing at the roof. Above them the elegant models stood on their plinths, dressed in camisoles and negligees, averting their eyeless faces like disdainful idols.

Some of the creations in there were unbelievable. They were designed to tempt men, so it made sense to put them on the same floor as Menswear. He'd apprehended one man, about his own age, respectable in his choice of casual wear, greying at the sides and balding on top, trying to cram an expensive Gossard scarlet basque into his inside pocket. He'd wanted to buy it – for his wife, he'd said at first, then had admitted later, when he'd got him in the cubby-hole, that it was for his mistress – but he'd felt too embarrassed to take it to a pay-point and hand it over to be wrapped. He'd begged him to let him off – poor man, in his Yves Saint-Laurent polo shirt. Maybe not so poor: he'd probably get off with a small fine or an admonishment, and although he was in his fifties, he had a mistress – one who would wear a scarlet basque.

The doors hissed together and he was shut in with the darkness again. She hadn't wanted to be cremated, in case the soul turned out to be located in the hypothalamus, or some other part of the body. She'd had some funny notions that way. She'd believed in an afterlife, having been brought up a good Catholic, but in her later life – maybe because of him, because he'd turned his back on the priesthood – she'd stopped caring what form the afterlife might take. Heaven or reincarnation – she'd settle for either. In the hospice, she had accepted the services of the priest, the vicar and the visiting humanist, keeping her options open. If there had been a rabbi and a Buddhist coming round, she would have signed up with them too. With more eagerness, maybe, because they would be new to her, and she had always believed in anything she didn't know about, as if the very fact that she hadn't heard of it gave it credence, so complete was her humility.

There was the gasp of the hydraulics as the lift was released and he felt himself sinking again. It all seemed to take much longer in the dark.

He had watched her body shrink into itself like a withering fruit, but she'd gone on smiling, determined to keep up appearances. He remembered the last demented thing she had said to him as she lay there, scandalised by her own condition, about her bedside locker being bugged, about the other patients and their visitors being spies. Then she'd urged him to eat the fruit in the bowl: 'Have a banana, son,' she'd said, then died.

He remembered the moment when the faint pressure of her hand on his had faded away completely, leaving a dead hand there with no touch left in it.

None of it had made any sense to him then, but it did now as he was lowered slowly through the darkness. She'd died in public, in a ward full of strangers. They weren't involved with her death, but they were watching it. She was right – they were spies. And her bedside locker, with its fruit and its flowers and its cards bearing tactfully optimistic messages – in a way, it had been bugged.

He hadn't eaten the fruit, but maybe he should have. She had wanted him to, but he'd remembered reading, at the seminary, about the sin-eaters, the people in ancient times who were hired at funerals to eat beside the corpse and so take upon themselves the sins of the dead.

If they buried people upright the graves would have to be deeper, of course, but they'd take up less horizontal space, which was what you were paying for, in the end. At the same time, the thought of people being buried in a standing position was ridiculous. It made him think of the dead standing in a queue, waiting to be served. They had chosen, and now they would have to pay the price. Think of the inscriptions: 'He was, and still is, a fine, upstanding citizen.'

He could hear a tannoyed announcement passing from under his feet to above his head. Where was he? Surely he'd reach the ground floor soon. Or maybe he'd gone past the ground floor and he was on his way back down to the Food Hall. The motion of the lift began to make him feel queasy, as if he'd lost control of his own movements and was part of the workings of the store. He felt as if he had been eaten and was now being slowly digested by a huge machine.

The lift came to a halt at last, but the doors didn't open. Where was he? Without the illuminated numbers above the door, it was hard to tell. In a dark lift, you could be anywhere. You could be in the confessional, except that there was no one to confess to. All you had was yourself. He felt the sweat trickle from his scalp and took the crumpled handkerchief from his pocket, but instead of dabbing his brow he brought it to his lips. It tasted faintly of salt. Then he felt himself begin to travel upwards through the darkness, like a slow missile launched into the night, or a soul departing the body.

A Date with My Wife

I WOKE UP a few seconds before the alarm clock went off, as if another clock inside me had been set to wake me up. In those few seconds I just had time to realise that although it was almost nine o'clock, I hadn't slept in. No – I had a day off work. I didn't have to get up. In fact, I had been looking forward to today all week, because today I had a date with my wife. We'd scheduled it a week ago. We'd arranged to meet, here in our bed, at noon – after she'd taken Jenny to school and gone to the gym and the library, after I'd gone for my swim. It had the excitement of a showdown. We were meeting for sex. I watched the luminous digits change from 08:59 to 09:00, then thumped the button with the side of my fist as soon as it began to bleep.

A day off – especially a day off with sex thrown in – was a rare pleasure to be savoured. Things had been getting pretty hairy at work. Although I was technically a self-employed copywriter, for the past year I'd been hooked up with Focus Marketing – a brash new company in the process of staking out its territory, shafting its rivals and fighting tooth and claw for every contract Jeremy, the guy heading us up, got a sniff of. Sometimes he called me up on Sunday mornings to ask if I'd done the work for some presentation for a TV ad. Even if I'd finished the work and left it with him, he'd call me up on Sunday morning and get me to describe the work to him, because what was important wasn't the work itself – which he usually hadn't looked at, anyway – but how we were going to pitch it to the prospective client. He wanted to know there and then how I was going to sell the ad to the suits in the boardroom when we went to meet them.

Jeremy never stopped working – he never sat down in the office, even to eat lunch – but a lot of the work he did was pointless. Yesterday, I'd got home from work to find three messages from him on my answering machine. The first was a frighteningly laconic and ambiguous message that still managed to sound like the end of my career: 'You've fucked up here, Craig, you've given the company bad breath in Mouthwash worldwide. You get back to me. We have to talk.'

He was talking about a couple of storyboards I'd put together for a series of mouthwash ads, just notional stuff to be sounded out in a company meeting – i.e. before we even talked to the client. The first storyboard outlined an animation using the St George and the dragon thing. St George was the one needing the mouthwash, of course. The message and the target audience were: everyone needs mouthwash (message), aimed at everyone (target audience).

Jeremy had gone for it and he'd shown the stuff to the client without talking it through with anyone. The client hadn't liked it at all. It was too general, too comic. They wanted something using science, and for years they'd been trying to expand into the teenage market, trying to convince teenagers that they should expect their parents to buy them mouthwash. Which was exactly the subtext of my second storyboard, the one Jeremy hadn't shown the client because he hadn't looked at it himself.

The second storyboard was indeed aimed at teenagers, using the kissing thing and totally giving over the message that this mouthwash was cool – cool in all senses of the word. It not only looked cool but tasted cool, and the coolest thing about it was that it was the one thing your parents wouldn't mind paying for – what parent would want their teenage boy or girl to have bad breath? Although the target audience was 13–17, there was a guilt undercurrent aimed at parents who didn't buy their kids mouthwash, didn't protect their kids' teeth from decay and plaque. The voice-over delivered the science, whatever that was – that was the trouble, clients never gave you facts in their product definitions or their product descriptions, all they gave you was their ideas about what the product was . . . Anyway, there would be some stuff about how plaque is like an evil, tooth-attacking virus/disease thing that was curable only with this mouthwash because this mouthwash had a new kind of fluoride in it. I envisaged the actual TV ad ending with the mum kissing her teenage son/daughter goodbye before he/she goes out on a date, then the son/daughter screws up his/her nose and grimaces and the mum checks her own breath. It didn't have to be the mum, it could be the dad. I hadn't decided this yet. It could be mum–son, mum–daughter, father–daughter or father–son. The father–son one was the one I was in favour of, moving with the times, so in the final frames of the storyboard I'd shown the dad saying goodbye to the son he'd bought the mouthwash for and then checking his own breath. Okay, it was shit, but if he'd read their brief Jeremy should have shown them that one, not the dragon one.

In other words Jeremy had fucked up, so he had to tell me I'd fucked up. That's what he had to do, because he was the boss. He had to kick some ass, but it was my ass he was kicking. His second message was less aggressive, maybe, but no less threatening – saying how he'd talked up my work on the phone to such-and-such a big cock in the mouthwash company and she'd eventually condescended to agree to look at a resubmission, so he wanted it on his desk by tomorrow morning. On his desk. That was a joke, because Jeremy didn't have a desk, or if he did I'd never seen it. There were desks in his room, of course, lots of desks, some with computers and phones and fax machines on them, some with draft presentations on them and Jeremy's memos to himself – which were usually written in huge felt-tip block capitals on white-boards, like lists of suspects. There were also desks with nothing on them at all. But there wasn't a desk that was *his* desk.

The third message was about looking at my second story-board and saying we could maybe do something with it.

So, three messages on my answerphone from Jeremy. In a way it was flattering – he was the alpha male, and he was paying me a lot of attention. In another way he was stressing me out, and what worried me was that he might be doing this deliberately because he wanted rid of me and this was his way of preparing the ground for the 'I'll have to let you go' speech. Whatever, I'd decided not to phone him back. I'd just let him hang there. If necessary, I'd tell him the truth: I hadn't got back to him because today I had a date with my wife. Maybe that would shock him so much that he'd get off my back.

I had a day off work, but this whole mouthwash thing was getting to me. I knew I was going to have to go in tomorrow morning and give Jeremy something that was seen to develop my second storyboard but didn't actually change anything in it, because that was basically what they wanted.

I turned over in bed and tried not to taste my own breath. There was probably footage of plaque doing its stuff on some teeth, using fast-forwarded film like those clips of flowers/ mushrooms growing or skies changing or the sun coming up/ going down. Maybe I could use something like that if they wanted the parent/science thing developed. But maybe the parent/science element was just not cool enough.

I was on my own in the house. It was the first time in weeks that I had been alone in my own home. I should be feeling a sense of luxury, but I felt guilty. Why did I feel guilty? What was I feeling guilty about? I was having a day off work, because they owed me fifteen days' holidays I hadn't taken. No guilt there. I'd stayed in bed while Vivienne dealt with the kids – was that where the guilt came in?

I'd been aware of her getting out of bed, doing the breakfast for the kids and having an argument with Jenny about her football boots. Vivienne was patiently explaining to her that she hadn't cleaned them because Jenny hadn't given her them to clean, and that if they needed cleaned she should give them to her the day before she had football. But Jenny was wailing and being difficult and blaming Vivienne for the state of her football boots. I had wanted to intervene. I had wanted to get up, confront Jenny and tell her: your football boots are your responsibility, not Mum's, but then it had blown over and I'd drifted back into sleep. Some time later I remembered George, our fourteen-year-old son, coming into the bedroom to look at himself in the long mirror on the wardrobe, adjusting his hair and his jeans and examining a few of his spots with forensic interest.

There should be no guilt in this, none at all. I'd done the breakfast-and-school routine the previous two mornings before going to the office, fobbing off Jeremy with the traffic as an excuse for my lateness. Jeremy didn't like it if the family was seen to encroach on his employees' time. Anything else was more acceptable.

I'd been picking up Jenny from football practice after school most Wednesdays for nearly a year now and none of my colleagues knew it. Vivienne couldn't pick her up that day, because she had a late class at the college where she taught. Of course, one or two of the guys at work sometimes questioned the stories I gave them – that I was meeting a client, feeling ill, attending a funeral, collecting a computer component, putting my car in for a service, keeping an appointment at the dentist's or the optician's, etcetera. After a while I'd let them believe what they seemed to be hell-bent on believing – that I was having an affair. Somehow this had made it so much easier to get away – even Jeremy had stopped expecting me to be there after four on Wednesdays. So here I was, lying through my teeth and thought to be an adulterer, having to suffer their nudges and innuendoes in the pub after work on a Friday, all so that I could collect Jenny from school.

It worried me that Jeremy let me go on a Wednesday afternoon. It confirmed my suspicion that he thought I was dispensable. I was the copy guy, the guy who came up with the captions, the words, the voice-overs, or the three or four lines of dialogue if it was that sort of ad. It was a difficult role to play in the team, because usually very few words are actually used in any television advertisement. They have to be carefully chosen. Everyone in the team recognised the importance of the words, but everyone in the team felt that they could do the words just as well as me. But the words aren't easy, especially when someone else is in charge of the script.

I'd volunteered to do the breakfast-and-school routine the past two mornings so that Vivienne could concentrate on getting herself ready and out to her conference – a two-day in-service thing she'd organised single-handedly for Business Management teachers – and she'd appreciated it. Last night she'd told me to enjoy my long-lie, enjoy my swim. So why did I feel guilty that I hadn't woken up, hadn't heard the kids shouting their goodbyes before they went out the door? I was in the clear. Plus, I'd gone to a lot of trouble to get this particular day off work, because Vivienne had a holiday.

We'd only recently decided to meet for sex in this way, at a prearranged time. There were few times when it was possible. Both our jobs were demanding and mine often involved evening or weekend work when there was a rush to get a particular package ready for a prospective client. Part of the reason for timetabling our sex was that, if we didn't, it was virtually impossible to fit it in to suit both of us. Everything else in our lives was timetabled, so it made a kind of sense. It wasn't ideal, of course. It wasn't exactly spontaneous, but on the other hand it did away with the doubts, the uncertainties: Is she in the mood tonight? If I make a move, how will she respond? It must be, I realised, similar for her: Am I in the mood tonight? If he wants it, how will I respond? The prearranged meeting was a practical tactic, but it also had some advantages: the anticipation before a date was something I had long since consigned to memory, but now here it was again. I hoped I wouldn't bump into Vivienne – the gym was part of the same centre as the pool – because that might defuse some of the anticipation.

I yawned and thought: good, it's not late, get out of bed now, have a leisurely breakfast, go for that swim. To hell with Jeremy and his demands. I smiled and closed my eyes. Everything was as it should be, everything was running according to plan.

I hadn't made it to the swimming-pool for months. This was meant to be the start of a new routine, a new effort to get fit or, at any rate, less unfit, at least to combat the rot that was setting in now that I was forty. The target I'd set myself was exactly that: forty lengths, one for each year of my life, at least twice a week – though the real target was four days a week. Like others who'd hit forty, I'd started to go loose around the middle. My once tight bum had spread from years of sitting on office chairs in front of drawing-boards and computers. The magazine articles all said it: from now on it was all down-hill, unless you did something about it. Vivienne had already started her own routine months ago, making it along to the gym at least three times a week. Now I had to get going on it, but as I lifted my swimming bag from the passenger seat, locked the car and turned to the swimming-pool, a feeling of dread seemed to add weight to my movements, as if I was already wading through heavy water.

The young attendant in the reception booth was on the phone, and had turned away from the counter on his swivel-chair. He wore a white open-necked short-sleeved T-shirt and black shorts and had his feet propped up against the wall, showing his suntanned and muscular legs. He held the phone propped between his chin and his shoulder so that he could leaf through *The Sun*. Though he spoke in a voice too loud to ignore, he was obviously talking intimately to a woman, a girlfriend, because he seemed to be arranging a date with her. Or maybe it was someone else's girlfriend, someone else's wife? What he was saying seemed to suggest this: 'Where's he gone? I like it. When'll he be back? That's cool. Don't worry, I'll be there. Steve can cover for me, no problem. Try and stop me.'

When he hung up he went on turning the pages of his newspaper. I had to clear my throat to get his attention. He swung round in the chair to face me. As he leaned towards me, his gold chain swung forward on his broad brown neck. He swept a plume of shiny black hair from his brow and flashed his brilliant white teeth in a smile.

'A swim, please,' I said.

As I paid my entrance fee I got the feeling that he was sup-pressing a scalding peal of mirth. I felt like reaching over the counter, grabbing him by the collar, pulling his face close to mine and growling at him: *you vain little bastard, you, you will never know the suffering you have caused.*

I pushed through the double doors into the pool area. The smell of chlorine, the wavering light, the elongated, echoing sounds usually made me feel good, but today everything seemed ugly and distorted. It was an old-fashioned style of swimming-pool, with the changing cubicles around the side. Along the women's side, above the shoulder-high cubicle doors, there were striped plastic curtains, all of which seemed to be closed. It was obviously busy, and I couldn't find an unoccupied cubicle on the men's side.

I found an empty cubicle, the last one on the men's side, shut the door and began to undress. I took off my jacket and hung it on a hook, removed my wristwatch and put it in one of the pockets, then I did the same with my glasses. I glanced over the cubicle door at the people swimming. There didn't seem to be any women in the water. Just men. That was very odd – especially as all the women's cubicles seemed to be taken. Had I stumbled on a 'men only' session? But they didn't have 'men only' sessions, they just had 'women only' sessions, 'mother and baby' sessions and '50 +' sessions. If they had a 'men only' session, wouldn't it quickly become a 'gay men only' session? Jesus, maybe that's what it was. As I hung my shirt on a hook, I looked again at the men swimming. None of them looked gay, or even heterosexual. None of them looked like a sexual being at all. Even without my glasses on, I could see that they all looked exhausted and overweight – unhealthy men doomed to swim lengths interminably as a punishment for letting themselves go. Men like me. But maybe it was a special session of some sort, because I noticed that the entire pool was divided into lanes, rather than just half the pool as usual. I stood on one foot to slide off my shoe, then the sock, which I crammed into the shoe.

I was doing the same with the other foot when I heard the crack of a starting pistol. Christ almighty, were all these men racing each other, as if they were taking part in some Olympic event? Would I be able to keep up?

I turned away from the pool and tugged the shower-gel and the towel from my swimming bag. My trunks – where were they? Had I forgotten them? I looked in the folds of the towel, but they weren't there. Jesus, I'd have to get dressed again and leave, leave without even getting in the water. Maybe that would be just as well, given the way they seemed to be running things nowadays, but my body felt hot and moist. I itched to immerse myself in the water. Then I saw my trunks – on the floor of the cubicle, under the bench. They had landed in a pool of water, and when I picked them up they felt cold and clammy. They wouldn't be pleasant to put on, but at least I hadn't forgotten them. The starting pistol cracked again. I peered over the top of the door and saw a woman attendant sitting up on that metal edifice – half chair, half ladder, except this one looked higher than the ones swimming-pool attendants usually used, this one was more like the kind of thing the referees at Wimbledon sat on. The woman was blonde, and she sat in a very straight-backed attitude, with one hand raised on a level with her ear, holding the starter pistol pointed at the ceiling. Something in her posture made me fish my glasses out of my jacket pocket and put them on. When she sprang into focus, I saw that my suspicion was confirmed: it was Vivienne. Why hadn't she told me she was working as an attendant?

She looked bored and rather scornful as she surveyed the men swimming up and down beneath her. I had to admit that she looked fantastically good, poised up there on that pedestal of chrome. She was wearing a black swimsuit. It was a one-piece, but briefer and tighter than the one she usually

A DATE WITH MY WIFE

wore, and it was boldly designed with a convoluted, rope-
like pattern like a twist of liquorice. She had definitely lost
weight – all those hours at the gym had paid off. It was what
the swimsuit concealed that filled me with such longing – I'd
be meeting her soon, very soon. After my swim, at twelve
o'clock, we had a date – in bed. I would lie down with this
woman whose poised body rose above the swimming-pool
like a dark question-mark.

I unzipped my jeans and pushed them and my boxer shorts
down to my ankles in one swift movement. My cock sprang
out, already semi-erect. I took it in my hand and tried to force
it down, but this only made it more insistent. I sagged on to
the bench, shut my eyes and tried to think of something
boring, not Vivienne out there in the black swimsuit – Jesus,
I'd be in bed with her soon! – something completely unstim-
ulating, the kind of thing you could use to postpone an orgasm.
Mental long division. Divide fifteen thousand by thirty-two.
Too difficult. Times tables. Nine ones are nine. Nine twos –

By the time I'd got to nine nines, I knew I could relax. I
hurried along to the men's showers, avoiding eye contact with
Vivienne. Maybe I'd wave to her once I was in the pool. There
were two men in the shower. I went to the vacant spray
between them. One was a guy with a broad-chested, slim-
waisted body. The dark hair on his muscular chest arrowed
down towards a tight stomach. He stood with his back to the
wall, naked, his long dark cock sprouting from the crevice of
his groin like an outcrop of rock in a waterfall. He stood there
staring directly at the sign on the wall opposite which stated
that the removal of swimming costumes was forbidden. How
come this Greek god was here? He was totally unlike the other
men I'd seen in the pool. On the other side, was an old guy.
A grey stubble above his ears was all that was left of his hair.
He wore a capacious pair of shapeless shorts, once white but

now yellowing, almost transparent when wet. They weren't even meant for swimming. They were enormous, and so was he – not in height, but in girth. He huffed and puffed as he showered energetically, soaping himself all over with the stuff from the dispenser. Unlike the naked satyr, this guy was having a real shower, shoving both his hands down into his shorts to wash his genitals thoroughly. His enormous, pale member flopped in and out of the baggy shorts like a French loaf that's gone soft.

I hurried out of the showers and dived quickly into the pool. Too quickly. I felt my trunks being pulled from my hips by the water, sucked down my legs and off. Jesus Christ, I was naked in the swimming-pool. I surfaced briefly to hear a shrill whistle, then ducked under the water again to search for the trunks. The chlorine stung my eyes and the shadows of the swimmers confused my vision. Then I saw them: sliding along the bottom of the pool like some deep-sea creature moving over the ocean floor. I swam down towards them, confused momentarily by a school of goldfish gliding by. Before I could reach the trunks, I had to come up for air. When I did, I saw that it was Vivienne blowing the whistle, but it wasn't hers. It hung from a chain around the handsome young attendant's neck. He was up there on the pedestal with her, leaning forward obligingly so that she could use his whistle, and the two of them looked to be in a position of delicately arranged intimacy. She was blowing on the whistle and shouting down at me as I treaded water. The water – what was wrong with the water? What was wrong with it was that it was pink. I had swallowed some of it, and now I spat it out of my mouth. It was mouthwash all right, but it tasted more like chewing-gum. It was mouthwash designed for teenagers, that's what it was, chewing-gum-flavoured mouthwash.

I sat upright in the bed. It was hot and airless in the bedroom, and I was sweating. Chewing-gum flavoured mouthwash. It was brilliant. We could go back to the client and say, yes, we can sell it to teenagers, all you have to do is change the product slightly. This was the right, aggressive approach. I felt like calling Jeremy there and then. I looked at the clock. It was eleven-forty. Jesus, I'd slept all morning.

I heard Vivienne moving around downstairs – her heels on the kitchen floor. Did she know I was here? Maybe she would have seen my swimming bag hung on a hook in the hall, packed ready last night, and know I hadn't gone. Or maybe she'd think I had gone, and just hung the bag back on the same hook. But she was probably too preoccupied to have noticed my swimming bag. As I listened to her moving about in the kitchen, somehow I knew she thought she was alone in the house. She made herself coffee, sat down at the kitchen table, then the phone rang and she hurried into the hall to answer it.

I strained to listen. I knew it was Jeremy by Vivienne's tone – deliberately evasive. No, she didn't know where I was. She didn't know when I'd be coming home. Yes, she'd give me the message. Of course, she understood how important it was. When she put down the phone she groaned, then came upstairs and went into the bathroom. I heard her flushing the toilet, showering, cleaning her teeth. Then I heard her gargling – I'd brought home some sample bottles of mouthwash the company had sent us. So now she was using it. She'd be surprised to find me here, already in bed. When I heard her opening the bathroom door and walking towards the bedroom, I wondered if I'd lie to her or tell her the truth.

The Start of Something

THE LETTER FROM Long John Silver was waiting for Bill Rafferty when he came home one drizzling morning in June after driving Lillian and Rachel to school and Julie, his wife, to the theatre where she was rehearsing for a new production. He was hoping to write something about a memory which had come into his mind as he was falling asleep the previous night: as a boy, going to the shows with only a couple of foreign coins in his pocket. It was just the start of something, he didn't know if there was a story there or not, but he wanted to describe the shows, and the boy walking round with the strange coins in his pocket. He didn't know what it was about, but he wanted to get started on it before it went the way some stories had gone in the past.

He reheated some coffee left over from breakfast as he went through the post without opening it. He threw aside a couple of bills and some junk mail with irritation, pausing over a card inviting him to the book launch of his friend Mike McGrane. Mike was doing okay. Not that great, but okay. About the same as Rafferty, maybe, but here he was with another book out. There was a letter from the BBC. One fat, handwritten envelope – a letter from an old friend. A few things for his wife . . . He put the post aside to pour his coffee and thought, just leave it till later, get down to work. On the other hand the one from the BBC might contain a small but meaningful cheque, or the promise of such later in the decade. Or maybe an acceptance, a rejection, even a request: 'Dear

Mr Rafferty, We are currently planning to run a series of short stories set in fairgrounds, preferably about young boys with Irish coins in their pockets . . .'

So they were Irish coins. Had he remembered that or decided it? Maybe it didn't matter. Maybe it was going to be one of those rare stories that virtually wrote itself, and all he'd have to do was take dictation. He picked up the BBC envelope and examined it with fetishistic interest. Sometimes he hung around at the window, watching the postman's progress along the street, anxious for something good to come his way. 'Dear Mr Rafferty, Having long been an admirer of your work, it gives me great pleasure to invite you to speak at the Sorbonne . . . I can offer you a fee of . . . You will be staying at the Hotel . . .' Sometimes when he'd sent things out and needed something back, he found himself waiting behind the door for the letterbox to open – Pavlov's dog, salivating for its dinner.

He sipped at his coffee, then recognised the letter from Long John: how could he have missed that slender cream envelope with the address in crisp, black print? The kind that might yield an expansively generous cheque but instead delivered a smug invoice. Silver's bills came quarterly, and if the first two were anything to go by, he wasn't cheap.

Long John was an accountant who had been recommended to Rafferty by his publisher. They nicknamed him Long John, as far as he could make out, because his surname was Silver and he was long – or rather, tall. Rafferty had taken his publisher's advice and made an appointment, and had driven in his battered Escort to Silver's elegant Georgian house in the New Town. The secretary had let him into a high-ceilinged drawing-room, told him Mr Silver wouldn't be a moment and asked him if he wanted coffee or something.

'Something,' Rafferty had said.

She had smiled with real understanding and opened the drinks cabinet. Rafferty pointed to a label he had sometimes admired from a distance and said he'd leave the measure up to her. She poured him a large one – I'll pay for this, he thought – and left him to look around the room. A bank of computers had put out their creepers of grey flex among the house-plants. He watched the screen-savers, wondered if the antiques were genuine and waited. Long John came in. A lean, angular character, dressed in jeans and a sweatshirt which looked worn but expensive. His pale eyes, magnified by thick, tinted lenses, looked both owlish and distant. He listened to Rafferty's story, nodding every now and then as if he'd heard it all before. The year he'd paid tax on the assessment but not submitted accounts. The year he was unemployed some of the time and the rest of the time writing book reviews, paid as badly as they were needed. Then there was the year in Canada on a cultural exchange fellowship, where he taught Creative Writing, whatever that was and – Rafferty sensed boredom in his listener, and threw in some local colour – caught a seven-pound salmon and non-specific urethritis.

Long John smiled a thin smile and told him everything would be taken care of. He knew the ways of the Inland Revenue. He had worked as a tax inspector himself. He would have someone go through Rafferty's papers and submit finished accounts within the month. The Canadian earnings could be written off: in the nature of a non-taxable stipend.

'If you have any hassle from the Revenue,' he'd added on the way out, 'Just pass it on to me.'

Rafferty opened the letter and sagged into a chair as Silver's words began to register. The inspector of taxes had not accepted the accounts which had been submitted. Furthermore he – Rafferty had always thought of the Inland Revenue

as 'it' or 'they'; now it was 'he', and he had a name: Mr Mason
– *he* was not prepared to concede that Rafferty's Canadian
earnings were 'in the nature of a stipend'. Moreover, he wanted
to see bank statements, building society books, remittances
and receipts. In short, Mr Mason wanted to take a close look
at Rafferty's financial affairs for the past six years. A casual
mention of the interviews, plural, he would have to schedule
with Mr Mason, then Silver ended his letter with a placatory
paragraph to the effect that there was nothing to worry about.
He would assign one of his assistants to the case immediately. He added that as a considerable amount of additional
accounting work would be involved he would invoice him on
a monthly basis until the investigation was concluded, if that
was all right.

Enclosed was a list of documents and information Mr
Mason required, and a booklet called *Inland Revenue Invest-
igations*, which Rafferty read the way you sometimes feel
compelled to read a bad thriller. This one was about interest
on tax unpaid, penalties, false accounting. It was full of sug-
gestive vocabulary: 'fraudulent or negligent conduct'; 'deliber-
ate evasion'; 'culpable duties'; 'voluntary disclosure'. The
denouement was a settlement or a court action.

He went to the corner of the living-room he used as his
study, switched on the anglepoise and the computer, created
a new file and stared at the blank screen.

The boy steps out of the surrounding night into the light
of the fairground. He can hear music, screams, laughter, a
noise that sounds like bubbles made of tin bursting one after
another. He can see the coloured lights spinning, flashing,
swaying in the wind. He can smell candyfloss, popcorn, hot-
dogs, machine oil and churned-up earth. He feels hungry but
doesn't want to spend his money on something to eat. In any
case, he's sure he can't pass off the Irish coins as real money

at the food stalls. He clutches the coins in his pocket, reluctant to spend them even if he can, because he likes them.
Both have a harp on one side. In his collection of foreign
coins – which he gets from his father, who works for the Gas
Board emptying the meters – they're his favourites, but they're
also the right size to be passed off as real currency in the slot
machines . . .

He wanted to go on but the tax thing was in the way. He
saved what he had, shut down the computer and started
searching in drawers and cupboards for his remittances,
receipts and bank statements.

He hadn't always been thorough about keeping remittances
and receipts. Sometimes he'd used the backs of them to write
shopping lists, or to take a light from the gas fire when he was
writing late at night and he'd run out of matches. He began
to notice items in newspapers and documentaries on TV
about the powers of the Inland Revenue. They could search
your home. They could take you to court. They could seize
your assets, make you sell your house. They were accountable
to no one, it seemed. It seemed they had more power than
the police.

He began to feel vaguely ill. There was a persistent, pul-
sating tightness in his left temple – a nerve, or a vein? Was it
neurological or vascular? The prelude to a stroke? Then there
was the breathlessness, the racing pulse. The writer in him
observed himself sitting in defensive attitudes, shoulders
hunched, head lowered, and entering rooms furtively, like a
child afraid of being scolded. His body bristled with aches
and discomforts, and often he would stop in the middle of
doing something to place a hand on his knee or his arm or
his neck, tilting his head and averting his eyes, as if listening
to someone over his shoulder.

It became difficult to sleep at night. He was used to staying awake late – often he liked to work during those quiet hours when the house, and sometimes the entire building, was sleeping. Now a different sort of work awaited him: to study his bank statements, trying to identify credits. Could £281 on 17 March 1995 possibly be the repayment of that lawyer's bill he'd paid for Graham, a friend who'd had to renegotiate his mortgage when his wife left him? It could. It was. But how could he prove it? Graham was still in a mess. He'd had a nervous breakdown and was in hospital. He couldn't go and ask a guy with problems like that to write a letter to the Inland Revenue explaining that Rafferty had once paid a lawyer's bill for him.

He began to invent stories to account for his pay-ins. This one was a gift from my father, who empties gas meters and brings home sacks of foreign coins. That one was the refund on a cancelled flight to Paris, where I had been invited to speak at the Sorbonne . . . I had to cancel the engagement due to an attack of laryngitis, an occupational hazard among writers who give public readings.

When he had sorted out, ordered and identified what he could, he stuffed everything into six large padded envelopes, one for each year under scrutiny, labelled them, strapped them into the passenger seat of the Escort and drove to Silver's. Long John came to the door himself, shielding his eyes from the sun with a pale hand.

'Ridiculous,' he said, as he took the bundle of envelopes in his arms, like an emaciated nurse bearing away a healthy baby, 'quite ridiculous. A chap like you, earning next to nothing. It's random, it's just something they do from time to time. We'll get it all sorted out, don't worry. I mean, you haven't *done* anything, have you?'

There was something almost camp, slightly theatrical, in the way Silver's magnified eyes opened in mock shock. Rafferty shook his head more vehemently than he meant to. He put his hand in his pocket and jingled his change. He thought of the boy with the coins in his pocket. What was going to happen to him? Who was he? Did he have a personality? Was he more than the victim of his circumstances? It was a bad sign that such questions were presenting themselves. The story was going to get away. He said goodbye to Silver and walked to the car. He climbed in but didn't start the engine.

Suppose the boy has moved away from the food stalls and is now looking at the rides: the dodgems, the waltzer, the ghost train, the big wheel. Most would cost more than he has, even if the Irish pennies were accepted. He wonders if the old man taking the admissions to the Crazy Mirrors tent would notice that his coins are Irish. He hangs around nearby. The old man sits on a stool, hunched forward, his arms dangling down on either side so that his fingers almost touch the ground. His cap droops over one eye and his jaw sags. He looks like a creature of a different species, a rare kind of ape. The old man notices the boy hanging around and growls the price at him. The boy holds out his two coins, the harp and the hen. The old man may not notice that they're Irish. If he does – what then? Does he chase the boy, cursing him and shouting? Or does he turn a blind eye to the boy's deception and let him into the magic mirrors?

He found himself wondering what Mr Mason looked like.

Rafferty took personal possession of a bottle of red wine as the sparse applause disintegrated. It was a depressingly small crowd for Mike McGrane's book launch, yet it felt crowded, sticky and airless in the book shop. Outside, it was a warm August evening.

Mike followed hot on his heels to the wine table, a cigarette already between his lips. 'Pour one in here while you're
at it.'

'You deserve it, after that.'

'Too right. I hate question time. Why is it somebody always
asks where you get your ideas from? I mean – what does it
matter where the hell they come from, as long as they come?
It's not as if stories start from ideas, anyway.'

'What do they start from, Mike?'

'Don't you start.'

McGrane wasn't enjoying his own launch. He looked
strained, tense. Book launches were like that. A weird mix-
ture of friends, family, other writers, editors, publishing
people, press if you were lucky.

Rafferty commiserated: 'Thought you'd get a better crowd.'

McGrane looked around and shrugged with resignation.
'So what are you working on?'

Rafferty was about to mention the story about the boy at
the fairground when he stopped himself. It wasn't written yet.
If he spoke about it, he would dispel it. How many unwritten
stories had gone that way in the past?

'Nothing much. Too busy with tax, my accounts.'

'A real work of fiction, eh?'

'Too true. I'm being investigated.'

'Really? You'd think they'd have bigger fish to fry. Who's
your accountant?'

'A Mr Silver.'

Rafferty saw Mike's glass stop on the way to his lips, then
his friend spouted smoke from his lips and looked at him
askance.

'Not Long John. No wonder they're looking at you.'

'Why? What's wrong with him?'

'Silver? Notorious. Ex-tax-office. The sheriff doesn't like it when his deputy decides to ride with the outlaws – know what I mean?'

Mike elaborated, citing various actors and writers who'd had Silver as their accountant. A playwright Rafferty knew vaguely who'd had to sell his house to pay the back tax and the interest and the fines. An actress who'd had some dental work done and was allowed to claim it on expenses, until a few years later, when they investigated her and decided it wasn't allowable after all. Ironically, according to McGrane, she'd had to do toothpaste ads to cover her arrears . . .

Someone took McGrane by the arm and led him to the table to sign books. Rafferty swilled a last glass of free wine and thought of the boy at the fair.

He must be thirsty by now. He must be getting tired, and maybe he was beginning to want to be home again, but there were the coins in his pocket. He knew he couldn't leave until he had spent them on something.

The letters he received from Silver began to assume the ominous significance of legal missives. Those slim, elegant envelopes with his name and address published neatly on their smooth cream skins made him close his eyes and bow his head before he opened them, as if trapped in a moment of private grief. The most recent ran to several pages, and pointed out the discrepancies for each year between his bank credits and his earnings. Could he account for these discrepancies? If not, they would be treated as earnings for which tax had remained unpaid. A date for the first interview with Mason had been set. He had a fortnight to worry about it. After studying his dog-eared bank statements for a week, Rafferty thought he could account for some of it – a refund from an insurance company, a gift from his mother-in-law, a book award, a few misfiled remittances . . . it went only so far.

One evening he was poring over faded receipts from unknown cash-registers in the past, when Julie came home from the preview night of the play she'd been rehearsing,

'How did it go?' he asked her.

'Don't ask.'

Rafferty opened a bottle of wine and tried to listen. The play was about a fisherman's wife who loses her husband at sea. The wind machine hadn't worked properly, or had worked too well, so that a poignant moment – with the wife standing alone on the beach and lamenting the loss of her husband – had become comic, because the wind machine had somehow got stuck on the wrong setting, at full blast, so that she had to struggle to make herself heard above the noise it made. Rafferty found himself laughing for the first time for ages.

'What the fuck's so funny?' his wife asked him.

'Just the thought of the wind machine . . . You have to admit, it's funny.'

'Funny if you're not expected to say your most plangent lines while you're being blown off the stage. It was demoralising.'

'I'm sorry.'

He seemed to be apologising to her a lot recently.

When she went to bed, he quickly put his bank statements in chronological order and followed her. Sex between them had been intense, lately. It offered a kind of escape for both of them, and they embraced each other with an urgency that was exciting at first, then troubling.

He slipped into bed beside her but didn't touch her.

'What are you waiting for?' she said.

'What's your hurry?'

'It's late. I'm tired.'

Rafferty complied, climbing into position immediately. There was a hunger in it that was new. He needed the sex to take his mind off the tax, and she needed it to take her mind off the show, but their needs eclipsed everything else. Even when they shuddered to a climax together, there was no sense that it had brought them closer to each other, and soon they rolled apart and turned from each other to their separate pre-occupations.

Rafferty needed it too often. He had become obsessed with orgasm – not his own, but hers. He felt troubled if he came but she didn't, as if in the currency of sex he dreaded getting into more debt than he was already. Sometimes he pestered her about this, asking her how it had felt for her, and she said that she needed to sleep and that if it was good no investigation should be necessary.

It was a sentiment close to his heart.

From such transactions between the sheets, Rafferty would rouse himself to don his dressing-gown and go into the kitchen, where he would strain his eyes looking at blurred numbers on crumpled pieces of paper.

What could a credit of £1,000 (one thousand pounds) on 14 July five years ago possibly represent? Had it been a present from his mother-in-law? If so, had he thanked her for it? Then there was a publisher's advance which had somehow escaped his accounts but not his bank statements, un-declared and untaxed, because it had been shoved into the 'Royalties' file, a slim one compared to the others. But there it was, an inexplicably undeclared amount. He felt amazed that he had ever received it. He couldn't remember paying the cheque in and coming out of the bank feeling that much richer, thinking that the next month or two would be a little easier and walking with a descriptively clichéd bounce in his step. If only he could relate the figures to concrete events, he might get somewhere, but the more he puzzled over long-spent pay-ins, the more elusive the whole concept of money became. The only money he could relate to was the money in his pocket.

The boy is still wandering through the fairground but he has given up watching the rides. Now he's looking at the stalls that offer prizes. The roll-a-penny stall. The hook-a-duck. The rifle range with the playing cards pinned up on the wall. But the boy realises that although he would like to roll the penny, hook a duck or shoot a rifle, he doesn't want a teddy bear, a coconut or a goldfish, so he wanders into the crowded amusement arcade.

The night before his first interview with Mr Mason, Rafferty was about to go through the figures for a particularly problematic year when Julie came into the room. He went on doing what he was doing, but she came up behind him and put her hand on his shoulder.

'Come on,' she said. 'Come to bed. The worst that can happen is they send you a bill.'

A bill I can't pay, he thought, but didn't say.

'You can't afford to spend more time on this. You have to write.'

'I can't concentrate.'

'It's good you got rid of the accountant, anyway. You'll meet the inspector tomorrow. When you speak to him face to face, it'll be okay. I mean, it's not as if you've got money stashed away in a Swiss bank account, is it?'

For a moment Rafferty thought his wife might be hoping he would say he had.

'Come on. Let's go to bed.'

Rafferty complied, determined not to run up debts.

The tax office is very dark, like a ruined castle inside, and the gaps in the outer walls allow the breeze to come in, making the coloured lights sway in the wind. There are corridors of a kind, with muddy carpets, and windows into offices full of teddy bears and coconuts and goldfish in plastic bags. There are doors too, with names on them: Mr Waltzer. Mr Big Wheel. Mr Dodgem. He stops at one door and reads the name 'Crazy Accounts Inspector'.

When Rafferty tries to knock, the door becomes a tent-flap and he pushes it aside. Inside, Mr Mason is sitting on a low stool, his cap drooping over one eye, his arms dangling down so low that his fingers almost touch the grassy carpet. The old man looks up as he enters and growls the price: 'Twenty thousand pounds, plus interest!'

Rafferty nods and smiles, anxious to let the old man know he's good for it, and digs into the pocket of his jeans. He brings out the two coins, his favourite coins, the ones with the harp and the hen, and offers them to the old man. The old man stares at them a moment, then rises from his stool to become enormous, a blisteringly angry giant of a man, and he chases Rafferty out of the tent, and Rafferty's frayed gym shoes are being sucked from his feet by the muddy carpet as he runs down the corridor, past the candyfloss stall, past the roll-a-penny, the hook-a-duck, out into the dark foyer, and behind him the giant is shouting, 'I'll catch ye!'

He woke up bathed in sweat and sitting upright in bed. His wife's voice came to him in the darkness as an urgent whisper, telling him to go back to sleep. He told her he'd had a nightmare about the investigation. She reassured him it would be all right in the end, then he lay awake and thought with longing about that time to come when it would all be over. He would look back on these tribulations in a mood of amused detachment. Maybe he would even write something about it. But such an experience wasn't the stuff of fiction, was it? No, it would have to be a piece for the paper. My experience in the hands of the Inland Revenue, that kind of thing. As he drifted back to sleep, he fantasised about threatening Mason: By the way, I should tell you that as a freelance writer I have access to the media. As a matter of fact, I have been commissioned to write a series of investigative pieces for a national newspaper on the Inland Revenue's methods, and it's only fair that I should inform you that this interview is being recorded, as have all the others. If you would like to see the transcripts, you'll have to go through my editor, my agent and my team of lawyers.

Mr Mason came to meet him in the lobby. A dark-haired, dark-suited man in his late forties, careful but not fussy in his dress – it was difficult to say if it was casual or formal. Rafferty found himself admiring the cut of his suit, but couldn't tell if it was expensive or cheap. Mason thanked him for coming in and smiled in an exasperated way. Rafferty noticed the incline of the head, as if he was used to peering at the world through a narrow opening. He shook Rafferty's hand, and introduced himself politely. As Rafferty followed him to his office, he noticed that Mason's trousers were slightly short, and tailored to slant downwards at the back in the French style. Expensive.

On the corner of Mason's desk there was a framed photograph of his wife and children. So he's human, thought Rafferty.

'Sorry about the smell in here,' said Mason. 'New carpets.' He smiled, and for a moment Rafferty thought he knew, somehow, about the muddy carpet in his dream.

They sat down.

'Now, Mr Rafferty,' Mason spread his fingers above Rafferty's documents, which were arranged, after a fashion, on his desk. Rafferty averted his eyes from the unsightly papers which had lain in his cupboards and drawers for years. He hoped he would never get them back. 'We have a few things to sort out here, don't we?'

Rafferty agreed and leaned back in the chair. He noticed a framed reproduction on Mason's wall. It was that Magritte thing of the pipe, and under it the words: *'Ceci n'est pas une pipe.'*

During the interviews which followed, over the weeks and months the investigation took up, Rafferty came to understand and loathe the implications of this picture on Mason's wall. He thought he understood what Magritte was saying: this is not a pipe, this is a *representation* of a pipe. But it was why Mason had chosen it that got to him: Mason dealt in duplicity, so he liked having a neat reminder on his wall that truth did exist, though it might not at first sight look like the truth. There was a motto-like quality to the picture in the context of a tax inspector's office which wasn't so very different from those wacky signs that said: 'You don't have to be mad to work here, but it helps.' At the same time, the simple contradiction of the Magritte picture seemed at times like an accusation, at times a reproach.

Rafferty had to admit that Mason treated him cordially, though sometimes he would look up from the documents on his desk and, from under cover of his bushy eyebrows, his keen blue eyes would ambush Rafferty with a piercing look of accusation. The questions came thick and fast: What were his assets? Where did he get the money to buy his house? What was its current value? How many bank accounts did he and his wife have apart from those already disclosed? Was he ever paid in cash? Did he own shares, savings bonds, antiques, works of art, jewellery? What was the value of the contents of his house? Did he own any properties abroad?

Where did he go on holiday? How often? How often did he and his wife go to the theatre or the cinema or out for a meal? Did he smoke? How many cigarettes did he smoke a day? How much did he and his wife spend on alcohol in an average week? Did he gamble?

'I don't want to worry you, but at the moment your lodgements for this particular year exceed your declared income by . . . and let's say it was the maximum penalty of one hundred per cent, then the fines and the interest would amount to . . . let me see . . .' Mason's fingers danced on the keys of his calculator.

It was April, the cruellest month for self-employed writers – the beginning of the new financial year. Rafferty's bank account still hadn't recovered from Christmas. He had to write something. He had to earn some money to knock a corner off the amount he had agreed was due in his letter of offer to Mr Mason. After a reading recently, during question time, someone had asked: 'What advice would you offer to younger writers?' and Rafferty had replied: 'Arrange to be paid in cash whenever possible, and keep track of your pay-ins.' What really got him was that it wasn't even a case of being sent a bill. No, you had to write a letter of offer, saying how much you owed them.

He had become it, and it had become them again.

Already Rafferty had two pristine files for his filing cabinet, one for receipts, the other for remittances. He had also bought a weighty ledger with four columns in which he could detail all moneys received. From now on, he would be able to date and identify everything.

He switched on the computer, formatted a new disk and created a new file. He selected a layout, set the tabs and created five neat columns: date; source; remittance number;

pay-in date; amount. Finally he set the decimal tab for the last column and hoped it would be a good year.

The boy has been so long in the fairground, now he knows that the moment has come when he must spend his coins on something. He has already wandered round the amusement arcade twice, examining all the machines carefully. The one with the silver ball you fire up into a spiralling track, then it drops into one hole that wins or one of six that lose. The Penny Derby with the spinning jockeys on horses under a glass dome. And the one called Penny Falls which he is peering into now. Behind the glass, a circular tray revolves slowly, and stacks of pennies have piled up on top of one another. Some are hanging over the edge of the circular hole in the middle. Your penny can cause the avalanche into the pay-out tray, then you've won. The boy takes a coin out of his pocket and rolls it down the chute into the machine. He watches as it rolls over the other coins and falls over. He does the same with the other, and watches as it almost causes an avalanche of coins into the pay-out tray, but instead ends by hanging precariously over the edge. It will be one of the first to go. The boy leaves the fairground and walks off into the darkness. He listens to the music and the noise of it fading with every step he takes. He walks home along a path over a dark hill, and at the top he turns to look at the fairground below. It looks so tiny now, he reaches out and cups it in his hand.

The End of Something

I WAS HEARING too much. There was nothing I didn't hear. The mice running up and down inside the walls. The wind gasping in the chimney. I heard the couple next door caressing each other in bed, or I thought I did. I'd become the opposite of deaf. It had got worse since I'd reverted to my bachelor existence, spending long days and nights without speaking to another human being, playing and listening, listening and playing, but there was always something to compete with.

They were at it again next door, shouting and yammering at each other. A door slammed and I felt the reverberations through the floor. Maybe it was their turn to split up. Or maybe they were just getting their own back for all the rows we'd had. I stopped playing and lowered the cello to the floor, laying the bow along its side. I reached into my waistcoat pocket and took out the earplugs I'd bought at the chemist's a few days ago. I squeezed them between my fingertips, trying to make cones of them as it had said to do in the instructions, then I pushed them into my ears with a twisting motion.

I stood up and walked around the room, feeling the foam expanding inside my ears. The neighbours were pushed into the background, but other things came into the foreground: the noises inside my body, my breathing, my throat swallowing, my heartbeat, the hum of my blood. I scratched my chin – a tenement being sandblasted. I hummed a few bars of the piece I was trying to finish and my voice boomed in my skull like the organ in a cathedral. It was no good – all they did was make my head feel like a drum.

When I took them out again and dropped them on the mantelpiece, the brittle outside noises sprang into the foreground: the yelled ultimatum from next door, the whisper of my own breath in the air of the room, somebody running down the stair, the traffic in the street five flights below. I could pick out each individual vehicle as if it was an instrument in an orchestra, tuning up. Even without looking out of the window I knew there was a jam. It wasn't that people were revving their engines or blaring their horns. No, they were crawling a yard at a time and then stopping. I could hear the brakes being released and then compressed. I could hear each growling engine. I began to hear the music of the traffic jam, instead of the piece I was trying to compose.

The same thing had happened last night, with the mice. The mice had moved in when Claire had moved out, and now they were multiplying. I'd been distracted by their squeaks in the kitchen – it sounded like they were having a party. I'd stopped playing and gone through, deliberately making as much noise as possible to scare them away. Even so I could hear them in the spaces beneath the kitchen units, running up and down inside the walls, scurrying behind the cooker.

I'd tried peering down behind the cooker, but it was too dark to see anything. Then I'd found a box of matches, lit one and tried to see into the narrow space between the wall and the cooker. The match had dropped from my hand and I'd heard a keen crackling noise as the dry paper and wood behind the cooker ignited. I grabbed the nearest thing to hand – my tennis racquet, which was lying on the worktop for some reason – and swiped at the flames behind the cooker. Then I remembered that the way to put out a fire was to stifle it with a carpet. So I rolled up the fireside rug and tried to stuff it down behind the cooker – the flames were licking up the walls and would soon be taller than me. It was only when the rug began to catch fire that I remembered water. It had taken pails and pails of water finally to douse the fire – by the end of it the kitchen was flooded. It was the kind of thing that would never have happened when Claire had been there.

I took up the cello and sat down on the upright chair. I played the last few phrases I'd written. It was getting there, but I kept hearing the traffic from the street below. I tried to go on from where I'd left off, but my playing had become edgy and frantic, as if the traffic noises had polluted the music. I went on, humming as loudly as I could to drown out the cars, but even my humming had become discordant and strident. I wrote the notes on the manuscript anyway, then played the piece through from the beginning. The last bit didn't go. The last bit was a traffic jam.

I scored it out. The doorbell rang. I started playing through the piece again from the beginning. When the doorbell rang again, I stood up, leant the cello against the fireplace and walked out to the hall. I opened the door and said: 'Oh. It's you.'

'If you're going to be like that, I'll go away.'

'Like what? Come in.'

I followed her through the hall into the living-room. She brought a breath of the cold night in with her. When I closed the living-room door, she was standing with her back to me, the violin case in her hand, looking around the room. I looked at it too. Shrunken, bare. All the pictures had been taken down and were leaning against the walls, tied together with string. They had left lighter shadows of themselves on the wallpaper. There were bags and boxes, some shut, some open, lying all over the floor. The window was curtainless and each pane was a dark mirror, reflecting the bleak room back in on itself. The cello leant against the empty fireplace as if trying to get warm.

When she put the violin case down and turned to face me, I looked at her. There were dark marks under her eyes. Her face looked honed by the cold. She didn't look happy, but in the bare light of the room – I'd packed the lampshade in one of her boxes – her features had a clean, stark beauty. I wanted to kiss her, but I didn't know how to any more.

'So you're packing,' she said.

'Nearly done. I see you brought your weapon.'

'Come off it, Gerry. You know I've come from Stephen's. Where were you?'

'I was here.'

She didn't say anything to that. I sat down on the upright chair, took out my packet of tobacco, rolled a cigarette and lit it. I smoked it, looking at the floor. 'I've been trying to compose something,' I said.

She still didn't say anything but just stood there willing me to look at her. I didn't. I went on smoking and looking at the floor. I could hear the anger buzzing inside her like a hot electric socket.

'You've been trying to compose something. Tell that to Stephen and James. Tell that to the audience on Friday night.'

Her voice, tight with anger, had a slight echo in the hollow acoustic of the room. She exhaled loudly, like a horse. It was meant to mean exasperation. There was almost a snort in it. The snort would have added derision.

She took off her coat and threw it at the couch, then walked up and down, her heels detonating on the bare floorboards.

I wished she would sit down. She was picking things up and putting them down again – things I'd packed and things I hadn't packed yet. She stooped to reach into one of the open boxes on the floor, yanked out my tennis racquet and plucked at the frazzled gutting. 'What happened to your tennis racquet?'

'It caught fire.'

Her fingernails plucked an impatient pizzicato on the remains of the gutting. 'How surreal. You're not taking it, are you?'

'I thought I could maybe have it restrung.'

She dropped it back into the box and clomped around again. She stopped at the mantelpiece, looked at the lighter silhouette of the mirror where the mirror had been, then she noticed the earplugs. She picked them up between the fingernails of her index fingers and her thumbs.

'What are these?'

'Earplugs.'

She dropped them on the mantelpiece as if they'd burned her fingers. 'Since when have you worn earplugs?'

'Since I started hearing too much.'

'How can you hear too much? People hear what they choose to. You told me that once.' She looked in the mirror that was no longer there and adjusted her hair.

'Did I say that?'

'Especially us, you said. Especially musicians. We select, you said. We have to.'

'I don't think I ever said that.'

One of her feet was moving in time to some music going on in her head, probably one of the pieces they'd been playing at the rehearsal.

'So you've taken to wearing earplugs. Disgusting things.' She moved away from the mantelpiece. 'Anyway, since you didn't show up, I'll go through the pieces with you. Let's start with the Gluck.'

She picked up the violin case, opened it, took out the violin and the bow and played a bit of the Gluck arrangement.

Orpheus and Eurydice. What is life to thee without me. Or what is life to me without thee. I couldn't remember which and I didn't care what people called it. It was one of the first pieces we'd played together in public. I didn't need to practise it. Now she was walking up and down the room between the bags and boxes all over the floor, playing it to our separated belongings.

'I don't want to hear it!'

I wasn't shouting, but I'd raised my voice. She broke off, laid the violin and the bow on the table, then leaned over the table to say quietly: 'So Gluck's out now, is it? Fine. Anyone else you want us to scrub from the repertoire? Haydn? Beethoven? Mozart? And if you don't want to practise the pieces, I'll go.'

'Fine by me,' I said.

I stood up and walked to the bookcase. There were a few books left on one of the shelves, waiting to be packed. I gathered them between my hands, upturned them like a squeegee concertina and dumped them in a pile on the table. I started going through them, throwing them into boxes labelled 'HIS' and 'HERS' on the floor. She turned to glare at me as if this was the ultimate insult.

'You seem a bit tense,' I said. 'Yours. Mine. Mine. Yours.'

She slapped her forehead with a hand, closed her eyes and put a sarcastic trill into her voice: '"A bit tense"? Do I? How strange!'

'Mine.'

'How utterly astonishing!'

'Yours.'

'I mean, why should I be "a bit tense"?'

'Yours. Mine.'

'We're on at the Queen's Hall on Friday. You don't come to rehearsal.'

'Mine.'

'You're obviously moving out and you don't even tell me.'

'Yours. Yours.'

'Yes, I suppose I am "a bit tense". Full marks for obser-
vation.'

'Yours. Mine.'

'What are you doing?'

'Packing the books. I hate packing, don't you? You accumu-
late such a load of old junk. Mine.'

She was leaning towards me across the table, looking
straight at me. When she stayed still I didn't have to hear the
shoes. They were new shoes – at least I'd never seen them
before. Maybe she'd bought them with a view to the concert
on Friday night. They were black and formal enough, with a
bit of a heel. I moved away from the table, then scuffed a box
across the floor with my foot, as if my leg was lame. I was
talking. I could hear myself talking.

'Most of it's useless, but you have to hang on to it all in
case something turns out to be invaluable one day. The best
of it is, half this stuff isn't mine.' I picked up the last book
lying on the table. It was a *Life of Mozart* I'd given her as a
present soon after we'd met and started playing together. 'I
don't mind my own junk. It's other people's stuff that gets to
me. I mean, look at this.' I held out the book to show her,
whirred the pages. 'A totally obsolete book.'

'Drop it.'

I dropped it into a box. Hers. 'Yours,' I said. 'That's the
books done, then.'

I stood there doing nothing and wishing I had something
to do. I wanted to be busy with something, instead of having
to stand there and listen as she paced up and down the room
picking things up and putting them down. Even when she
stood still, she kept scraping one heel along the floor and

tapping the toe of the other shoe in time with some rhythm in her head.

'So,' she said. 'You're moving. You've found somewhere, then.' She picked an ancient cheesegrater out of a box, looked at it with incomprehension, then put it back. 'So where are you moving to?'

'Morningside. Sit down.'

'I don't want to sit down,' she said. Now she'd picked an African mask carved out of wood from one of the boxes labelled 'HIS' and was frowning at it as if she thought it might be hers.

'All right, then,' I said, 'we'll go on standing, if that's the way you want it.'

'If you want to sit, sit. I'm not stopping you.'

'Your shoes. They're new, eh?'

'Not that new. Why?'

'New to me, though. Take them off, eh?'

She looked at me askance. 'What!'

'The shoes, I mean. Just the shoes.'

She dropped the mask into the box and put both hands on her hips. 'What the hell are you trying to do, Gerry?'

'I'm not trying to do anything. I just thought you might want to take off your shoes. Make yourself comfortable –'

'Make myself at home? No thanks.'

She stamped around, making as much noise as she could. When she went to pass where I was standing, I caught her by the arm. She tried to pull away but I drew her towards me and held her tight and whispered in her ear: 'They're nice shoes, they're lovely. Don't get me wrong – I find your shoes very attractive –'

'You're hurting me! Let go!'

I let her go. 'It's the noise they make. It's my hearing. Please!'

She shook her head at me, then unfastened the shoes and kicked them off – one and then the other. In other circumstances, it could have been the prelude to something.

'Please sit down,' I said, as if we'd only just met, as if she was some kind of distant acquaintance who had arrived unexpectedly. To show her that I wasn't trying to 'do anything', I sat on the upright chair, leaving the couch to her. She moved her coat out of the way and sat down.

'I'm sorry I didn't come tonight,' I said. 'I've been meaning to talk to you about the quartet.'

'Oh, have you? That's big of you. Talk to Stephen and James. They're both feeling pretty miffed!'

Miffed. The word made me want to laugh. It was exactly the right word to describe Stephen's face when he didn't get his own way. Miffed. He thought he was Pinchas Zukerman as soon as he put the tux and the bow-tie on. I could imagine him wearing them at home, conducting imaginary orchestras in front of the mirror. As for James, he was getting worse. The way he acted the shy little boy who's nervous about doing his party piece. Then when the audience applauded, the way he beamed at them! It was sickening.

'I just want out,' I said.

She slapped her forehead with a hand and looked at the ceiling. 'Not this again. Last time it was a month before the concert. This time it's a week – no, less than a week – five days. What'll you do next time? Announce it to the audience when we've finished tuning up? "Sorry about this folks, but I've decided to leave the quartet"?'

'Maybe I will. Maybe I'll do just that.'

That shut her up for a while. She took a deep breath, leaned forward and put her elbows on her knees. Her long pale fingers clawed at her hair. 'Look, I know this isn't easy, this playing together. I know we lived together for a while –'

'We lived together for four years! You make it sound like we sat together on the bus one day!'

'But we have to be professional.'

'Professional. Oh yes, at all costs.'

'Sometimes things have to change, that's all.'

'That's what I'm trying to tell you – I want out.'

'There are other cellists looking for work.'

'Get one, then.'

'All right, but we can't get one before Friday. And you know we'd rather go on as we are – with you.'

'We never play my pieces – not good enough for Stephen. "A bit avant-gardey," he says.'

'That's unfair, Gerry, and you know it. We've performed a few of your pieces.'

'Only when James makes a pig's ear of the Prokofiev and it has to be ditched. Or when Stephen wants to get some grant or other for original compositions. Then he apologises for it before we play it: "This is a little experiment, composed especially by our own cellist . . ."' I could hear my own voice going on and on in that snide way and I didn't like it. 'Shh. Listen.'

I could hear them again. The people next door moving around each other, avoiding each other. The silence growing between them, the tension building. I leaned forward on the chair and sat perfectly still.

'What is it?' Claire said. 'I can't hear anything.'

'The people next door. Shh. Listen.'

We both sat still, listening.

'They were having a row before you came,' I whispered. 'Now this. Silence.'

'That could mean anything. They've probably gone out.'

'Oh no, they're in. She's lying on the bed, face to the wall.

She's pulled the cover over her face. She's angry, silently fuming. Her eyes are wide open in the dark.'

'How can you tell it's dark?'

'Sounds are different in the dark.'

'They could be reading. Sitting in front of the fire.'

'The room is in darkness. He's standing by the window, looking out. She's on the bed. There's been an ultimatum. He's told her to leave then, if that's how she feels. They've reached a deadlock, that's obvious.'

'Maybe it's not like that at all. Maybe she's sitting up in bed. She's turned the bedside light on. She's asking him to turn round, speak to her, but he won't.'

'He's stubbing out his cigarette, turning round. They're going to make it up. It's become tediously predictable. Then they'll go out for a meal, drink too much, come home, put their music on, kick their shoes off, throw themselves on the bed –'

She sat up. 'You're talking about us, aren't you?'

I didn't say anything. I stood up and walked over to the window. I took the tobacco out of my waistcoat pocket, rolled a cigarette and started smoking it. Yes, they'd throw themselves on the bed and I'd have to hear them making love. No hour of the day or night was safe from them. I heard their whispered intimacies, their kisses, their breathing in each other's ears.

'It's us you can hear, isn't it?'

I heard Claire moving across the couch, reaching for her coat. I kept my back turned as she put it on and pushed her feet into her shoes. The violin and the bow went back into the case. I closed my eyes and waited for the snap of the catch.

The Night

JOE WAS SITTING at a table by the window, reading one of the pub's newspapers. He pointed the top of his head at the pages, so that he had to look upwards at the print. His fair hair was cut short, but if this was someone's idea of neatness it hadn't worked: it spiralled from the flat crown of his head to stick out like the splayed bristles of a ruined paintbrush. He wore baggy denim work jeans – the kind with a long pocket on the outside of one leg for a folding ruler or some other technical instrument – and a loose-fitting navy-blue pullover. A grey duffelcoat hung over the back of his chair. He licked the tip of his middle finger before turning a page, making a low, growling noise in his throat. He wore a thick, digital wrist-watch which he checked regularly, pulling the sleeve of his pullover up his arm to read the digits and announcing the time to nobody in particular. Occasionally he was distracted by the sound of someone's voice in the street outside, and he would look up, suddenly alert, and cock his ear in his hand.

Most of the men who stood at the bar were dressed in oil-stained work clothes or muddied boilersuits and boots, and had come straight from work for a drink before going home. A few wore jackets and ties, but it was clear from the way the men chatted easily to each other and to the barman that they all knew each other and were regulars in the pub. At the other side of the bar, which was in the shape of a horseshoe, a few younger men played pool and sometimes nodded their heads in time to the music on the jukebox.

155

Joe scanned the newspaper, licked his middle finger, turned a page and made the growling noise in his throat. Suddenly he said aloud: 'The night. What about the night?' Then he turned to stare at the men standing at the bar, as if waiting for their opinion. None of them seemed to have heard him, or if they had they paid him no attention. Joe kicked the empty chair next to him, not with anger or irritation, but as if it was just something else to do, like looking at his watch and announcing the time.

He closed the newspaper and let it fall across the table in front of him. Then he moved it aside to find his pint glass, which was almost empty. He picked up the glass and closed one eye to peer into it with the other eye. There was a little beer left in the bottom. Joe swirled it around, then brought the glass to his mouth and upturned it. When the beer had trickled into his mouth, he shook the glass to get the last drops of liquid from it, then he put it down carefully on the table, wiped his mouth with his sleeve, and looked out of the marbled window.

'Cannae see a thing through they windaes,' he said, to nobody in particular. He put his hand behind his ear and cocked it to listen. What was there to hear outside? Traffic was going by on the road and there were people's voices at the bus stop, but Joe was listening for something else. After a few moments, he said to nobody in particular: 'There it is. Ah can hear it.' He smiled, nodded, pulled up his sleeve, looked at his watch and announced the time.

He delved into the pocket of his jeans with his short, stubby fingers and tugged out a small, brown leather purse. He looked around the bar warily before unfastening the popper of the purse and opening it. He lowered his face to peer inside it, then counted out some coins very carefully. He touched each of the coins with his index finger as he counted them, as if he knew each one personally. When he'd counted out a certain number, he arranged them neatly in a column on the table, then he smiled with satisfaction as he tipped them into his palm, picked up his glass and walked to the bar. The barman turned from the cash register and ambled towards him. He was a loosely built man in his late forties with quizzical blue eyes and a frizz of red hair receding from his broad forehead. His chin and cheeks showed a fuzz of reddish stubble. His shirt, rolled up at the sleeves and unbuttoned to the chest, looked too tight for him.

'Lager, Joe?'

'Lager, *please*,' said Joe.

'How's the Co-op, Joe?'

'Co-op's fine.'

'Still likin it, are you?'

'It's a good job.'

'That's good.'

'Ah look efter the trolleys,' said Joe.

The barman nodded.

'Ah look efter the trolleys an the baskets. It's a good job.'

The barman opened his mouth to say something, but Joe went on: 'Ah used tae look efter the pigs.'

The barman put Joe's pint on the bar in front of him and asked: 'What pigs?'

'The pigs on the ferm. Ask Bert.'

Joe pointed with his short index finger at a tall man in a boilersuit who stood at the far end of the bar smoking a cigarette and watching the TV.

'That's right,' said the barman. 'I forgot you worked up there with Bert.'

'Ah looked efter the pigs,' said Joe.

'So you did,' said the barman. 'Eh . . . one pound ninety-five pence, please, Joe.'

'They were braw pigs,' said Joe, as he placed the column of coins he had counted out of his purse on the bar and looked at the barman bluntly, as if challenging him to check that the amount was correct. The barman took the coins, turned to the cash register, pressed one of the keys and sorted Joe's coins into the different sections as he dropped them into the open drawer. As he was doing so, Joe said: 'It's good money.'

The barman shut the drawer of the cash register and turned round: 'What's that, Joe?'

'At the Co-op. Lookin efter the trolleys. Better money than the pigs.'

'Is it? That's good, then.'

'Aye, it's a good job,' said Joe.

The barman nodded, his quick eyes dancing along the bar to see if anyone needed serving. He was about to move away when Joe reached over and tapped him on the arm with a finger. He motioned to the barman to come close so that he could whisper something to him. The barman smiled, folded his freckled arms on the bar and leaned towards him. Joe spoke into his ear through his cupped hand. 'Ah'm different,' he said.

'We're all different, Joe,' said the barman.

'No you're no,' Joe said. 'No like me.'

'Whatever you say, Joe,' said the barman, straightening up and glancing along the bar, but again Joe reached over to prod him with his finger and motioned him to come close. The barman stifled a yawn, then smiled and leaned over the bar again.

Through his cupped hand, Joe whispered something into the barman's ear.

The barman stood up quickly and fixed Joe with his eyes. His mouth opened and shut, as if he'd thought better of smiling. 'You're no supposed to call it that nowadays, Joe. You're supposed to –'

'Shh!' Joe opened his eyes wide and put a finger to his lips. 'Ah'll tell ye somethin else,' he said to the barman, 'Ah'm no bothered ma erse what anybody calls me.'

The barman smiled and nodded. 'Good for you, Joe.'

Joe covered his mouth with his hand as he let out a squeaky, wheezing chuckle. 'Ah'm different, me. It's true.'

'Whatever you say, Joe,' said the barman. He was smiling with his mouth but not his eyes. His eyes were looking around to see if anyone needed serving. He noticed that one of the pool players at the other side of the bar did, so he went to serve him.

Joe sucked the froth from his pint of lager before lifting it up, then he drank a little more. He carried it back to the table, taking great care not to spill any of it. He sat down, opened the newspaper and scanned the pages, making the growling noise in his throat. He licked his finger, turned a page, then brought the top edges of the pages to his mouth and moved them from side to side between his lips. When the paper bent and fell away from his lips, he looked startled, straightened out the pages and brought the edges to his lips again. Then he licked his finger and turned another page.

Suddenly he said aloud: 'The night. What's on the night?' He pulled up his sleeve, consulted his watch, announced the time, then went back to the newspaper. One of the pool players passed him and said: 'Hi, Joe.'

Joe grunted in answer, not even looking up from the newspaper. He was studying a photograph of a woman holding her baby to her cheek and smiling. He moved his pint of lager in order to flatten out the page on the table, then he began to tear the picture out of the newspaper very carefully. He brought his face to within an inch of the photograph as he tore it out – painstakingly, his tongue probing the corner of his mouth.

The man called Bert stopped at Joe's table on his way out of the bar, stood with his feet apart and rocked on his heels a little. 'How's Joe?'

Joe shut the newspaper hastily, as if he'd been caught doing something he shouldn't. 'Yes, Bert.'

'How's your mother keepin, Joe?' said Bert.

'She's bein kept in the hospital,' said Joe. 'How's the pigs, Bert?'

Bert put his hands in his pockets and tilted his head back, as if he was looking into the distance. 'Oh, the pigs are doin fine, Joe, just fine. So you're lookin after yourself, then, are you, Joe?'

'Lookin efter masel, yes, Bert. An the trolleys.'

'What, Joe?'

'The trolleys an the baskets. At the Co-op.'

'Oh aye, at the Co-op. Very good.'

Bert nodded and rocked on his heels. Joe swayed forwards and backwards a little as he watched him, his eyes flicking from Bert's boots to his head and back again quickly. For a few moments neither man seemed to have anything else to say.

'Well, I hope your mother's better soon, Joe.'

'Thank you, Bert.'

Bert rummaged in his boilersuit pocket, brought out two pound coins and tipped them from his palm onto the table. 'Have one on me, Joe.'

'Thank you, Bert.'

As soon as Bert had gone, Joe tugged the purse from his pocket and put the money away, then he opened the newspaper and resumed tearing out the photograph of the mother and the baby. When he had torn it out, he carefully ripped it into long, narrow strips, each of which he curled up in his hand and dropped into the ashtray. When he had disposed of the entire photograph in this way, he picked up his pint of lager and drank it until it was half empty.

He put the glass down, wiped his mouth with his sleeve and said, 'There's nothin on the night.' He kicked the leg of the chair next to him repeatedly, making it jiggle from side to side and move along the floor a little.

He picked up the newspaper, folded it shut, turned it over, folded it again and smacked it down on the windowsill. Then he picked it up again, unfolded it, turned it over, re-folded it and smacked it down on the windowsill again.

'Nothin in that paper,' he said, to nobody in particular. He pulled up his sleeve, consulted his watch and announced the time. He cocked his ear with his hand, listened intently, then smiled and said: 'There it is. The river.' He looked out of the marbled window. It was beginning to get dark, and the whorled glass of each window pane had turned a deep blue colour, reflecting the yellow lights and everything inside the bar, as if the night was turning the glass into a whirlpool, sucking everything into it.

'The night,' said Joe. 'What about the night?'

He turned to stare at the men standing at the bar, as if waiting for their opinion.

Bad Boy

IT WASN'T BECAUSE he broke it, because nobody knew he broke it, nobody even knew it was broke, because he hid it away in the secret place in the cupboard with the hot tank in it, the warm cupboard nobody ever went into except to get towels or sheets. But only his mum went into the warm cupboard to get towels or sheets, except sometimes she went in to put his dad's wet work shirt on the hot tank so as to get it dry for work in the morning, and when she took it off the tank in the morning it was that dry it was hard and it was that hard its arms stuck out at the sides like it was remembering being worn and was getting ready to be worn again. It was the same when the shirt froze on the line when it was freezing cold in the winter and the grass was hard and white and spiky and even the ground under the grass was that hard it was like iron. Then his mum took the shirt off the line and laughed because it was as stiff as a board. How could the hot tank and the frost both make the shirt go as stiff as a board? And what was it like to go to work wearing a hard shirt? He imagined his dad meeting the other workmen and smiling, proud of his hard shirt. But maybe his dad wasn't proud of it. Maybe he would be trying to hide the hard shirt under his jacket, in case anybody saw it.

The other time his mother went into that cupboard was to put the dough in there to rise, and it did rise, because when he went into the cupboard to hide the thing he broke, he saw it. The dough in the big brown bowl had grown in the warm dark cupboard and now it looked like a giant's thumb. But she never looked in the secret place because she didn't know it was there, only he knew it was there. He'd not said a word to anybody about the secret place behind the hot tank, not even when he licked the pipe above the tank and tasted the hot copper on his tongue and his tongue remembered licking a battery. Maybe there were giants. Maybe the giants in the stories were true and there was a giant inside the pipe and inside the battery. Maybe the giant was so big he could be inside different things like that, because he was so big that everything was in him, even the house, even the sky. Everything could be inside the giant because he was so big that the whole street could fit inside his pinkie.

If it wasn't because he'd broken it why did he get sent to his room? It must be because of something else he did, but he didn't know what it was even if he did it. Sometimes you didn't know you did wrong even when you did it. But some-times you did something and you knew it was wrong, like when you tied the cat's ears shut with elastic bands and cut his whiskers off with the scissors, or when you woke up in the middle of the night needing and you just stood up and did it down behind the bed, because you didn't want to go into the upstairs landing to the bathroom with the teeth in the tumbler on the windowsill in case they jumped out of the jar and bit you. You knew it was wrong and you shouldn't do it but you did it anyway, because you were a bad boy and you didn't care if your dad went to prison because you didn't wear your glasses, because you smashed them on the first day you got them, because nobody was going to call you four-eyes.

Or if you didn't own up to something you did wrong that you knew was wrong, that was wrong as well and you knew it was wrong as well. But he didn't know what he did wrong, so how could he own up to it? But he must have done it or they wouldn't send him to his room even though he didn't mind being in his room. There was nothing bad about being sent to your room, because then you could be by yourself. That was the good thing about getting sent to your room because your room was good because it was yours and it was your room and when you were by yourself in your room you could do whatever you wanted. You could even do something wrong if you wanted because nobody knew about it and nobody could send you to your room for it either because you were in your room already.

The glass tank that used to have a goldfish in it was full of cars and soldiers and marbles and aeroplanes that had all been his big brother's but now he had them. They were his now, but they were all broken and didn't work any more, because the cars didn't have their wheels and the aeroplanes were missing their propellers and the boats had holes in their hulls and the soldiers had all been melted and had lost their bayonets and their helmets. There were no working things in the tank any more, just broken things, and there was no goldfish in the tank any more either. There used to be a goldfish in the tank a long time ago, but it died and stopped swimming and swelled up and turned upside down in the water, then his big brother fished it out with the net and buried it in the back garden beside the old gas cooker, then the cat dug the goldfish up and ran away with it in its mouth.

Maybe if he put the broken thing in the tank with the other broken things nobody would see it. But they would see it because it was bigger than the other things in the tank. He opened the cupboard and leaned down to get his hand into the place under the hot tank, then pulled out the toy he'd got for his birthday. You drew on the screen with a pen that wasn't a real pen and a black line came on the screen where you took the pen. You could draw anything you liked on the screen, even a scribble, because then you slid the button along and it wiped the scribble away. When he first went to school his sister told him he would get a jotter for rough work and you could draw or write anything in it, you could even scribble all over it if you liked. But when he got his rough work jotter and scribbled all over every page, the teacher gave him a row. Now there was a crack down the middle of the screen but it still worked at the sides. He wanted to find out what was under the screen that made the line under the pen you could wipe away. He wanted to know what was inside it, he wanted to know how it worked.

He put the Magna-Doodle on the floor and stamped on the screen. It cracked under his shoe and some of the bits of it broke off. He picked up one jaggy bit in his hand and looked at it and saw the bubbles, like the plastic bubbles in the stuff that came out of parcels and you could burst the bubbles one by one with your finger. But these bubbles were hard, because you couldn't burst them with your finger, and inside them they had black dust. He stuck the one of the points of his big brother's dividers into one of the bubbles in the bit of broken screen, then he turned it upside down and poured the black dust out on the floor. It must be the black dust that made up the lines when you drew them on the screen, but how did it do that? He took the pen in his hand and crouched down on the floor and moved the pen in the black dust. Some of it stuck to the pen, and some of it followed the pen along the floor. Then he dropped the pen and the dividers on the floor and they moved. The dividers stuck to the pen. He bent down and pulled them away from each other and he felt it: the dividers were pulled to the pen. When he held them close to each other, they stuck together, because the pen must be magic.

And it was a magic pen, because it stuck to the metal lock

on the windowsill, and the hot tank in the cupboard, and the radiator, and the dividers, and it pulled the black dust along the floor and it made the black dust stand up on end, like the cat's fur when it saw another cat in the back garden. And when he licked the pen his tongue remembered licking the hot pipe and remembered remembering licking the battery. He saw the three holes in the wall where his mum plugged in the hoover and tried licking them to see if they tasted like a battery, but they tasted like plastic and dust. Then he put the magic pen in one of the holes, but nothing happened. Then he picked up the dividers.

He cried as loud as he could because the giant in the pipes had hurt him with the dividers and the magic pen and the three holes and he was inside the giant and it made him shake all over and he could still feel it running up and down his arm and because he didn't know how it worked how the hard shirt froze on the hot tank or the black dust stood up like angry cat fur on his fingers or the giant's thumb in the warm dark cupboard swelled up like the dead goldfish upside down in the cat's mouth in the cracked fish tank in the smashed glasses with the broken toys like the Magna-Doodle that didn't work any more and now he would never know how it worked because he broke it because he was a bad boy and because if he cried loud enough he knew somebody would come.

A New Alliance

I

A Better Place

DOUGIE DRANK HIS tea standing up and sang along to The Animals on the radio – '*We gotta get outta this place, if it's the last thing we ever do.*'

His mum came into the kitchen and turned the radio off, her scandalised eyes magnified by the thick lenses of her glasses. 'Damned rammy!' she said.

She had taken her curlers out and now she began to brush her hair, peering into the wee round shaving mirror on the windowsill. It was a circular mirror that swung round on a hinge. One side of it was convex, the other was concave. He'd learnt that in physics. The concave side was cracked. His dad used the mirror to shave. His sisters used it to put on their make-up and do their hair. All these things were done in the kitchen rather than the bathroom because the kitchen was warmer. He wondered if other families used the oven with the door open to heat the kitchen in the morning. It didn't seem like a normal thing to do.

Dougie lifted his jacket from the back of the chair and put it on. 'Ah better go,' he said.

'Is that you away? Have ye packed everythin ye'll need?' She pulled his bag across the kitchen table, unzipped it and started to rummage through it. 'How many pairs of underpants have ye packed, Douglas?'

'Ah dunno. Three.'

He wished she wouldn't ask him questions about his under-pants. His underpants were private, even if she bought them for him. He wished she wouldn't go through his bag. He chucked the rest of his tea in the sink and looked out of the window. It was beginning to rain. There was no sign of Maureen Todd yet. She was late.

'Ye'll need more than three, Douglas. Ye're goin on holiday for a week.'

'Plus the pair Ah've got on makes four. That's plenty, Mum. Anyway, Antoine's mum'll wash them.'

'Will she?' She looked worried at the thought of that. She unzipped his bag and started rummaging among the contents – his rugby strip and boots, his clothes and his records. He had never had to pack a bag before. He had never really gone anywhere on his own.

'Antone – is that his name?'

'It's French for Anthony. Here, he'd probably be called Tony.'

She pulled his white shirt – the one with the tab collar and the pin through it – out of the bag. 'Oh, Dougie, ye're no takin this, are ye?'

'Leave it,' he told her. 'Ah like it.'

'But the cuffs are frayed. Why no take the checked shirt Ah bought ye out the catalogue? Ah mean, look – it's no even clean. At least let me iron it.'

'Mum – the bus leaves at half past. Ah'll be late!'

'It'll only take a minute.'

'Mum!'

But she was determined to iron his shirt before he went to France. It wasn't clean – she was right about that – but that was because he'd worn it for three days running. He wanted it to look a bit dirty, like Keith Richards' shirt on the cover of *Out of Our Heads*. Being a bit dirty was what it was all about.

'And pack that tin in your bag.'

'What tin?'

'That tin there.' She nodded towards a huge biscuit tin on the kitchen table. It was covered in wee Scotty dogs wearing tartan tammies on their heads and tartan ribbons round their necks. He lifted the tin from the table. It weighed a ton. He shook it. The contents made a rumbling noise.

'How? What's in it?'

'It said in the letter to take things for a present they don't get in France, like the sweeties we get here. Ah've put in Milky Ways, Crunchies, Mars Bars, Caramacs, Edinburgh Rock, Soor Plooms –'

'Mum, Ah cannae take this – it'll never fit in ma bag!'

She was folding his shirt and rummaging through the stuff in his bag again. 'There's plenty room. Ye've just packed yer bag harum-scarum. Ye're no taking this auld camera?'

'Yeah, Mum. Ah've got a film in it and everything.' He took the camera out of her hands and dropped it back into the bag.

'What are ye takin all these records for?'

'Leave them, Mum, Ah'm supposed to take them. It said in the letter. Remember? Look, Ah've got it here –' He took the letter out of his pocket and read some of it aloud: 'There is no better passport to a French teenager's bedroom than a selection of top twenty pop records . . . and a stamp album. The teenagers can listen to each other's favourite hits while swapping their stamps.'

'Ye've no packed yer stamp album.'

'Mum! Antoine's two years older than me. He's sixteen. He'll no be wantin stamps! Anyway, Ah gave mine to Neil ages ago.'

'Well, if ye're takin records, ye should mibbe take a record for Antone's mum and dad as well. A wee present from me.

Wait there a minute.' She went out of the room to get it.

'Mum, Ah'm gonnae be late!'

He looked out of the window then and he saw her. Maureen Todd. She was doing his paper round for him while he was in France. He wondered if he fancied her. She was okay-looking apart from all the spots – curly brown hair, freckles, blue eyes – but she was so shy that it was hard to talk to her. When he'd taken her round with him the morning before to show her the route, the only bit of conversation they'd had about anything apart from the route and the papers had gone:

'So Ah'm away to France the morra.'

'What time d'ye go at?'

'The bus leaves at half past seven.'

'Ah didnae ken ye could get a bus to France.'

He'd explained that the bus – or luxury coach, as Peezle, the gym teacher, had called it – took them to Dover, then they'd get a ferry, then a train to Paris, then another bus to Sense, Dryburgh's twin-town in France. Her face had flushed red and she hadn't said anything for the rest of the round.

His mother came back into the kitchen with a very old-looking record in her hand. It was inside one of those brown cardboard inner sleeves with the hole in the middle and he could see the dog and the old gramophone on the label.

'Aw, Mum, what is it – Frank Ifield? God – it's an old seventy-eight! Ah cannae take that!'

'It's no Frank Ifield, although there's nothin the matter wi Frank Ifield – he can fairly yodel. This is Paul Robeson. Ah bet ye they like it in France.'

She was squeezing it into his bag on top of the biscuit tin. When she zipped up the bag he grabbed it and said, 'Right – Ah better away!'

Before he could get to the door she unclasped her purse

and took out some money. 'Here, son, here's a wee something to spend in France.'

He took it and stuck it in his pocket. Although he'd saved nearly three months' paper-round money, some of the others in the team were taking a lot more cash than he was. They'd made it by selling tablet in the lunch-hour at school. He'd got his mum to make tablet too, but it had never hardened because she had a gas cooker and she couldn't cook it slowly enough, or something. Nobody had wanted his soft tablet. He'd had to eat it himself or give it away. Why couldn't his mum have an electric cooker like Neil's mum? It was yet another example of all the things that just weren't good enough in his life.

'Cheerio, then, son.'

'Cheerio, Mum.'

Dougie wasn't sure if he was supposed to kiss her or not because he'd never gone to France before, so he didn't.

He was running hell-for-leather with the wind in his eyes and the rain streaming down his neck as he turned the corner to the school and saw the bus outside the gates. Everyone else was on board. He saw his friend Neil's carrot-red hair and freckled face halfway along the bus. He was pressing his nose and tongue against the glass and crossing his eyes. Peezle was standing in the open doorway, his starey blue eyes swollen with fury, the long strands of hair he combed over his baldness standing on end in the wind as if even they were angry. He bawled at Dougie just the way he did from the touchline: 'Come on, MacLean, step on it – you're supposed to be a winger! If we miss the ferry to Calais I'll be holding you personally responsible! Get on, get on! Here – give me the bag. What've you got in here, laddie – a year's supply of Forfar bridies?'

They gave him the slow hand-clap, jeering at him as he

made his way up the aisle. He sat down in the seat Neil had kept for him and tried to get his breath back.

Neil said, 'Dougie, remember that stamp album ye gave me? Look at it now.' He held it up for him to see – he'd covered it neatly with bright blue paper adorned with colourful stamps and had printed 'DOUBLES' on the front. Neil's own album, which lay open on his knees at 'France', was a more serious, ring-bound affair, with a thick spine and alphabetically indexed pages like an address book.

Dougie was too out of breath to tell his friend to shut up. The bus driver closed the door, started the engine and they were moving. The school slid out of view, then the dim streets of Dryburgh blurred through the rain-spattered windows, as if the town they lived in was already becoming a memory.

He'd been asleep and dreaming about Maureen Todd del- ivering all his newspapers to the wrong houses when Neil nudged him awake. Peezle was standing up at the front of the bus, making a speech.

'As you know, normally this twin-town exchange is offered to the most academic pupils in the school. This year, I don't mind telling you, I have stuck my neck out and said that I would be prepared to accompany the third-year rugby team. You lot. All right. We'll shortly be arriving in Dover to take the ferry to Calais –' The cheers were half-hearted. Everyone was tired of being on the bus. 'We will be taking a train from Calais to Paris, and a coach from Paris to Sense. I mean *Sawns*. As I'm sure Mr Quinn, your French teacher, will have pointed out to you, it is pronounced *Sawns* . . .'

He tried to get back to sleep. He wanted to go over the route with Maureen again to make sure she got it right. In the dream she wasn't so shy. She was talking about pop groups – the ones she liked and the ones she didn't like – but it was the opposite of what he'd expected of her: she didn't like The Hollies, she liked The Yardbirds. And The Animals – God, it was hard to believe that Maureen Todd, who wore hand-knitted cardigans and pleated skirts, could like a band as wild as The Animals . . .

'I hope you've all been brushing up your French. I've certainly had a few private lessons from Mr Quinn –'

Someone whooped at the back of the bus. Mr Quinn, the French teacher, lisped when he spoke, wore pale tan moccasins, and had his blond hair coiffed like candyfloss at the front. Everyone called him Flossie.

'Who did that? Come on – which one of you whooped? Oh, it may surprise some of you that Mr Quinn and I, your humble PE instructor and rugby coach, have something in common, but we do, and I can tell you what it is in one word. Anybody? Typical. Nobody. This is the raw material I have to deal with. That one word is "rugby". I want you to remember at all times that you are the third-year rugby team from Dryburgh High School. As such, you are ambassadors not only for the school but for Scotland. You've heard of the Auld Alliance, I hope, between Scotland and France. Well, this exchange will be a New Alliance. How many of you have been to France before? Raise your hands. What – nobody?'

Norrie Townshend, the class clown, shouted something about Little France, the wee place outside Edinburgh, and there was some jeering laughter.

'All right, how many of you have been abroad? Not one of you? Yes, boy?'

It was Norrie again, his monkey-like face with the joined-up eyebrows and the wide, toothy grin, jumping up and down on his seat and waving an arm in the air.

'Sir, Ah've been to Arran.'

'Arran is not abroad, you pea-brained ignoramus! Has no

one ever been on holiday abroad? Good Christ, this is the raw material. Surely some of you have been on holiday, at least? Don't your mums and dads take you anywhere in the summer holidays? You, boy, where was your last holiday?'

Dougie sat up in his seat and looked around, as if Peezle's finger must surely be pointing at somebody else. 'Who, me, sir?'

'Yes, you, MacLean. I'm not pointing at anyone else, am I? Answer the question.'

'Well, eh . . . Ah went to ma Auntie Annie's last summer, sir.'

'Your Auntie Annie's? And where, pray tell us, does your Auntie Annie live?'

'Craigmillar, sir.'

It was true – he'd been sent to stay with his Auntie Annie in Niddrie Mains while his mum and dad went away for a week to Ireland. An ugly, jeering laughter had erupted all over the bus, and Peezle had to shout to restore order before he could go on, weighting each of his words with measured incredulity as he came along the aisle to where Dougie sat.

'Are you seriously asking us to believe, MacLean, that the only holiday you've had in your entire life has been to . . . *Craigmillar*?' Peezle leaned over the seat in front and glowered at him, puckering his tight mouth as if he'd tasted something sour.

Dougie felt the shame warm his cheeks and neck and ears as he answered, 'No, sir.'

'Well, where else have you been? Come on, spit it out.'

'Portobello, sir.'

Peezle stared at him for a moment, then his thin mouth curled into a tight smile. He stood up straight, flung his head back and gestured with his hands like an Italian. 'Ah, Puerta

Belli, the famous Italian seaside resort – just along the road from Prestonpans!'

There was more of the ugly laughter that always happened when Peezle singled someone out for sarcasm. They were all glad it wasn't them, but scared it might be them next. Even Neil was covering his mouth with a hand and pretending to look out of the window.

The French boys they were going to be staying with, their headmaster and one or two of their teachers had come to meet them outside Sense's town hall. The street was noisy with passing lorries and mopeds, and Peezle was having to raise his voice to read his speech: '. . . *et alors, je veux dire un grand merci à Miss-your LeBlonk, le principale de l'Académie de Sense, pour sa bienvenue chaude. Merci beaucoup.'*

The French, who had listened with pained amusement to Peezle's attempts at French pronunciation, applauded with obvious relief.

Peezle took another sheet of paper from his coat pocket and unfolded it. '*Maintenant, excusez-moi, mais je dois parler anglais, parce que je ne parle pas le français très bien.* It only remains for me to get down to the nuts and bolts of the job, introducing each of our Scottish pupils to their French hosts. Neil Pringle? Step forward, boy, make yourself seen. Your opposite number is . . . Christian Char-bone-ear. *Où est* miss-your . . . is it "Char-bone . . . er"?'

A gaunt young man with sallow skin, a long nose and black hair hanging over one eye stepped forward and said: '*Oui, monsieur.'*

Dougie noticed that his hair hung over the tops of his ears and that he was wearing a black poloneck jersey under his jacket. He envied Neil for being paired off with him.

'*Ah. Vous êtes ici,*' said Peezle. 'How d'you say your name, gar-son?'

'*Mon nom? . . . Ah, Charbonnier.*'

'Char-boney-ay. Very good, Christian Char-boney-ay, this is Neil Pringle, who'll be lodging with you and your family for the week. As will I. Your family have kindly offered to act as my host for the week.'

The boy called Christian did something expressive with his lips and eyebrows. He made a 'pff' sound with his mouth and shrugged. '*Ah . . . je ne comprends pas, monsieur.*'

Peezle looked at the French boy suspiciously, as if he might have just said something cheeky, then turned to the Scottish boys and said: 'Oh, dammit, is there a decent French speaker among us? We need an interpreter. You, MacLean, Mr Quinn told me you've got a half-decent French accent. Step forward.'

Dougie felt himself flush as Peezle tugged at his sleeve and positioned him in front of the assembled French.

'Come on, then, laddie, don't just stand there gawping. Translate!'

'*Monsieur Barbour a dit . . . qu'il va . . . rester . . . avec Neil . . . chez vous –*'

The boy called Christian flicked the hair from his eye and spoke in rapid French: '*Ah, oui. Ma mère attend à leur arrivée – tous les deux, oui.*'

Peezle turned to him and asked suspiciously, 'What did he say?'

'He says . . . the sea is waiting for the hour to come. No, wait a minute. He says his mum's expecting . . .' Dougie could hear the barely stifled laughter from the crowd of Scottish boys behind him.

Peezle turned to them and barked: 'Cut out the tittering. You're not the hockey team, you're the rugby team. And remember: you are all ambassadors for Scotland.' He turned back to Dougie and said: 'And?'

'He says she's expecting the both of yous.'

'Very good. Now, MacLean. We may as well pair you off with your French counterpart while you're in the spotlight. Antwan . . . Le-boof?'

A boy dressed in a black blazer with silver buttons, grey trousers, a white shirt and striped tie stepped forward. 'Good afternoon, sir. I am present.'

His thick black hair was brushed back from his forehead so neatly that it looked stuck on. He stared straight ahead through wire-rimmed glasses and wore a fixed smile. He reminded Dougie of one of the puppets in *Thunderbirds*.

'Aha, Antwan – so you speak English?'

'Yes, sir. I am learning to speak English.'

'Excellent. Right, here's your Scottish counterpart, Douglas MacLean. He is also learning to speak English.'

Dougie heard the ugly laughter behind him but tried to ignore it. He held out his hand.

Antoine shook it firmly and said: 'I am pleased to make your acquaintance, Dog-lass.'

'Eh . . . *oui. Moi aussi*, Antoine. My friends all call me Dougie.'

'Doggie?'

'Dougie.'

'Doogee. Okay, Doogee. I welcome you into the bosom of my family.'

The housing blocks were a dirty white colour, four storeys high, surrounded by dusty reddish ground with the odd patch of dried, worn grass. To Dougie, they seemed a far cry from the houses in Dryburgh, which had front and back gardens. These were more like the tenements in Craigmillar, except that they had wee balconies and shutters on the windows. Antoine and Christian lived in the same building. As they went in, Antoine made a big thing of apologising to Peezle because the lift was broken and they would have to use the stairs.

'That's all I need,' said Peezle. He was sweating and breathing hard from carrying his heavy suitcase. On the way from the town hall, both French boys had offered to take a turn of carrying it, but Peezle had scorned their offers and told them he was as fit as a fiddle. Now he dumped the suit-case at the foot of the stairs, opened his duty-free cigarettes, lit one up and coughed a weak '*Merci*' when Antoine and Christian began to lug his case up the stairs between them. Dougie and Neil followed.

When they came to the first landing, Christian said: '*Nous sommes arrivés chez moi.*'

Antoine interpreted: 'This is the house of Christian. Neil and ah, you, sir, you go with Christian. My house is on the next, ah . . . one storey more.'

Peezle wiped the sweat from his forehead with his hand-kerchief and nodded.

Dougie listened to Antoine and Christian having a short conversation in rapid French. It sounded like they were arranging to meet up again later on, but their French was so completely different to any French he'd heard at school that he couldn't be sure. Then Antoine translated: 'After the dinner, we meet again – in the house of Christian. Okay, Doogee?'

'Oh, yeah. Good.'

'*Très bien,*' said Neil. '*Au revoir, Antoine, au revoir, Dougie.*'

Dougie answered with a puzzled nod. It wasn't like Neil to be confident enough to talk in French, but ever since they'd stepped off the ferry at Calais, he'd noticed something diff-erent about his friend. It was hard to put a finger on what it was, but he could see it in the way Neil was looking around at everything, wearing a pleased little smile on his lips, as if everything he was seeing and hearing confirmed some idea about France he'd always had.

Peezle still hadn't got his breath back, but he nodded to Christian to lead the way and said: 'Oh-revv-wah, as you say here in France.'

'Yes, goodbye, sir,' said Antoine.

On the way up to the next landing, Antoine asked: 'Your teacher . . . Monsieur — what is his name?

'Barbour. But he's called Peezle.'

'Peaz-elle, *oui*?'

'It's his nickname.'

'Nickname? What is this?'

'Eh . . . I'll tell you later, Antoine.' Dougie was gasping for breath because of the weight of his bag.

When they came to the door, Antoine took a key from his jacket pocket, opened it and said, 'Enter, please.'

Dougie stepped into a small hallway with a wooden floor. There was French accordion music playing on a French radio somewhere inside the house and he could smell French polish and French food smells he didn't recognise. Antoine shouted to his mother and she came scurrying out of the kitchen, wiping her hands on her apron. She was a small woman with frizzy black hair in a side parting, held away from her forehead by a clasp. Her top lip curled the way Antoine's did — up at both sides and down in the middle — as she smiled at him and clapped her hands together.

'*Maman, c'est Doogee*. Doogee, may I introduce my mummee.'

Dougie put down his bag and said, '*Bonjour, Madame*, eh —'

'*Ah, bonjour, uh . . . Du-qui? Bienvenue.*' She stepped up to him and put her hand on his arm, then she kissed him on the cheek. Dougie felt the colour rising in his face, then she did it again on the other cheek. She clasped her hands together, tilted her head and smiled, speaking to him in a sing-song voice: '*Bienvenue chez nous. Si tu s'enlèves les chausseurs, s'il te plaît. Tu as fatigué, je crois, après le voyage? Tu veux un petit café?*'

He could just about understand the last bit about the coffee, but the rest had been and gone before he'd had a chance to hear it. '*Ah . . . je ne . . . comprends . . .*'

She bent down and patted one of her feet with a hand. '*Les chausseurs. Si tu voudrais s'enlever –*'

'*Chausseurs?*' Dougie couldn't imagine what on earth she was trying to tell him. She kept gesturing and lifting her foot in the air and touching her shoe with her hand.

'My mother ask you to, ah . . . take off the shoes,' said Antoine. '*Regarde, comme ça.*' He bent down and began to unlace his own shoes, which were black, highly polished, and had squared toes.

Dougie didn't want to take his shoes off. His socks probably had holes in them, and after the journey he'd had, they'd smell like a siver. Still, it seemed like he had to. He took them off and the mother laughed and clapped her hands.

'Oh-kay! *Voilà!*'

Then she said something he didn't understand to Antoine and Antoine translated: 'You have, in the bag . . . les *pantouffles?*'

'*Pantouffles?*'

'I don't know this English word. I will show you.' Dougie watched as Antoine opened a cupboard and took out a pair of leather slippers. He held them up and said, '*Pantouffles.*'

'Ah, slippers.'

'*Ah, oui?* Slippers. You have the slippers in your bag?'

'Eh, no. I don't have the slippers.'

The mother looked worried. '*Il n'a pas de pantouffles?*'

Antoine shushed her and said to Dougie: 'It's okay, Doogee.'

'*Oui, oui,* is okay!' said the mother.

'I will borrow you this slippers,' said Antoine. 'I have another slippers. You take. You must . . . wear these slippers, please. Because you see my mother has a very expensive floor – *tu comprends?*'

Dougie took the slippers and put them on.

The mother tilted her head and clapped her hands again. 'Oh-kay! *Voilà! Et maintenant – du café? Viens dans la maison, uh . . . Du-qui. Viens. Tu veux un petit café?*'

Antoine, who had taken off his blazer and carefully hung it on a coathanger in the cupboard, hurried his mother away with: '*Oui, Maman – arrête. Bien sûr, il a besoin du café. Allez, allez.*'

The cake was like no cake he had ever eaten. The nearest thing to it in Scotland was called a vanilla slice – a sort of slider made of two slabs of flaky pastry with a dollop of custard between them and icing on top. The cake he was cramming into his mouth was maybe made along the same lines, maybe it was the French version, but it tasted totally different. The layers of pastry were crisp and thin and tasted of honey and nuts. The custard in the middle wasn't just custard but had a soft, creamy feel and tasted of something – maybe it was real vanilla.

When he had finished it, he said to Antoine: '*Très bon, ce gâteau. Je n'ai jamais mangé un tel gâteau . . .*' He didn't quite know how to say 'in my whole life' in French.

Antoine lowered his eyelids and looked at Dougie with amusement. '*C'est de la pâtisserie française . . . bien sûr, c'est bon.*'

'*Ah, oui . . . pâtisserie. Très bon.* Mmm.'

'You have eaten the cake, Doogee. Now you must taste . . . *le café.*'

The trouble with the coffee was that it was in a bowl.

'What is wrong, Doogee?'

'The coffee . . . it's in a bowl.'

'A boll?'

'Yeah, eh . . . Ah mean, there's no handle.'

'Hand-elle? *Ah, oui, je comprends.* You drink it like this.'

Dougie watched as Antoine took the bowl of coffee between his hands and raised it to his lips.

'*Oh. Oui. Comme ça?*'

Dougie took the bowl between his hands and raised it to his mouth. When he tried to tip it to his lips, the way Antoine had, he tipped it too far. The hot coffee spilled over the rim of the bowl, scalding his mouth and his chin. He dropped the bowl on the table and the coffee exploded over his legs. He could feel it burning his thighs as he stood up and held his trousers away from his skin. Antoine jumped to his feet and shouted something in French. Then the mother was there with a cloth in her hand.

'*Oh, mon Dieu,*' she cried, '*regardez les pantalons!*'

Dougie started trying to apologise, but he was still manoeuvring his trousers to stop them coming into contact with his legs.

The mother was fussing around him with her cloth, trying to wipe the table, the floor and his trousers with it as she tutted and gasped and cried, '*Mon Dieu!*' She spoke rapidly to Antoine: '*Ah, regarde la tache! Je dois laver les pantalons – vite, Antoine!*'

Antoine frowned, folded his arms and said: 'Doogee, you must remove the wet trousers. My mummee must wash this trousers quick. You must give to her this trousers.

Take your trousers off, Doogee.'

Suddenly Dougie felt very tired. It had been a long journey and now he had arrived. He was in France. France was a place where the cakes were great and they drank coffee out of bowls and asked him to take his shoes off – and now his trousers. He turned his back to the mother, hoping she'd go away, but she didn't. He took his trousers off quickly and handed them to her, saying, 'Sorry. *Excusez-moi.*'

For the first time she looked at him without smiling. She shrugged. '*Pas du tout.* I wash. I wash. It's okay.'

'Ah'll go and get ma jeans, in ma bag,' he said to Antoine.

Before he could do so they heard the front door opening and Antoine's father cursing as he tripped over Dougie's bag in the hallway.

'*Ah, papa!*' Antoine called out.

The father came in muttering '*Merde!*', then he saw Dougie and apologised.

'Papa,' said Antoine, 'this is Doogee. Doogee, may I introduce my father,'

Dougie thought he could smell aniseed on the father's breath as he shook his hand. He was a short, stocky man with a pock-marked face, heavy stubble and a receding black crew-cut. Under his oil-smeared boilersuit, his thick body hair was matted like the fur of an animal.

'*Bonjour, eh . . . Monsieur Le-boof.*'

The father moved from foot to foot and said, '*Ah, oui, bonjour, uh . . . Du-que. Je suis . . . le "daddee", mais je m'appelle Jean.*'

'*Oh, oui,*' said Dougie '*Eh . . . en anglais, c'est "John".*'

The father laughed heartily, as if Dougie had made a joke. He thumped his own chest with his fist and cried: '*Ha! En anglais – je m'appelle Jon!*'

The mother reappeared from the kitchen with Dougie's

washed and wrung-out trousers in a basin. '*Jean. Tu es rentrer, enfin.*'

The father winked at Dougie and replied: '*Oui, enfin.*' Then he turned to her and lowered his voice: '*Le garçon écossais – il n'a pas de pantalons?*'

'. . . And so, Doogee, on the day when you depart, Christian and I must do . . . the *baccalauréat.*'

'What's that?'

Dougie moved the last piece of steak around on his plate and hiccupped. The meal had been good, especially the chips, but although Antoine had said his steak was '*bien cuit*' there was still blood oozing from it when he cut into it. Still, they'd given him wine to drink, and Antoine kept refilling his glass.

'We must have the examination. If we pass, we will go to the university. I have already one older brother, Pierre, at the university in Paris. He will be the engineer. Me, I prefer to be the professor. *Un peu de vin?*'

Dougie nodded, laid his fork and knife across the plate and drank some more. He thought he should try to speak to the father, who had said nothing during the meal apart from '*Merde!*' when his knife had fallen on the floor.

'*Et vous, Monsieur . . . Jean, qu'est-ce que vous faîtes, pour travail?*'

The father went on chewing energetically as he spoke. '*Moi?*'

Antoine intervened: 'My father is, ah . . . in charge of the very large garage . . .'

The father mopped the bloody juice from his plate with a piece of bread and said to Antoine: '*Ah, monsieur le professeur, je peux répondre moi-même, merci.*' Then he winked at Dougie, popped the bread in his mouth, washed it down with some wine and said: '*Je suis mécanicien, Du-que. Tous les jours, je répare beacoup, beacoup de voitures, de camions, de –*'

Antoine said, '*Oui, Papa – je crois que Doogee comprend "mécanicien".*'

The father banged his glass down on the table and began to protest, '*Mais il m'a demandé –*' but the mother shushed him, smiled at Dougie and began to gather up the plates.

'*Alors*, Doogee,' said Antoine, 'you like the French cooking?'

'*Oh, oui . . . c'est très bonne.*' This didn't seem to say enough, so he gulped some wine and tried again: '*Merci, Madame Leboof, c'était un repas . . . très, très bon. Eh . . . magnifique.*'

The father, who was picking at his teeth with a toothpick, laughed and cried out: '*Oh, entendez – "un repas magnifique!" a dit le gourmet sans pantalons!*'

The mother shushed him again and said in her sing-song voice: '*Oh, pas du tout. Merci, Du-qui.*' She cut a triangular slice of something yellow with white skin, laid it on a plate with a couple of biscuits and put it in front of him.

Antoine said: 'And now we complete the meal . . . with the cheese.'

Dougie looked at the thing on his plate. The smell of it rose to his nostrils and he began to feel queasy. He had thought it was a kind of pudding, and still he found it difficult to believe that it was cheese.

'*C'est le fromage, Antoine – oui?*'

'Yes, of course. *Le fromage.* You like the Camembert?'

'Eh . . . Ah've never had cheese like this before.'

The mother asked, '*Il n'a goûté jamais le fromage?*'

Antoine translated: 'Doogee . . . my mother ask . . . you have never, ah . . . tasted the cheese?'

'Oh, oui . . . but in Scotland the cheese is hard . . . *le fromage est dur, et . . . orange.*'

The mother looked puzzled. '*Orange?*'

'*Ah, oui, je comprends,*' said Antoine. '*Le "Cheddar" – c'est ça.*'

'*Ah, oui, le fromage d'Irlande!*'

'But now you must taste the Camembert, Doogee. Taste, eat. One more glass of wine with the cheese.'

Dougie waited while Antoine poured more wine into his glass.

'*Attention, Antoine,*' said the mother. '*Trop de vin! Il n'est pas habitué –*'

'*Oh, Maman, un peu de vin.* Taste, Doogee, taste.'

It was only when he had put the cheese in his mouth that Dougie realised what a mistake he had made. All three of them were looking at him, waiting for him to give his verdict. He gulped some wine and hoped that it might dilute the taste of the cheese.

'You like?'

'Mmm, eh . . .'

The father, who had finished his cheese and was cutting another slice for himself, said: '*Le Camembert ne plaît-il, le gourmet sans pantalons?*'

'*Jean!*' said the mother. '*Arrête, s'il te plaît.*'

When he started to gag on the cheese he stood up suddenly, overturning his chair.

Antoine sprang to his feet. 'Doogee! What is wrong?'

He wanted to tell them he needed the toilet, but he didn't dare open his mouth as he rushed out of the room, hearing the father's booming laugh behind him as he cried out: '*Ah, ha . . . trop de vin pour le petit ivrogne écossais!*'

Dougie was still feeling queasy when Antoine took him downstairs to meet Christian and his family. Christian's parents were taking Peezle out to a café, leaving the four boys to listen to records. They were going to be the teenagers who could 'listen to each other's favourite hits while swapping their stamps', except that Neil was the only one still interested in stamps. Dougie found his friend sitting on a camp bed that had been set up for him in Christian's bedroom, looking through a stamp album.

'Look, Dougie, Christian gave me all these stamps – he says he's stopped saving them.'

Dougie rolled his eyes to show his boredom and sat down opposite Neil on Christian's bed. They could hear Peezle trying to talk in French to Antoine, Christian and Christian's parents in the hallway.

'What's wrong wi you?' said Neil. 'Did ye no enjoy yer French tea? Great chips, eh?' He turned a page of the stamp album and said: 'The Belgian Congo. Funny the way they serve out everything separate, eh? They put some salad on the table first. Ah thought that was all Ah was gettin for ma tea, so Ah ate two plates o it. Then they gave me this fish . . . it wasnae in batter, and Ah'm tellin ye, Dougie, it still had the heid on it!'

'Shut up, eh?'

'It's true. Ah couldnae eat it. It kept lookin up at me from the plate! Then came the chips and the meat . . . Ah dunno what kinda meat it was, Ah've never ate meat like it before. It was pink in the middle. Then this cheese –'

'Shut up, Neil, eh?

'It was soft, like jelly in the middle, and it smelled like –'

Dougie thumped him hard on the arm.

Neil cried out, clutched his arm and said, 'What's the matter wi you?

'Ah threw up after the meal. Mibbe it was the wine they gave me.'

'Yeah? They offered me some, but Ah said Ah was too

young.' Neil flicked through the pages of the album. 'There's some good African stamps here. See.'

'Put that away, Neil. Ye're fourteen, for Christ's sake.'

They heard Antoine, Christian and Peezle saying their goodbyes and *au revoirs* in the hallway, then Antoine's precise voice saying quite clearly, 'Goodbye, Mister Peaz-elle. I hope you enjoy your evening.'

Peezle said: 'What? Who told you to call me that, boy?'

They heard Antoine say Dougie's name. The bedroom door opened and Peezle stepped into the room. He had his suit and tie and coat on and his paisley-patterned scarf with the shiny fringe and he'd slicked his hair over his bald head with brylcreem.

'MacLean, if I hear you bandying that nickname about again, you'll earn yourself a punishment exercise in Sense Academy instead of a trip to Paris on Friday. The PE teacher here is just as keen on circuit training as I am. Understood?'

'Yes, sir.'

When Peezle stepped back into the hallway, Neil went into a fit of sniggering. Dougie told him to shut up. They heard Christian's parents saying their *au revoirs* before they went out and the front door closed.

Antoine and Christian came into the room. Antoine was frowning. He marched up to where Dougie sat and said: 'This is not his name – "Peaz-elle"?'

Neil had gone into a spasm of silent laughter, exposing his big yellow teeth and scarlet gums.

'It's his nickname,' said Dougie, 'but ye don't call him it to his face.'

'Face? Nickname?' said Antoine. '*Ah, oui, c'est comme le soubriquet.* And, ah . . . what does it mean?'

Neil could hardly say it for laughing: 'It means bull's wullie.'

Dougie noticed the muscle at the side of Antoine's jaw

moving out and in, as if he was clenching his teeth. It seemed to annoy him when things like this, to do with the meaning of words, were not clear. '*Comment?* Please translate, Doo-gee.'

Dougie didn't know the French for 'penis', so he resorted to pointing at his own.

'Ah. So I have called your teacher . . .? *Mon Dieu!*'

Christian whistled, let out a throaty chuckle, then pointed his finger at Antoine and mimicked: '*Bonjour, Monsieur "Queue du Taureau"!*'

'*Ta gueule, Christian!*' Antoine turned to Christian, pushed him roughly against the wall, shook his fist in his face and said something ugly in French. Dougie and Neil watched as Antoine took his friend's ear between his fingers and twisted it. Christian turned his body to try to lessen the effect of the ear-twisting. Between his cries of pain he kept shouting '*Arrête!*' and apologising. Eventually Antoine let him go, turned to Dougie and Neil and said: 'I do not like to be made the fool – you understand?'

Neil was quick to nod and reply, 'Yeah. *Oui, je comprends.*'

'Ah, Neil – so you like the stamps, yes?'

'Yeah, it's ma hobby.'

Antoine sat down on the bed beside Neil. 'I have many stamps. I can show you. Tomorrow. But now, let us play the discs. Doo-gee? You have brought some Scottish discs?'

He put on 'Not Fade Away' by The Stones – Christian seemed to have his own record-player in his room – and they all sat and listened to it. Then Neil put on one of his favourites – 'She Loves You'. When it was finished, Antoine said that he preferred The Beatles.

'Me too. *Moi aussi,*' said Neil.

Antoine nodded, pleased to have gained an ally. 'You see, Doogee? Neil also prefers The Beatles.'

Dougie was used to this, but he knew there was no real

point in arguing with them about it. 'What about Christian?'

Christian, still sulking after his painful humiliation, shrugged his shoulders and said, '*Pff. Sais pas.*'

Antoine said: 'You must decide, Christian. Which do you prefer – The Rolling Stones or The Beatles?'

Christian spouted some air from his mouth, then he caught Dougie's eye and saw a chance to disagree with Antoine and form a new alliance. 'The Rolling Stones.'

Antoine wanted to get an argument going between the two sides, but there was a quiet knock at the bedroom door and a girl's voice called out Christian's name. Christian opened the door and let his sister in. She carried a tray with a coffee pot, cups and a plate of biscuits. Dougie looked at her. She had dark eyes and black hair and sallow skin like Christian, and the same long nose, but somehow the nose looked good. It looked French, that must be it. He noticed the way she had her hair behind one ear but not the other, and he liked that. On the lobe of her small ear she wore an earring with a pale green stone.

Antoine took charge of the situation: 'Ah, Doogee. I shall introduce you. This is Christian's young sister, Marie. Marie – Doogee.'

Dougie stood up awkwardly. Should he shake hands? 'Hi, eh . . . *bonsoir*, Marie.'

'*Bonsoir*, Doogee.'

'No, Doogee. *En France*, you must kiss. When we meet, we kiss. Like this.' Antoine held Marie by the arms and kissed her on the cheeks. Although she squealed and tried to push him away, she was smiling. 'You see?' said Antoine. 'First this cheek, then this cheek. Now you, Doogee.'

Marie looked at Dougie shyly. He took a step towards her, smiled, placed his hand on her shoulder and kissed both her cheeks quickly, but not so quickly that he missed the scent coming from somewhere behind her ear. To his amazement, she now placed a hand on his arm and kissed him on both his cheeks. It was the feel of her hand on his arm and the coolness of her lips on his skin and the way her hair fell against his neck and the perfume . . . all these things mingled and went on mingling inside him even after she had run out of the room. Christian was putting on a French record. Neil was looking at stamps. Antoine was applauding and saying, 'Very good. This is how we meet in France. You like, Doogee?'

Dougie nodded and smiled and went on nodding and smiling as Françoise Hardy's husky voice told him that all over the world, tonight, people were falling in love.

Though Dougie found excuses to go downstairs to Christian's house whenever he could, Marie never seemed to be there – or, if she was, she was doing something in another room, usually the kitchen, with the door shut. Once, he caught a glimpse of her coming out of the bathroom in her dressing-gown, a towel wrapped around her head, but she hurried to her room and closed the door. He didn't see her again for three days. It was after one of the rugby games which Peezle seemed determined to make them play almost every day. They had been thrashed as usual, and it was only as they trudged from the field that Dougie saw her, standing with Antoine and Christian on the touchline. She was wearing a wee blue anorak like the kind girls wore in Scotland. Although Dougie didn't like it, at the same time it gave him hope: although she was French, she was just ordinary.

'Forty-three eleven – they massacred us,' Neil moaned. Dougie didn't care about losing. What mattered was that for once he had scored a try – and Marie had seen him.

'Bad luck!' Christian said to them as they walked from the pitch.

Antoine said, 'Perhaps your national team will do better against France – but perhaps not!'

Dougie felt himself redden when Antoine said they'd seen him score the try. He nodded to Marie and tried to get his '*bonjour*' exactly right.

'*Salut,*' she replied. '*C'était très bien – ton but.*'

'Eh? *Comment,* Marie?'

Antoine translated: 'She say that it was a very good goal you score, Doogee.'

'Ah. *Oui, eh . . . merci,* Marie.'

They walked towards the school in a group. Dougie hung back so that he could walk alongside Marie. It was hard to think of what to say. '*Tu aimes . . . le rugby,* Marie?

'*Oui . . . un peu.*'

'*Moi aussi,*' he lied.

'*Mais . . . J'aime mieux le football.*'

'Yeh? *Oui – moi aussi.*'

He searched in his mind for the words to explain that he really loved football and that the only reason he played rugby was because Peezle made them all play rugby instead of football at the school, but before he could find any of the words Antoine turned round to speak to him.

'Doo-gee, after you and Neil will change, we can go for something to drink. We go to the café, yes?'

It was noisy with pinball machines and coffee machines and somebody called Johnny Halliday on the jukebox. A lot of people were chattering and laughing. It was great to be here, in a real French café, except that Marie hadn't come along.

Dougie could see that Neil was lapping it all up. Neil had never drunk beer before – or, if he had, Dougie had never seen him do it. Now he seemed to be doing it as if it came naturally to him.

'Come on, Antoine,' he was saying. 'Ye're pullin ma leg.'

'Pulling – what do you say?'

Dougie watched Neil gulp the beer, hiccuping and grinning as he tried to explain: '"Pulling my leg", it means . . . You're joking. *Tu rigoles*.'

Antoine seemed amused: '*Pas du tout*, Neil. It is true. You may ask Christian.'

'Christian – *ce n'est pas* . . . *vrai*, eh?'

Christian looked as bored with it all as Dougie was. '*Si, c'est vrai*.'

Neil drank some more beer and went through it all again: 'What, ye mean they actually charge ye *more* if ye sit down?'

'Yes, yes, Neil. *En France* – many things different. The food, the cafés, the girls . . . the beer. But what is wrong with Doogee? Why don't you drink the beer, Doogee? You don't like the beer of France?'

'What? No . . . *c'est bonne*.' He picked up his glass and drank some of it.

'But you drink only a little. Look – I have finished. Neil has finished. Christian – *vite, mon Dieu!*'

Neil hiccuped and laughed. 'Ah think Ah'll stand up for the next one. See if it's true that it costs less.'

Antoine clapped his hand on Neil's shoulder and grinned. 'Yes, Neil. You and me – we stand for another beer. You will see. It is less expensive this way.'

Christian frowned at Dougie over the table. '*Qu'est-ce que c'est*, Doo-gie?'

'Eh? Nothin. *Rien*.'

'*Ça va?*'

'*Oui, ça va bien*. Eh, where's . . . Marie?'

'Marie? *A la maison*. She . . . must help my mother with the cook.'

'Oh, yeah.'

Antoine elaborated: '*En France*, the young girl must learn the cooking. This is the same in Scotland, no?

'Not my big sister,' said Neil. 'The only thing she can cook's a fried egg.'

Dougie told Neil to shut up, but Antoine intervened: 'No, Doogee. Let Neil talk. Your sister – what is her name?'

'Doreen.'

'Daurine? I like this name. Daurine. And now, let us have another beer.'

'Ah'll get them,' said Dougie. He stood up before Antoine could object and walked over to the counter. He had to practise his French. He had to be able to deal with things like ordering a drink in a café if he was going to have a hope of talking to Marie. He stood at the bar, but the barman didn't seem to notice him. He was washing cups and glasses under the counter while talking to an old man who sat on a stool at the bar smoking a yellow cigarette and drinking a pale green drink. Dougie was watching the way the man gesticulated with the hand holding the cigarette as he spoke. Maybe if he bought some of those yellow cigarettes and moved his hands around a lot when he spoke it would help with Marie . . .

'*Oui?*'

The barman had turned to him so suddenly that it took Dougie a moment to remember what to say, even though he'd been rehearsing it in his head.

'Eh . . . *quatre bières, s'il vous plaît, eh . . . monsieur.*'

'*Pression?*'

'*Eh . . . Comment?*'

He was lying in bed listening to a dog barking and a moped droning away in the distance, thinking about her dark eyes again, her black hair tucked behind her ear, the earring with the pale green stone, the perfume, the touch of her lips . . .

'Tomorrow, you go to Paris, Doogee.'

'Yeah.'

'And I must study for the examination. We must sleep now. Goodnight, Doogee.'

'*Bonne nuit*, Antoine.'

'Goodnight.'

Antoine switched off the bedside light and moved around in his bed.

'Antoine?'

'*Oui?*'

'What age . . . is Marie?'

'Marie? Oh . . . fourteen – the same as you, I think. Why you ask?'

'Ah just wondered.'

'You are in love with Marie?'

'Nah. Ah just wondered what age she is.'

'*Oui, je comprends. C'est l'amour.*'

'Nah, it's not. *Pas du tout.*'

He heard Antoine shifting in the bed and laughing softly. 'Goodnight, Doogee.'

'*Bonne nuit*, Antoine.'

They were going to Paris to see the Eiffel Tower and he'd slept in. Antoine came into the bedroom with a half-eaten croissant in his hand and shouted, 'Hurry, Doogee. It is eight o'clock. You must go to the station at eight and a half past.'

Antoine walked over to where Dougie's bag lay at the foot of the wardrobe. The zip was partially open and the biscuit tin with the wee Scotty dogs could be clearly seen. 'Doogee, what is this, ah . . . great round box in your bag?' he asked.

Damn that biscuit tin. He had felt too embarrassed to give it to Antoine's mother and had tried to keep it hidden in his bag. '*C'est un cadeau . . . de ma maman.*'

'A gift of your mummee?'

'*Oui.*'

'What is it?'

'Ah dunno. Sweets. *Les bonbons.* They told us to bring them.'

'But, ah . . . why did you keep it inside your bag for many days?'

'*J'ai oublié . . . pardonne-moi.*'

'Shall I give this box to my mummee?'

'Yeah, please.' He unzipped his bag, lifted the tin out and handed it to Antoine.

'*Mon Dieu, c'est lourd, eh?*'

Dougie pulled the old seventy-eight from the bag as well. He might as well get it all over with at once. 'Oh, and, eh . . . she sent this as well.'

'This disc is from your mummee also?'

'Yeah. For your . . . *maman.*'

'*Ah, merci. C'est ancien, je crois.* And now you must hurry, Doogee. You will miss the train.'

He nearly did. It was ready to pull away from the station when he jumped on. Peezle stared at him steadily, shaking his head and muttering the word 'hopeless'.

In the Louvre they were given half an hour to look round on their own before meeting up at the Mona Lisa. Dougie and Neil wandered from room to room until they found the shop. While Neil went in to see if they had any Mona Lisa stamps, Dougie tried to look at a big oil painting in a gold frame. Maybe he could tell Marie about it if he got a chance to talk to her before they left, but that was beginning to look unlikely – they were leaving the next day. Anything would be better than what he'd said to her last time. That '*tu aimes le rugby?*' made him wince every time he thought about it now. He might get a chance to kiss her on the cheeks again when they left, but then he'd be gone and she'd just be a memory. The painting was of a few nude women in a pond in a clearing in a wood. It looked like they'd been washing their hair. But they'd been interrupted by a guy with a bow and arrow. He had a few dogs with him, and the nude women were all turning away from him and trying to hide their tits. Except one big fat blonde woman who was wearing a crown. She looked really annoyed with the guy with the bow and arrow. The funny thing about him was that he seemed to have a pair of antlers growing out of his head. He could say to Marie, '*J'ai vu un . . .*' – he'd have to look up the word for 'painting' – '*qui s'appelle "Diane et Actaeon"*. . .'

Neil reappeared with a postcard of the Mona Lisa in his hand. 'Ah couldnae see any stamps. Let's sit down for a minute, eh? Ah've got a stitch.'

They sat down on a long leather seat and watched the crowds of people walking past. Neil bent over, pressing a hand to his side, and unlaced his shoes, complaining that his feet were sore from walking.

'Stop moanin,' said Dougie.

'It's okay for you. Peezle had me up at seven in the morning, daein press-ups and knee-bends. You wouldnae like it.'

'At least ye get to see Marie.'

'Ye fancy her, eh?'

'Well . . . she's nice, eh?'

Neil shrugged. 'Ah feel a bit sorry for her.'

'How?'

'Well, she's Christian's wee sister, but the mum and dad . . . all they talk about is Christian. How he's doin this big exam, this back-a-lorry-ah thing. It's all they talk about. Marie has to set the table, serve out the food, then clear up after and do the dishes. You wouldnae catch Doreen doin half the stuff she does. And they're always gettin on at her. But they're sayin she might get to go to Scotland wi Christian, if she's good, like.'

Dougie couldn't believe what he was hearing. 'What – you mean Marie might come to Dryburgh? Ah thought it was just . . . rugby teams this year?'

'Naw. That's just us, because Peezle brought us. The French folk are comin owre wi their English teacher, no their PE teacher – lassies as well.'

'Yeah? That's great.' Dougie tried not to show what he was feeling, but Neil was watching him closely.

'Ah bet ye're hopin ye get Marie to stay wi ye instead of Antoine, eh? Ye'd like sharin a room wi her, eh? Specially at night, eh?'

'Shut up, Neil. Come on, or we'll miss the Mona Lisa.'

It wasn't a very big room, or maybe it was just too crowded because everybody wanted to see it. A guard stood on either side of it and there was a rope around it to stop people getting too close. Peezle was counting them and getting them to stand in two lines heel-to-toe in front of the picture.

'Stay together now, boys. Form a line-out here. Tallest at the back. Try not to obstruct the passage of the other sightseers.' When he'd accounted for everyone and arranged them in two lines, he said: 'Right, then. I'm no expert on art, but this is of course the Mona Lisa, by Leonardo da Vinci. The woman in the picture is of course famous for her e-nig-mat-ic smile. E-nig-mat-ic. Who can tell me what it means? Yes, boy?'

Norrie had his hand up. He was wearing a beret and a striped T-shirt he'd bought and he looked more clownish than ever.

'Stretchy?'

Peezle pursed his mouth. 'No, stretchy isn't it. Good try.

Anybody else? It means . . . that nobody knows what it means. Got it? Good, let's proceed in an orderly fashion to the exit. Follow me.'

At the foot of the Eiffel Tower, among the pigeons and the other sightseers, Peezle made them sit cross-legged on the grass in a semi-circle as if he was giving them a team talk at half-time. 'This is the Eiffel Tower. Or, as Mr Quinn would say: "LaTour Eff-elle".'

There were a few 'Ooh-la-las' about that and everyone could hear Norrie mimicking Flossie's voice.

Peezle clapped his hands for order and went on: 'Boys, boys – show some respect. We are in the heart of Paris. At the foot of the Eiffel Tower.' He consulted a leaflet he had in his hand. 'It was built in 1889 and was named after its builder Alexandre Gustave Eiffel. It's three hundred metres tall – if you can imagine three full-length rugby pitches end-on-end, boys – and it's composed of two platforms resting on four supports called pylons. Look at it, boys – it is an impressive structure, a great feat of engineering. Yes, boy?'

Norrie had his hand up. 'Sir, what's it for?'

They waited as Peezle glanced at the leaflet in his hand. After a moment he crumpled the leaflet, stuck it in his pocket and said, 'What does it look like it's for, Townshend? It's for climbing. Now, once you've been up and come back down, you can have some time to explore the surrounding area in groups of two or three. You can get yourselves something to eat. Meet back here at two o'clock. You've all got your maps. I'll show you where we are . . .'

'That was great, eh? Great chips. Great *oeufs sur le plat*.' Neil drank the last of the red wine in his glass and smacked his lips. 'Great *vin rouge* as well. Ah could go another glass or two.

Fancy gettin another wee giraffe? Ah'll pay ye back, Dougie.'

'You drank most of that one,' said Dougie. 'Anyway, Ah've no got much money left . . . we better leave a franc or two as a tip.'

'Come on, Dougie, it's dead cheap. Just one, eh? Lend me twenty francs, eh?'

'Ah've still to get my souvenirs.'

'Ah've got a souvenir for you. See, Ah've had ma photaes developed.'

Dougie watched as Neil tugged the packet from his pocket, spilled the black-and-white prints over the table and started to sort through them. Most of them were just grey sea and grey sky and a tilting horizon – the first sight of France, taken from the ferry.

'Ah don't want any of them.'

'No even this one?'

Neil held the photograph an inch from Dougie's face. Dougie sat back and snatched it from his hand. It was of Marie, sitting on her bed in her room, with her legs crossed, her elbow on her knee and a hand supporting her chin, smiling.

'It's yours for the price of a carafe,' said Neil.

When Dougie had packed his bag for the next morning Antoine told him his mother had something to give him. He followed Antoine into the living-room and recognised the record that was on the gramophone. It was all scratchy and there was a man singing in a very deep voice. He started to say he was sorry it had scratches, but Antoine's mother interrupted: '*Pas du tout, Du-qui.* Thank you for this . . . *disque. Paule Robeson est un chanteur formidable, il a une voix très forte. Alors, si tu dis merci à ta mère pour moi –*'

Antoine started to translate but Dougie told him he could understand.

Then the mother picked up an LP with a glossy sleeve and held it out to him. *'Ce disque ici de Charles Aznavour – c'est un cadeau de moi pour ta mère. Voilà.'*

'Merci, Madame Leboeuf.'

It had been arranged that because they had a long journey ahead of them, she would make a cooked English breakfast for him and Neil and Peezle before they left. Antoine and Christian had already gone to Paris to sit the first part of the *baccalauréat*.

'Bacon 'n' eggs,' said Peezle. 'Can't beat it – eh, lads?'

They mumbled in agreement.

'Come on, boys, get it down you – we've got a train to catch. *Madame, eh . . . Le-boof?'*

The mother turned to Peezle, wiping her hands on her apron, tilting her head and speaking in her sing-song voice: *'Oui? Le petit déjeuner anglais – c'est . . .* ok-ay?'

Peezle put his fingers to his lips in a gesture of appreciation. 'Mmm. *Très bon. Très, très bon.'* To Dougie and Neil he added in an undertone: 'The best cooks in the world, the French, but they don't know how to fry an egg.' He cleared his throat and turned back to the mother. *'Merci pour votre hospitalité, Madame Le-boof.'*

'Ah, pas du tout. Merci, Monsieur Barberre. Alors –'

Peezle rose from his chair and announced that it was time to go.

Dougie picked up his bag. *'Au revoir, Madame Leboeuf. Merci . . . pour tout.'*

'Au revoir, Du-qui.' She kissed him on both cheeks. This time, he knew to do the same.

When they went downstairs to Christian's house, it was Marie who opened the door to them. Christian was away, and she explained that her parents had already gone to work. When

Peezle and Neil went into the house to collect their bags, Dougie was left at the door with her.

'Marie?'

'*Oui?*'

'*Tu va . . . venir? En Ecosse?*'

'*Oui. J'espère.*'

'*Moi aussi. J'espère aussi.*'

She asked him to come into the hallway. There was a clock on the wall, ticking away the precious seconds he was with her. It was as well to get the goodbye over with now, when they were alone.

'*Au revoir, Marie.*'

'*Au revoir, Doogee.*'

He kissed both her cheeks, she his, but he didn't let go of her. He looked into her eyes and she didn't look away. He heard his bag land with a clunk on the floor as he pulled her towards him and kissed her on the mouth. She kissed him back. They were still kissing when Peezle pushed Neil into the hallway, telling him to get a move on.

'Ah hah,' Peezle said, puckering his mouth. 'Your French has obviously improved, MacLean. I wish I could say the same for your conversions.'

Neil already had his stamp albums laid out on his bunk in the sleeping compartment. Dougie climbed onto the top bunk, stretched out and took the photograph from his pocket.

'Antoine gave me this album,' Neil was saying. 'Christian gave me that one. Ah can't believe it. Ah took two stamp albums to France and Ah'm comin back wi four!'

Dougie didn't bother to reply. He was looking at the way her eyebrows arched.

'Look at what else Ah've got.' Neil pulled a bottle out of his bag and waved it in front of Dougie's face. 'Real French brandy. Ah bought it in a shop. They didnae even ask me ma age or anythin.' He unscrewed the cap and took a swig from the bottle. Then he passed it to Dougie. Dougie sat up, took the bottle, drank from it and winced.

Neil said: 'Good stuff, eh?'

'A bit rough, is it no?'

Neil looked hurt. 'It's genuine French brandy. Gi'es it here.' He gulped some more of the brandy, then put the bottle on the floor and opened up one of his stamp albums. 'Look at these. Some of these stamps from the Congo look like they might be quite valuable.' He turned a few pages of the album. 'Sierra Leone. Ah dunno where it is, but their stamps are great.'

Dougie didn't say anything, but went on looking at the photograph of Marie. He had kissed that mouth, he had felt those lips press against his . . .

Neil picked up the bottle, stood up, took another swig and said: 'Can you no think about anythin except her? It's borin.'

'It's just something about her . . . when we were saying *au revoir* –'

'Ye'd think she was the only girl ye've kissed. Ye've kissed plenty lassies in Dryburgh –'

'Yeah, but this was different. Ah've never had a kiss like this before.'

'How – what was different about it?'

'She put her tongue . . . in my mouth.'

'Eh? Away – she did not!'

'Ah'm tellin ye, Neil. She did.'

'Ugh. That's disgustin.'

Dougie put the photograph carefully in his pocket and jumped down from his bunk. He looked at himself in the mirror on the wall. His hair was getting longer at the back and was beginning to hang over his ears at the sides, like

Christian's. He took his comb out of his pocket and combed it down at the front. Neil drank more brandy and went back to his stamps. There was a rap at the door and they heard Peezle ordering them to open up. Dougie grabbed the bottle from Neil's hand, found the cap and screwed it on, then reached up and shoved it under the pillow on his bunk. There was another rap at the door before Neil had time to open it. Peezle stepped into the compartment.

'Lights-out time, boys.' He froze, puckered his mouth, sniffed the air. 'I smell alcohol. Produce it.'

There was no point in trying to deny it. Dougie climbed up on his bunk, moved aside the pillow and handed the bottle over.

'I see. Brandy, eh? You have opened my eyes more than once during this cultural exchange, MacLean. Don't think I didn't notice you canoodling with, eh . . . the Char-bon-ey-ay girl in the hall. I trust it didn't go any further. I'm con-fiscating this, and I'll be reporting your behaviour to Mr Webster on our return. Now get to sleep.'

They lay in their bunks in the dark compartment, listening to the steady rhythm of the train as it sped through the night. After a while Dougie heard Neil moving around in the bunk below.

'Dougie?'

'What?'

'Thanks for no lettin on it was mine.'

'It's okay.'

'My mum and dad would've killed me.'

'Yeah. Goodnight, Neil.'

'Yeah. *Bonne nuit.*'

He had shut his eyes and was nearly asleep when he heard Neil moving around in his bunk again.

'Dougie?'

'What is it now?'

'What d'ye think it'll be like?'

'What?'

'When the French folk come to Dryburgh. It'll be different, eh? Imagine goin to Dryburgh – for a holiday. Ah mean – what is there in Dryburgh? But mibbe for them . . . it'll be like goin somewhere really foreign, like . . . Sierra Leone.'

Dougie turned over and shut his eyes again. 'Yeah, sure,' he said. 'Or the Congo.'

2

See My Friend

DOUGIE WASN'T SURE how the exchange thing worked exactly. The French party was twice the size the Scottish one had been, so some of them were staying with people who hadn't even gone to France – Marie was staying with a girl he didn't know in fourth year. Maybe the Scottish families who hadn't sent anybody to Sense got paid something for acting as hosts. It was a drag Marie wouldn't be staying with Christian at Neil's house just along the street. That would have been magic.

Antoine arrived in Scotland looking exactly the same as he had when Dougie had first met him in France: the blazer, the striped tie, the pressed grey trousers, the stuck-on hair. Nothing had changed. It was a hot afternoon. By the time Dougie and Antoine reached the corner of the street, Neil and Christian had already reached Neil's front door. Antoine stopped, put his heavy case down on the pavement, took a folded handkerchief from his blazer pocket and dabbed his forehead with it.

Neil and Christian waved to them before going into Neil's house.

'This is the house of Neil?' said Antoine. 'Who is this girl in the window?'

'That's Neil's big sister, Doreen.'

Doreen had come to the window to take a look at the

French guys arriving. Dougie watched in amazement as Antoine started blowing her kisses and calling out to her, *'Bonjour, Daurine!'*

Doreen turned away from the window quickly.

'Like the deer in the forest,' Antoine said, 'she is there and she is gone.'

Dougie wondered what Antoine was talking about. The idea of Doreen Pringle being like a deer in a forest . . . it was nuts.

'Ah'll take a shot of yer case, Antoine.'

'Shot? What does this mean?'

'A turn.'

'Turn?'

'Ah mean . . . Ah'll carry it now. Ah'll take a shot of it.' He picked it up – it was heavy – but Antoine made him put it down again.

'No, Doogee. You must not. You are not enough strong for this. *Attend un moment.*'

Dougie leaned on a garden fence to wait. 'Ah saw, eh . . . Marie, Christian's sister, gettin off the bus.'

'Ah yes. I forget you are in love with Marie.'

'I am not, Antoine.'

'Ah yes, I remember. But, ah . . . Marie is older now.'

'No that much older.'

But although it was only four months since he'd seen her in France, when he'd watched her getting off the bus he'd thought she looked different. Maybe it was just the clothes that had changed. She was wearing tight white jeans and the anorak had gone – now it was a fitted blue jacket. The hair was longer, but that wasn't it – it was the make-up, that's what it was. Eye-shadow. Mascara. Lipstick. She didn't look the way he remembered her at all.

'How can I say? Marie . . . she is changed.'

'Changed?'

'Yes, yes, Doogee. Changed. Like the bug. The bug . . . you know this? *C'est la métamorphose.* The bug, it change, it become the butterfly.'

Dougie didn't know what Antoine was talking about, but he nodded anyway.

'But, ah . . . Marie is not the butterfly,' Antoine continued. 'Marie, she is change into the little *araignée* – the, ah . . . spider, yes, this is the word.'

'A spider? What – Marie?'

'Perhaps you shall find this out, Doogee. Shall we go?'

Dougie remembered stepping into Antoine's house for the first time and now, when he opened his own front door, the sounds and the smells seemed strange to him: the budgie chirruping in its cage in the living-room; the radio playing some demented Scottish country-dance music in the kitchen; his mum clattering pots; the smells of boiling soup, mince, cabbage . . .

His mum came hurrying through when he shouted to her, wiping her hands on her wrap-around pinny, a fag in her hand.

'Oh! Is that you, Douglas?'

'This is Antoine, Mum.'

'I am very pleased to make your acquaintance, Mrs MacLean.'

She smiled at Antoine and said, 'Come in, son. Welcome to the living-room. Ye'll be in the same room wi Douglas. Ye can sleep in Eddie's bed – that's Douglas's big brother. He's in Doncaster, runnin a bingo hall. Ye'll be tired, son, with the journey from France. Sit down on the settee.' She turned to Dougie. 'Would he like a wee cuppa tea?'

Dougie cleared his throat. He'd never spoken French in his own house before. '*Antoine, veux-tu . . . du thé?*'

'*Du thé?* Okay, yes please. I like the cup of tea. Thank you.'

Dougie's mum looked at him and nodded meaningfully. 'Oh my,' she said. 'We'll have to watch our Ps and Qs.'

Antoine drank his tea – no milk, no sugar – standing up, making clucking and whistling noises into the budgie's cage.

'*En français,* this bird is called *une perruche.* What do you call it in English, Doogee?'

'A budgie.'

'Bu-jee?'

Dougie wished Antoine would pay attention to things that were more important, like *Jukebox Jury.*

See my friend, see my friend, way across the river . . .

Antoine kept walking up and down with his hands in his pockets. He hadn't taken his blazer off. 'I don't know this pop group, The Kings. You like, Doogee?'

'Yeah, The Kinks, they're great. Listen.'

*Now she's gone and there is no one else to take her place . . .
'cept my friend, way across the river . . .*

Antoine sat down on the settee. He sat with his knees apart, looking around the room and frowning. 'What shall we do this evening, Doogee?'

It was something he'd been wondering himself – what to do with Antoine. There was nothing organised for the first night. On Wednesday, Flossie was taking them all to Edinburgh to see the Castle. On Friday Peezle had organised a dance in the youth club. Apart from that, what was there to do?

'Ah could show you the town, and that.'

'What is there to visit in Dryburgh?'

'Well, no much. There's the fleapit – the picture-house.'

'*Qu'est-ce que c'est* – fleepeet? Which house?'

'The cinema – films.'

'*Ah, ciné, oui.* Which film shall we see?'

'There's nothin much on this week, just some film for kids. They might change it at the weekend.'

Antoine shrugged and made the 'pff' sound with his lips. '*Alors.* What shall we do? Shall we go to a café?'

There was a café in the High Street. Lemetti's. But it wasn't open at night.

'We could go and see Neil and Christian, take some records.'

Antoine blew some air out of his mouth in a display of exasperation. Then he seemed to think again. 'Mmm. This is a good idea. Let us visit the house of Neil.'

Dougie heard the front door opening and his father coming in, stumbling against Antoine's case and saying 'What the hell's fire –?' When he saw Antoine he said, 'Oh. Hullo there. Ah thought it was Eddie back frae Doncaster –'

'This is Antoine, Dad. Antoine, this is my dad.'

'I am pleased to make your acquaintance.'

'Aye, same here, eh . . . An-tan.'

His dad stuck his hand out and grinned at Antoine. Dougie almost laughed, because suddenly he saw his dad in a new way, as if he was an illustration of something: here is the typical Scottish workman, with his smiling red face and jaunty blue eyes, his bunnet tilted to the side of his head and his haversack containing his piece-tin and his flask over his shoulder.

'You have been at the workplace, Mr MacLean?'

'What, An-tan? Aw, aye, the workplace. The pit.'

'Ah, what is this – "pit"?'

'The mine. Coal.'

'Ah, you are the coal-miner. I understand.'

'Uh-huh. Right-o. You, eh . . . make yerself at hame, An-tan.'

'Thank you, Mr MacLean.'

Dougie watched his dad going into the kitchen for a cup of tea. He knew there was something odd happening in the kitchen – there was a silence in there, coming from his parents. Then he thought he heard his mum mimicking Antoine's question under her breath – 'You have been at the workplace, Mr MacLean?' – and his dad wheezing and coughing as he stifled his laughter.

'Now, Antone, you sit yourself down there, that's it. Douglas, turn that TV off, for heaven's sake.'

Dougie turned it off and looked at the table. It had a checked tablecloth on it and the place-mats she had brought back from the holiday in Ireland. In the middle of the table there was a doily with a jar of mustard, a butter dish, salt and pepper and bottles of sauce.

Antoine sat down and said: 'And, ah . . . where is Mr MacLean?

'Here he's comin now, Antone.' They heard the stairs creaking as Dougie's dad came downstairs. 'He likes to get a wee nap after his shift – he's been on the night shift lately and he's that used to sleepin durin the day. Here he is.'

Dougie saw his dad come into the room the way he always did when he'd had a sleep, his shirt unbuttoned and his braces hanging loose, but it was as if he was seeing it for the first time. His dad scratched his armpit, yawned and said: 'What's aw this, then?'

His mum tutted. 'We're having our tea in here the night, Jimmy. We've got Antone here, remember. Tuck yer vest in, for heaven's sake, and button up yer shirt.'

She placed a bowl of soup in front of Antoine and said to him: 'Ye'd think we never had a guest. We usually just eat in the kitchen. It saves carryin things through.'

When they were all sitting at the table, Antoine began to explore the soup with his spoon. He lifted a spoonful to his lips and looked at it. 'Ah, this *soupe* is . . . It is a Scottish soup, yes?'

'Aye. Scotch Broth. There's plenty left in the pot. Jimmy'll have another bowl. Ah'm sayin, ye'll have another bowl – ye like yer broth, eh?'

'Mmh? Oh, aye. Rare soup, Jean.'

For Antoine's benefit, she said: 'It's made the old-fashioned way, wi a knuckle of beef and a bit of lamb shank.'

'Rare?' said Antoine. 'Aha, like the steak in France.'

Dougie tried to explain: 'No, Antoine, it just means "good" in Scotland.' Then he tried to explain to his mum and dad: 'In France, if ye ask for yer steak "rare", it's like hardly cooked, when ye cut into it ye see the blood.'

'Fancy that. D'ye hear that, Jimmy?'

'Hmm? Oh, aye. Ah like a steak.'

Dougie cringed as he heard his mum telling Antoine: 'Jimmy likes his steak braised, wi ingins.'

'Ingins? *Qu'est-ce que c'est*, Doogee?'

'Onions,' said Dougie.

'*Ah, les oignons, je comprends.*'

His mother laughed and put a hand to her mouth. 'Oh, sorry, Antone, Ah'll have to watch ma English. Of course, you French, in yer cookery, use a load of onions, don't yous? Ah remember when we lived in Park Street, there used to be this wee French fellae came round on his bike sellin strings of ingins. "Onion Johnnie", we cried him.'

Dougie dropped his spoon into his bowl and put a hand over his eyes. He wanted to tell her to shut up. Here they were with someone French at their table and she was talking about Onion Johnnie.

'*Ah, les oignons,*' said Antoine. 'Very important in the

French *cuisine*. In the *soupe*. There is the *soupe à l'oignon*. And there is the *bouillabaisse* – the fish soup. Also, the *bourride* – this is the soup with many fishes in.'

'Oh, my. Ah don't think I'd like that. Ah'd think they were swimmin about in ma bowl.'

Dougie winced.

Antoine went on: 'And *les consommés* – the clear soup. In France, we make many soup.'

'Oh, aye. Here as well, mind you. There's leek and tattie, lentil, there's that fish soup here as well. What's it cried again? Cullen Skink. Ye make it wi a smoked haddie, tatties, onion, milk –'

Dougie had to stop her: 'Aye, Mum. Ye dinnae need to gie us the bloomin recipe.'

'What? Ah'm just sayin, Ah ken how to make it.'

'Ye never make it for us, though. Or onion soup – ye never make that. It's always this . . . bloody broth.' Dougie dipped his spoon into the soup, then emptied it back into the bowl.

'You wouldnae like onion soup. Huh. D'ye hear him, Jimmy? Swearin at the table – in front of Antone.'

His dad looked up, his spoon on its way back to the plate, and sputtered at his son through a mouthful of soup: 'Ah'll swear ye, ya bloody wee ungrateful sod ye, talkin to yer mother like that.'

'Some folk would be glad of a bowl of broth. Antone's eatin it.'

'This soup is very . . . very interesting, Mrs MacLean.'

His mum smiled. 'It's just ordinary broth, son.' Then she turned to his dad and said, 'D'ye hear that, Jimmy – Antone fairly likes his broth. He says it's "interesting".'

His dad, only half-listening, said, 'Aye – the quizz-een, eh?'

Antoine leaned towards Dougie and pointed to something in his spoon. 'Doogee, what are these . . . small eyes?'

He heard his mum whispering to his dad to tell him to try to make less noise eating his soup.

'That's barley,' said Dougie. 'Just leave it.'

Antoine frowned and sniffed. He made sure Dougie's mum wasn't listening before he said: 'Bar-lee? *Il y a beaucoup de sel dans la soupe. J'ai soif.*'

His mum asked, 'What's Antone sayin, Douglas?'

'He says he's thirsty.'

'Ah'll be makin a pot of tea in a minute, Antone.'

Antoine looked at Dougie in disbelief. 'Again the tea?'

'Unless ye'd like lemonade? Douglas, get Antone a glass of lemonade. There's a bottle in the cupboard. Now, who'd like another bowl of soup?'

They had listened to some of The Animals LP and now it was time to discuss it. Antoine picked up the sleeve and looked at the photograph of the band. 'I prefer The Beatles.'

'Me too. *Moi aussi,*' said Neil.

Dougie took the stamp album out of his friend's hands and threw it on the floor.

'Hey, watch it, eh?'

'Ye're no a kid any more, Neil, for Christ's sake.'

Neil looked hurt. 'It's ma hobby – what's wrong wi that?'

Dougie rolled his eyes. He turned to Christian. 'What about you – did you like it?'

Christian made the 'pff' noise, shrugged and said, '*Sais pas.*'

Antoine said, '*Christian, on doit parler anglais.* We are in Scotland, Christian. Therefore we must speak English. What is your opinion of The Animals?'

Christian put his hand out for the sleeve and Antoine passed it to him.

'Look at this hair they wear,' Antoine said. '*C'est comme une fille.*' Christian made an interested sound in his throat. Antoine went on: 'They are called The Animals and they look like the animals.'

'*Oui,*' said Christian, '*Et moi aussi, je suis un animal.*' Christian barked and howled like a dog. Dougie laughed.

Antoine shouted: '*Arrête! Christian – ta gueule!*'

He tried to grab Christian by the ear, the way they'd seen him do in France, but this time Christian was too quick for him. The two of them grappled with each other, fell on the bed and started wrestling. Antoine got Christian's head under his arm and began to squeeze him by the neck until he begged for mercy. When he let him go, Antoine said: 'That will teach him to behave like an animal. And now I shall play my French *disque* – a song by Johnny Halliday.'

They sat and listened to it.

'This is good,' said Neil. He had that pleased-with-everything look on his face, as if he was in France again. 'Naw, really, Ah like this. Ah like this better than The Animals, anyway.'

'*C'est comme la merde,*' growled Christian. 'It stink.'

Antoine grabbed Christian by the arm and shouted: '*Ta gueule, traître! C'est la musique française.*'

He pushed Christian back on the bed, stood up and strode to the window.

Christian mimicked him: 'Speak English, please, Antoine. *Nous sommes en Ecosse. On doit parler anglais!*'

Dougie heard the front door opening and closing and heels clunking down the garden path.

'Christian,' said Antoine, '*Viens, tout de suite!*'

Christian hurried over to the window. Dougie followed

him and they looked out of the window with Antoine.

'*Regardez*,' said Antoine.

'*Oui, c'est Daurine*,' said Christian, '*La soeur de Neil.*'

'*Oui, je sais, je sais*,' said Antoine. '*Elle est belle. Regardez ses cheveux, ses yeux, ses lèvres . . .*'

Dougie watched as Doreen opened the garden gate. She was wearing a short black jacket, a grey mini-skirt, white tights and shoes with cuban heels. He'd never thought of her as being beautiful, maybe just because she was Neil's sister and she had the same big teeth, freckly face and carrot-red hair.

'*Et les jambes*,' said Christian. '*Le derrière.*' He let out a low wolf-whistle and Antoine punched him on the arm. Doreen looked up as she shut the gate. She tossed her bright red hair to the side – it looked like she'd just ironed it – and smiled up at the window.

'*Elle a souri!*' Christian cried out. '*C'était à moi! Oui, Daurine! Je t'aime!*'

But Doreen was already walking away along the street.

When they turned from the window they saw that Neil had pulled a chair over to the wardrobe and climbed up on it. He opened a box and pulled out a stack of grubby-looking magazines.

'If it's girls ye're interested in, Ah've got these *Parades*.' He threw the magazines down on to his bed.

'*Qu'est-ce que c'est?*' Christian picked up a magazine and began to flick through it. Antoine did the same.

Neil jumped down from the chair, then crouched on the floor and reached under the bed. He pulled out one or two jigsaws and a Meccano set and rummaged further under the bed. 'Guess what else Ah've got,' he said, pulling out a half-bottle of whisky.

★　　★　　★

Dougie lay on his bed in his pyjamas, reading the Hibs supporters' magazine. Antoine paced around the room in his
dressing-gown and leather slippers, leafing through the
Parade he'd taken home from Neil's. Dougie had brought
the radio up from the kitchen – he'd never thought of doing
that before – and Radio Luxembourg came and went in the
background.

'These English girls,' said Antoine. 'They are not very
sexing to me.'

He'd asked Dougie to correct him whenever there was a
mistake in his English, so Dougie said: 'Sexy.'

'Sexy, yes. They are not sexy, these girls. Look at this
one . . . You see, Doogee? She is ugly like a pig. Look at
her chests. *Ce sont les bloblos.* These are not the chests of a
French girl. A young French girl has the chests . . . *comme
les pommes.* Like apples, Doogee, the small young apples,
sweet to taste. Mmm, mmm . . . Not like these chests, look
at them, Doogee, look!' Antoine held the magazine up to
show him.

'Ah've seen them,' said Dougie. 'Let me read ma magazine, eh?'

'What is this you read?'

'It's the Hibs supporters' magazine.' He held it up to show
Antoine a photograph of Pat Stanton. 'See him? Ah got his
autograph when he played for Dryburgh Thistle.'

'Pff. Football, football. It is all you know. This and the
pop music. *Jamais le sexe.* You see, Doogee, the chests of this
girl –'

'Breasts.'

'*Comment?*'

'They're called "breasts", not "chests".'

'Ah, *breasts.* Thank you, Doogee.'

'Or "tits".'

'Tits?'

Dougie laughed. Somehow the word just didn't sound right the way Antoine said it.

'Why do you laugh, Doogee?'

'It's just the way you say it —'

'What is wrong with the way I say it? Tits. Tits. This is the slang vocabulary, I think. The correct word is "breasts" — yes?'

Dougie couldn't help laughing when he heard Antoine repeating the word — it just came out of his mouth sounding wrong. 'Well, yeah,' he said. 'But if ye were talkin about a girl here — to another guy, like — ye wouldn't say "breasts".'

Antoine turned a few pages of the *Parade* impatiently. 'Yes, yes. I understand. You say: "She has the marvellous tits." But look at these English tits, Doogee. They are not like apples, they are like big potatoes. You see, the French girls they have the space . . . the space *between* the tits. The tits are . . . *séparés*, you understand?'

'Separated? What, ye mean like . . . two . . . different things?'

'*Exactement*, Doogee. The French tits are like two different things. This one, it points to the east, and that one, it points to the west. It is more beautiful this way. Not like these English potatoes. Look at her. Her tits are both together, *comme un gros derrière* . . .'

'Eh?'

'*Un gros derrière*. They resemble a big fat bottom, Doogee. Look.'

Antoine threw the magazine to him. Dougie's face flushed as he looked at the woman's cleavage. It was the sort of thing he might look at with Neil, but it didn't feel right to be doing it with Antoine.

'You see, Dougie?'

'Yeah, well . . . sort of.'

'And what do you think of the tits of Marie? You like the tits of Marie?'

They heard his mum coming up the stairs, bringing them their supper. He just had time to hide the magazine under his pillow before she got to the door. She called out, 'Douglas, open the door, son! I've got a tray in my hands.'

Antoine opened the door and ushered her in with a flourish of his hand. 'Ah, Mrs MacLean, enter, please.'

'Oh! Antone. It's nice to see somebody has manners. No like some. Ah've brought yer supper up, boys – cocoa, toast and marmite, and Ah thought ye might want a wee biscuit.' She pushed the radio aside to lay the tray on top of the chest of drawers.

'Ah, Mrs MacLean, this supper is super!' said Antoine.

Dougie's mum looked at him and opened her eyes wide. 'Oh, d'ye hear that, Douglas? Your English is fairly improving already, Antone.'

Antoine said it again, as if he was the teacher in an elocution class: 'The supper is sooooper!'

Dougie's mum rearranged the things on the tray. 'Ah'll leave it here and yous can help yourselves. They're custard creams.' As she turned from the tray she looked at Antoine and said, 'Oh my, that's a very fancy dressing-gown, Antone.'

Antoine held out his arms and turned round, so that the dressing-gown, made of some shiny material like satin and covered with a paisley pattern, could be seen in all its glory. 'Ah, you like? Is elegant, yes?'

'Oh yes, very elegant. Did ye not remember to bring any pyjamas with ye, son?'

'Pyjamas? . . . Ah, no. I don't, ah –'

'Oh, we'll have to get ye some pyjamas. Douglas's got a spare pair ye can borrow, Antone. Douglas, get up and find Antone a pair of pyjamas, for goodness sake.'

Dougie turned a page of the Hibs supporters' magazine and said, 'He doesnae want them, Mum.'

'Douglas. Get up off your bed and get some pyjamas for Antone this minute.'

'Mum!'

It wasn't like her to get on to him like this. Maybe it was because Antoine was here. He went over to the chest of drawers and looked for the pyjamas.

Antoine was protesting: 'Mrs MacLean, it's okay, I don't need the pyjamas of Doogee.'

'Ah don't want ye catchin a cold, son. Yer mother wouldn't like it if ye went back to France wi a runny nose now, would she?'

'Arunne . . . nose? I don't understand.'

'Douglas, what's the French for "a runny nose"?'

'I do not know this expression,' said Dougie, in a French accent. '*Peut-être . . . un nez snottaire?*'

His mum gave him a strange look, flapped her hand at him and said to Antoine: 'Never mind him. Enjoy yer supper, Antone. Have a custard cream. Look at the mess of this bed, Douglas.' She started straightening up his bed.

He found the pyjamas and held them out to her. 'Here they are, Mum.'

'Give them to Antone, then, don't just stand there. They're clean, Ah hope. What's this?'

Dougie shut his eyes and turned away. She'd found it. She'd found the *Parade* under his pillow. He pretended to be busy at the tray, stirring sugar into his cocoa.

'*Douglas.* Imagine wasting your paper-round money on

filth like this. Ah'm takin it away and showin it to yer faither. He'll have somethin to say about this. A damned disgrace, so it is. What will Antone think of you?'

He couldn't look at her. He kept his back turned and bit into a piece of the toast.

'He's not usually like this, Antone. He's got in with a bad crowd at school. You just tell me if he's up to no good.'

When she'd gone Dougie dropped the piece of toast and flung himself on his bed. Antoine collected his supper and brought it to the bedside table, humming a tune. Dougie watched him picking up a slice of toast from the plate and sniffing it.

'What is this *merde*?'

'It's toast.'

'Toast, you call this, all covered with this – *qu'est-ce que c'est*, this *merde*?'

'Marmite.'

'You call it this. In France, we call this *merde*, Doogee.'

'Ye don't have to eat it.'

'What else am I to do with it, this piece of burned bread covered in shit? And what is this, this cup of mud?'

'It's cocoa.'

'Co-co, pff. This is the name of a clown, co-co. Not the name for this . . . this cup of mud.' Antoine sipped at the drink and said, '*Ah, c'est le chocolat*. But it is not enough sweet for me.' He stood up and went to get more sugar from the tray. 'What is wrong, Doogee? You don't want to eat your supper?'

Dougie got off the bed and went to get it, then he took it and laid it on the bedside table next to Antoine's. 'Ye really landed me in it there, Antoine. Thanks a lot,' he said.

'Landed me in it? I do not know this English expression. Give me the French translation, please.'

'Aw . . . Ah don't know. *Tu m'as fait tomber . . . dans le merde.*'

'*La merde.*'

'*La merde*, then. How come, in French, everything has to be *le* or *la*, masculine or feminine? Why can't ye just say "the"?'

'Because life is the man and the woman, without *le sexe* there would not exist life. Don't you know about the birds and the bees yet, Doogee?'

'Pff. It's a pain in the neck trying to remember if a table or a chair is *le* or *la*. Ah mean, it's just a thing. Anyway, *tu m'as fait tomber dans la merde.*'

'You are angry with me, Doogee. Why?'

'My mum thought the *Parade* was mine, my own mum.'

'Ah, I see.'

'Oh yeah. As if ye didn't know.'

'But you can tell her it is Neil's.'

'Aye – and that it was you who borrowed it.'

'As you wish. I am not afraid. It is you who are afraid, Doogee. What will your father do? Will he beat you?'

'At what?'

'No, Doogee. I mean, will he beat you, with his belt?'

'Pff. Naw. Course not. He'll probably be glad to get his hands on a *Parade* – it might cheer him up.'

Antoine laughed. Dougie had seen him laugh before, but not like this. He had seen him laughing when he was expected to laugh, when somebody made a joke. But he'd never seen him laughing like this, as if he couldn't help it. Dougie watched him taking a bite of the toast, still shuddering with laughter.

'Mm-hmm. It is not so bad to taste, this, what is it called?'

'Marmite.'

'Mar-*merde. Oui. Bon appetit.*'

*   *   *

Dougie came in from his paper round and dropped the sack in the hall. He could hear Antoine singing in the bathroom upstairs. The night before, Antoine had come back late from his day-trip to Edinburgh reeking of beer. He'd eaten a sandwich with nothing on it except two slices of raw bacon and had fallen asleep in his chair. He'd stayed in bed most of the day today, and now he was having a bath and getting himself ready for the dance.

When Dougie went through to the kitchen, his mum was doing the dishes. She held a rubber-gloved finger to her lips and whispered: 'Is he still in the bath?'

Dougie shrugged. 'Sounds like it.'

'Huh. He's been here nearly a week and that's the first bath he's had. And he's drunk twenty bottles of lemonade, Douglas. He's drinkin four bottles a day, it's costing a pretty penny.'

'Mum, in France they had wine on the table every night. And beer – and lemonade, if ye wanted it.'

'Well, this isnae France, is it? It must be cheaper there. He'll have to have tea, like the rest of us.'

'Mum, he doesnae like tea.'

She took off her rubber gloves and threw them one after the other on the draining board. 'Well, he's no gettin wine here. He shouldnae be drinkin at his age. What'll Ah gie him?'

'Ah dunno. Water?'

'Ah didnae think of that. That's what Ah'll do. Ah'll fill a lemonade bottle with water and put it on the table beside his place. Listen, c'm'ere. Look at this, son.' She took a postcard of Edinburgh Castle from her apron pocket.

'Is that Antoine's?'

'Shh! He asked me to post it for him. Tell me what it says, Douglas.'

'Mum! Ye cannae read that.'

'Ah know – it's in French. Ah need you to translate it out of French.'

'Ah cannae do that. That's somebody else's private correspondence, Mum.'

'It's just a postcard son, no a letter. Ah just want to know what he thinks about . . . Scotland.'

He took the postcard from her hand, pulled out a kitchen chair and sat down. He turned the postcard over and translated it for her: '"Dear Mum, Scotland is very cold, although" . . . no, eh . . . "*despite* the summer. The people are so poor. They have no elegance. They drink with the food no wine, but tea, tea and more tea. They have no coffee, only Nescafé. It is all the time boiled chicken, boiled meat, boiled cabbage and boiled potatoes. Fried fish, fried potatoes, fried eggs. They serve with the food no sauce. How my stomach suffers. How I miss the cooking of you. With love, Antoine."'

When he handed the postcard to his mother he saw the stunned look in her eyes. She snatched it from his hand, shoved it back into her apron pocket and said: 'Nae sauce! That's a barefaced lie. There's been sauce on that table every night.'

They heard the ice-cream van playing its wobbly version of *Greensleeves* in the street outside. She found her bag, fished inside it for her purse, unclasped it and took out some money.

'Here, son,' she said. 'Go and get a bottle of Vimto from the ice-cream man. We better keep the bugger in the style he's accustomed to!'

Dougie leaned in the doorway watching Antoine getting ready for the dance. He was fitting his square silver cufflinks into the cuffs of his striped shirt, all the time looking at himself in the mirror above the chest of drawers and singing along to the record on the dansette – *Needles and Pins* by The Searchers.

When the record came to an end, he adjusted his cuffs, opened the fingers of both hands and said: 'I am bee-oo-tee-fool. No? Doogee?'

Dougie laughed and said, 'Ye look French, Antoine.'

'*Je suis français, évidemment.* Am I elegant? Am I bee-oo-tee-fool?'

Dougie laughed again and shook his head.

'You laugh, Doogee? Why you laugh? Why is this you believe funny?'

'It's just . . . ye don't say "beautiful" when ye're talkin about yerself. Only girls can be beautiful. Either that or they're hackit. Or else ye might say "beautiful" to talk about somethin like . . . a view.'

'Avu? What is this avu?'

'A view. Like, if ye look out a window, ye see a view.'

Dougie saw the muscle on Antoine's jaw moving out and in as he looked out of the window at the back garden, with its clothes poles and its coal bunker.

'Pff. I see no avu.'

'Y'know . . . A view. Like, a landcape.'

'Ah, *landscape*, I understand.'

'So, ye can say a girl is beautiful, or a view of a landscape . . . things like that. But ye don't say it about yerself. Or about . . . another guy, like. It means, like, really –'

'Yes, Doogee, I understand what is the meaning of the word "beautiful". In France, I have all the time the beautiful girls. But what is this "hack-it"? Please translate.'

'It means . . . well, ugly.'

'I do not know this "hack-it". It is not a proper English adjective, I think. Why do you not speak the proper English, Doogee?'

'Well, Ah'm Scottish, amn't Ah?'

'And so you speak Scottish? What is the Scottish language?'

Dougie had never thought about it. 'Words like "hackit" instead of "ugly", saying "ken" instead of "know" or "wheesht" instead of "shh".'

'Ah yes, but this is dialect. We have this in France. En France, we have seven dialects. How many dialects are in Scotland?'

Dougie thought for a minute, then shrugged.

'You don't know, Doogee? The Scottish dialect is not the same as the Scottish language, I believe. Does this exist, Doogee?'

'Ah think there used to be. .. a Scottish language. Ah think it was the Picts that spoke it. But now it's just . . . well, some words are still Scottish.'

'Which words are these?'

'Ah dunno. Words like "glaiket" . . . or "eedjit".'

'What do these words mean?'

'Well, if Ah said, "Ye look like a glaiket eedjit" it would mean . . . ye look . . . Ah'm tryin to think of the French. *Très elegant. Un jeune homme très elegant.* Ah think that's the translation.'

Antoine tied his maroon cravat, which was printed with a pattern of yellow fleurs-de-lys, and tucked it into the collar of his shirt. 'Glaeket. Idi-ette. I remember these words. *Alors,* help me with *mon veston, s'il te plaît.*'

Dougie took the blazer from the coathanger in the wardrobe, passed it to him and watched him putting it on.

'I am elegant, no?'

'Yeah, dead elegant . . . As square as they come.'

'*Comment?*'

'Square – very elegant.'

Antoine unscrewed the cap of his bottle of cologne, poured a little into his palms and dabbed it on his face. 'Skware. I am this, yes?'

Dougie nodded. 'Dead square.'

'Dead skware. This is Scottish dialect, Doogee?'

Dougie hesitated. He was beginning to see how this could go all wrong. 'Eh . . . yeah, Ah think so. Only, it's just young people who say "dead square". If ye said "dead square" to my mum or my dad, they probably wouldn't know what ye were on about.'

Antoine nodded. He held out the bottle of cologne, offering it to Dougie. Dougie shook his head. 'But why not? Smell, Doogee, smell the elegant scent. It will make the girls at the dance go crazy for you. Think of Marie. Think of the tits of Marie.'

'Ah'm no wearin perfume.'

'You are a fool, Doogee. It is not *parfum*. It is cologne.' He put the cap back on the cologne bottle and turned to look at Dougie. 'Doogee, you must finish getting ready.'

'How d'ye mean? I am ready.'

'You go to the dance like this?'

'Yeah, why not?'

'With the denims? I don't think you can enter the dance wearing these denims, Doogee.'

'Yeah, Ah'll get in okay.'

'But you must wear a tie, Doogee. You may borrow this one of mine if you wish. Look – it is "dead skware".'

Dougie pointed out that he couldn't wear a tie because he was wearing a poloneck.

Antoine told him he should change. He picked up the sleeve of The Searchers album. 'Look, Doogee, you see this pop group you like, they all wear the tie.'

Dougie picked up a magazine and leafed through the pages

until he found a photograph of The Rolling Stones 'See, they've all got polonecks on apart from Mick Jagger, and he's just wearing a vest.'

'This is not elegant, Doogee. Not skware. And the hair – they look like the hackit girls. I prefer The Beatles. The Beatles wear the shirt and the tie.'

'No they don't.' Dougie leafed through the magazine until he found the picture of their new album sleeve. 'See? Four black polonecks. Long hair.'

Antoine raised one eyebrow. 'Pff. Yes, but the hair is . . . *comment on dit . . . comme ça?*' Antoine took a comb from his inside pocket and combed his hair.

'Combed?'

'Yes, this hair is combed. Not like these Rolling Stones. *Voilà*. Comb your hair, Doogee.'

They went into the living-room to say goodbye to his mum and dad. Dougie's dad was slumped in his chair, watching the news. Antoine sat on the settee and tried to have a conversation with him: 'The three most important things in France, Mr MacLean, are the food, the wine and the bed.'

Dougie saw his dad nod and scratch his head, embarrassed. 'He means, they just like eatin and drinkin and sleepin, Dad.'

'No, Doogee,' said Antoine. 'You do not understand. You are too young to understand what is meant by "the bed".'

His dad cleared his throat, coughed and said, 'Ah-huh. So . . . where is it yous are off to the night, then?'

'We go to the dance, Mr MacLean,' said Antoine. 'We meet the Scottish girls.'

His dad rummaged in a pocket and brought out two half-crowns. 'Well, here. There's half a dollar each. Enjoy yersels.'

Dougie took the money before Antoine could refuse it.

His mum came into the living-room with a pot of tea and cups on a tray and said, 'Are yous no away yet? Ye'll be late for yer dance. Look at yer hair, Douglas. Please get a haircut – for my sake. At least comb your shed in. Look at Antone. Look how smart he looks.'

Antoine stood up, smiled and turned round slowly. 'Thank you, Mrs MacLean. Am I a glaiket idi-ette?'

Dougie pretended to be concentrating on 'the news' but out of the corner of his eye he could see the baffled look on his mum's face.

'Douglas, what's Antone sayin?'

'He's asking you if he looks smart, Mum.'

'Oh, yes Antoine. Very smart.'

When they came to the youth club – a flat-roofed, concrete building surrounded by a low wall – Dougie saw right away that they would have to run the gauntlet of Vincent McGeechan and his pals. Vincent had left school the year before to work in the carpet factory. Recently he'd cut his sideburns down and had given up his teddy-boy hairstyle and now back-combed his fair hair at the top. The black bowling jacket with the red and white stripes down the side and the skin-tight ice-blue jeans had gone too – now it was a 'shortie' white raincoat and grey, tailored trousers. All he needed was the right shoes to be a mod. He was still wearing the winkle-pickers with the laces up the sides, but that was probably because he hadn't been able to afford new shoes yet.

Vincent was standing with his legs apart, smoking a cig-arette and blocking their way. They could hear *Louie Louie* coming from inside the youth club.

'Look at whae it isnae,' Vincent said. 'Dougie MacLean. Whae's the tailor's dummy?'

His mates laughed. One of them jumped up on the wall

and sat on his hands, as if to get a better view of what was going to happen next. The other one sang along to *Louie Louie* and kicked a stone around the pavement.

Dougie said, 'Hi, Vincent. This is Antoine. He's, eh . . . French.'

'Ah can see he's French, Dougie, Ah'm no blind.' Vincent patted Antoine's shoulder with his hand and said, 'Hullo there, An-twan, Ah like the blazer. What d'ye think o the jaiket, boys?'

The mates laughed with derision.

'Vince, let us through, eh?'

But Vince ignored him and crouched down on his hunkers to look at Antoine's shoes. 'Aw, look at the shoes. An-twan – where d'ye get the shoes?'

Dougie could see that Antoine was nervous although he was trying not to show it. He raised one eyebrow and said haughtily: '*A Paris.*'

Vincent was examining Antoine's shoes closely. 'A Paree, eh?' He stood up and smiled at Antoine. 'They're dead mod, pal. Ah like the square taes, ken?' He turned to his mates and said: 'Watch at the shoes, boys.' They nodded and made interested noises.

Antoine, realising that he had been paid a genuine compliment, moved his feet this way and that so that they could see his shoes from different angles. 'My shoes are, ah . . . dead skware, yes?'

Vincent smiled and frowned at the same time. 'Eh? Aw naw, An-twan. The shoes are great. They're the kinda shoes Ah'm lookin for. But the jaiket and the tie – *dead* square.'

Antoine frowned, making the muscle in his jaw move out and in. 'My jacket is dead skware . . . but not my shoes?'

'Nah. The shoes are great – eh, boys?' The mates nodded and made noises of agreement.

'But my jacket, my tie . . . these are not great?'

'Well . . . nah, they're, eh . . . dead square. Ah mean, Ah wouldnae be seen deid in a jaiket like that. As for the tie –'

Dougie tried to intervene: 'Vince, we have to get into the dance now –'

But Antoine went on: 'What does it mean – this "dead skware"?'

'Well . . . like, no in fashion, ken?'

'Vince –'

'Shut up, Dougie, eh? Ah'm just talkin tae An-twan for a minute.'

Antoine turned to him and said: 'Yes, shut up, Doogee.' Vincent laughed and the mates joined in on cue. Antoine went on: 'So it is not good, "dead skware"?'

'Naw. It means, like . . . auld-fashioned. Really *square*, ken?'

'I see. Thank you for the language instruction. And now I must enter the dance.'

'Aye. On ye go, pal.' Vincent moved aside to let Antoine through the gate, but when Dougie tried to follow, Vincent stopped him with a hand on his chest. 'Wait a minute, Dougie.' They waited there, until Antoine had opened the door of the youth club and had gone inside.

Vince said, 'Dig the Roy Orbison haircut, eh?' The mates sniggered. Dougie tried to side-step Vincent and run through the gate, but Vincent grabbed him by the neck and pushed down until he was bent double. Then his arm was being twisted up his back. Dougie begged for mercy but Vincent wasn't listening. In a matter-of-fact tone of voice, he was saying: 'Listen, Dougie, they're no letting us in – Ah ken it's just a dance for the French folk and yous that went ower there. But, see, there's this wee French burd in there – Ah spoke to her before she went in, like. Ah think she fancies me. See when ye get in, just go for a pish and eh . . . leave the windae open, okay?'

'Ahhh! Aye, okay!'

Vincent let him go.

Dougie took a few steps towards the door, then turned and said, 'Wait till Eddie gets back from Doncaster.'

That wiped the smile off Vincent McGeechan's face. 'Aw c'mon Dougie. Just open the windae, eh?'

He went into the dance. Peezle stood behind a table in the hallway, supervising Maureen Todd who was taking the money and giving out the tickets. When Peezle saw Dougie he shook his head and said: 'Late as per usual, MacLean. Your French counterpart is already in there, boy. I've told your friends out there to beat it, pronto, or I'm calling the police. No-hopers, the lot of them. I washed my hands of them the day they left the school. I hope I won't be saying the same about you in a year's time, MacLean. What are your plans?'

'I dunno, sir. I'm hoping to get a start at Ferranti's. Trainee draughtsman.'

Peezle looked at him askance and spouted some air from his mouth. 'Huh. You'll need a haircut for the interview.'

Dougie paid. He saw that Maureen had tried to straighten out her hair and had started using eyeliner and a pale, nearly white lipstick. She still had the spots, but she'd covered them with make-up. The knitted cardigan had gone. Now it was a T-shirt, jeans and a reefer jacket. She looked a lot better, he thought. He smiled at her as she handed him the ticket.

He went into the dance. It was crowded and somebody had thought of turning most of the lights off to make it more atmospheric. It took him a while to find Antoine who was standing in the corner with his arms folded, watching the dancers sternly as if they were kids in the playground and he was the teacher at the staff-room window.

'Antoine, there you are. What d'you, eh . . . think of the dance?'

'I think it is good. *Dead skware.* I think it is bad. *Dead skware.* The English language it is a very fantastic language. This phrase, this "dead skware", it means very good, very elegant, but it also means very bad, very old-fashioned.' Antoine turned to glare at him and grabbed him by the neck of his jersey. 'I think you make the fool out of me.'

'No, Antoine, really. It's true. Some people think "square" is . . . well, elegant, and some think it means like . . . well, old-fashioned. It can mean both, Antoine, honest. Listen, ye look fine, Antoine. You heard what the guys outside said. They thought yer shoes were dead mod.'

Antoine pushed him away, folded his arms and glared at the people dancing. 'Mod. It is short for *moderne*, I believe.'

'Yeah. Probably. Listen, eh . . . Ah've got to go to the toilet, Antoine.'

He knew he had to open the window for Vincent, or he and his mates would be waiting for them outside after the dance.

The narrow window was up at the ceiling and he had to stand on the sink to reach it. When he got it open he heard Vince calling up: 'Dougie, is that you?'

He poked his head out of the window and saw Vince standing there below. He seemed to be on his own – that was good. 'Aye, Vince. That's the windae open, okay?'

'Wait, Dougie. Wait there a minute!' Dougie watched as Vincent jumped up and caught hold of the metal edge of the window and pulled himself up the wall. He reached out with his other hand. 'Gie us a hand in, eh?'

Dougie clasped Vincent's hand and pulled his arm through

the open window. Then a leg came through and Vincent sidled and wriggled his way in. He jumped down on to the floor beside the sink and took a comb from his back pocket and started to adjust his hair. Dougie clambered down from the sink.

'Ta, Dougie. Ye're a pal. Is ma hair okay at the back?'

'Yeah. If Peezle catches ye in here –'

'Ye think Ah'm scared o Peezle? He's a bumptious wee nyaff. Some of these French burds are nice, eh? This yin Ah talked to. Marie –'

So it was her.

He stood in the corner with Antoine, Neil and Christian. Neil had a bottle of something in his inside pocket and he was either drunk or pretending to be. 'What d'ye think, Antoine. Good dance, eh?'

'Yes, Neil – is your sister Daurine here?'

'Nah. She's away to a dance in Edinburgh.'

'Ah. I have been to visit Edinburgh. The Edinburgh Castle. The Camera Obscura. The Scottish Monument. Neil, I wish to meet with Daurine.'

'Yeah? Okay. Come round tomorrow. Ah'll introduce you.'

'Thank you, Neil.'

Neil belched and said, '*Pas du tout,*' and laughed. He turned to Dougie, still smiling, and said, 'What's the matter wi your face?'

Dougie was watching Vincent McGeechan wrapping his arms round Marie and necking with her while they danced.

Antoine said: 'You see, Dougie? Marie is changed. She is dancing with your friend, Vincent. The spider has catched the fly.'

'Caught,' said Dougie.

When the song ended, Dougie walked over to Marie and

asked her to dance. Vince put a hand on Dougie's chest, pushed him backwards and said: 'Can ye no see she's busy? Blow, Dougie.'

When it came to the ladies' choice, Maureen Todd appeared and asked him to dance. It was a slushy Beatles song, and he hated it, but it was slow and it was having the right effect on Maureen Todd. She was leaning her head on his shoulder and he was moving his hand down her back as the words of the song whispered, 'Here, there, and every-where . . .'

Antoine had gone into Neil's house to be introduced to Doreen. Dougie waited in his own garden and kicked a ball against the side of the house. He had asked Maureen Todd to go to the pictures with him. In three days' time they'd be sitting together in the dark cinema. Maybe he would try the hand.

He headered the ball against the wall and, when it bounced back to him, he'd trapped it under his foot. Christian and Neil came out of Neil's house and walked across the street to join him. They passed the ball to each other, then had a game of three-and-in. After a while they sat down on the doorstep at the back door.

Dougie said, 'He's been in there a while, eh?'

Neil looked at his watch. 'Fifteen minutes,' he said.

'Ah wonder what he's sayin to Doreen.'

'Oh, *Je t'aime, je t'aime, je t'aime*,' said Christian. 'I love you, I love you, I love you.'

Dougie laughed at the thought of Antoine saying that to Doreen. He turned to Neil. 'Mibbe Doreen would like that?'

'Ah doubt it,' said Neil. 'She's met a guy in Edinburgh at that dance on Friday. He's twenty. He's got a Lambretta.

Wears a parka. He looks dead like Roger Daltrey from The Who.'

Then they saw Antoine coming out of Neil's house, banging the front door behind him. He walked rapidly up the path, and when he couldn't get the gate to open they heard him say, '*Merde!*' He kicked at the gate then jumped over it and ran across the road towards them.

Christian jumped to his feet and shouted: '*Attention. Il est fâché!*'

Dougie saw that Antoine was glaring at him as he ran into the garden and crossed the lawn. Dougie rose to his feet. He heard Neil's voice sounding strange and far away as he asked, 'How'd it go, Antoine?' Dougie felt a stunning punch on the side of his head as Antoine flew at him with both fists. The anger rose up inside him, making a swarm of black dots appear in front of his eyes. He lashed out and caught Antoine on the side of the jaw, making his glasses fly off his head. He could smell the cologne in Antoine's hair as he grappled with him and pushed him to the ground. They rolled over and over, hearing Christian and Neil shouting their names – *come on Dougie come on Antoine come on Dougie come on Antoine* – and wasn't it Neil who was shouting for Antoine and Christian who was shouting for him? He had Antoine's face trapped between his knees on the ground under him and could have finished him off, but then he heard his mum's voice.

'Douglas! Stop that this minute!'

Somebody pulled at his sleeve and he stood up. Antoine stood up too and started brushing the dirt from his trousers and his jacket.

His mum stood in the doorway with her pinny on. She wagged the two fingers holding her fag and said: 'Wait till yer father hears about this, Douglas. Ah don't understand you at all. Ah'm going back in the house. Ah've made some soup, if yous want some.' She went back in but left the door open.

Dougie felt Christian's hand on his shoulder. '*Calme-toi,*' he was saying.

Dougie watched Neil picking Antoine's glasses out of the grass and handing them back to him. Antoine took the glasses, put them back on squint and glared at him. Dougie started laughing. Antoine's tie was twisted, and the collar of his shirt was askew. He was breathing hard through his mouth and his lips were twisted. He pointed at Antoine and said: 'Mad French bastard.'

He heard Christian's voice in his ear: '*Alors, arrête. C'est fini.*'

Antoine spat the words at him through his twisted lips: '*Oui, je suis fou.* I am mad. I am a glaiket idi-ette. I am dead skware. Everything you teach me is wrong. You teach me this word "tits". This word "tits" you say. I kiss Daurine . . . *Oh, mon Dieu, c'était un coup de foudre* . . . And we kiss and we caress and then I say to Daurine: "Daurine, you have the marvellous tits."'

Dougie felt Christian's hand gripping his arm as he tried not to laugh. He saw Neil's big, stupid mouth opening up to show all his yellow teeth and his scarlet gums as he laughed. All three of them couldn't help laughing.

Antoine glared at them fiercely, then he straightened his glasses with a hand, looked at Neil and said: 'Ah, you laugh, Neil, but I love Daurine. I am – how you say? – I am in love with your large sister. But she slap my face, she tell me to fockoff! Yes, go on, laugh. Laugh at me as I despair.'

Neil tried to stifle his own laughter with a hand as he guided Antoine to the doorstep and they both sat down. Dougie felt Christian leading him by the arm over to them.

Dougie said: ' Antoine, Ah know she's the same age as you, but Neil says she's goin out wi a guy who's twenty and who looks like Roger Daltrey'.

'Twenty?

Neil said: '*Oui. Il a vingt ans.*'

Antoine leaned against the door and asked: 'Is he very 'andsome? Very *elegant*? Dead skware? Is he "mod"?'

'He sounds it,' said Dougie. 'Neil says he wears a parka and he's got a Lambretta.'

Neil told Antoine: 'He still looks like a glaiket eedjit.'

Dougie's mum came back out to the door. 'Ah don't understand yous. Yin minute ye're fightin, the next minute ye're laughin thegither. Come in and have a bowl of soup.'

'*Ah oui,*' said Christian. 'Let us eat some Scottish broth.'

As they all went into the kitchen after her, Dougie was amazed to hear his mum say: 'Naw. It's *soupe à l'oignon* the night.'

Christian looked interested. '*Soupe à l'oignon.* With the *croutons*?'

His mum said: 'Eh?'

Dougie explained to her that croutons were wee bits of fried bread that they put in the soup in France.

'Fried bread? Pff. I can fry up some bread for ye if that's what ye want.'

Christian nodded. Antoine sat down and stared at the table.

'What's wrong, Antone? Are ye okay, son?'

'He is in love,' said Christian.

Dougie saw his mum pat her hair as she dropped the bread into the frying pan. 'Oh, is that what's wrong wi him? Who's the lucky lady, Antone?'

Dougie put on his French accent to tell her: 'Daurine!'

His mum looked puzzled. 'Neil's big sister? She's a bonnie

lassie. Mibbe she's just no for you, though, Antone. Ye'll meet other girls in France, I daresay. Douglas, away an put on that French record Antone's mum sent me. Let's have a bit of music.'

He went through to the living-room and switched on the gramophone. He found the French record and put it on. He waited until it dropped on to the turntable and the arm moved over and the needle hissed in the groove.

He went back through to the kitchen. His mum had put the bowls of soup on the table and now she was dropping slices of fried bread into them.

As Charles Aznavour strarted singing, his mum put her hand on Antoine's shoulder and said: 'Yes. Ah like this . . . What's his name again?'

Antoine, lifting a spoonful of soup from his bowl, said with pride: 'Charles Aznavour.'

'Charles Aznavour. Oh, yes. Your mother's got good taste, Antone. It's a lot better than that Perry Como.' She began to sing along to the song.

Antoine said: 'Mrs MacLean, this *soupe* . . . *c'est très bonne*. I love the *soupe* of you.'

Dougie heard his mum say: '*Merci beaucoup*, Antone.' Then she hummed along to the song and sighed. 'Oh, listen to that voice,' she said. 'He can fairly make a woman's heart ache.'